BLEEDING EDGE

ELLIOT SECURITY SERIES

EVIE MITCHELL

ACKNOWLEDGEMENT OF COUNTRY

I acknowledge the Traditional Custodians of the lands on which I write, the Ngunnawal people, and pay my respect to elders both past and present.

I acknowledge the continued and deep spiritual relationship of the Australian Aboriginal and Torres Strait Islander peoples' to this land, and their unique cultural and spiritual relationships to the land, waters and seas and their rich contribution to society.

Always was, Always will be.

*To every woman who has faced her fear and said,
"Not today, Satan."*

*And to my favourite husband, thanks for creating a life with me
that is more beautiful than any I could write.
You know which scenes are for you.*

EMMIE
PRESENT DAY

They say no good story starts with a salad but mine did. So, here goes.

It started with a salad. It wasn't even a good one like with feta or pear or chicken. No, limp soggy leaves sat sadly in a bowl surrounded by three evil looking prawns, their buggy eyes stared out at me. I *hated* prawns with the fiery vengeance of a thousand suns. This was one salad I did *not* want to make friends with.

I hadn't planned or even wanted to go out. Addie, the executive assistant at the security firm where I worked, had pestered me until I'd acquiesced. Addie had style with a capital cool. A total glam babe – I'd never seen her in anything less than full pin-up vintage. Despite my protests, she'd convinced me to attend Thursday night trivia.

We were at a small bar just down the street from my office. I'd had a burger for lunch and convinced myself I should make an attempt to be healthy and order something light for dinner.

Immediate regret.

I reached for the menu, looking back over the description. Yep. No mention of prawns. My nose wrinkled in disgust as I stared at my salad, gingerly poking a crustacean with the tines of my fork.

"Just saying, that looks horrible," Addie commented, taking a giant bite out of her deliciously decadent burger. She moaned, rolling her eyes in exaggerated joy.

I grunted, holding up a limp leaf for closer inspection. "Maybe if I–"

"Swap it." The deep voice interrupted.

I glanced at my boss, Luc, my cheeks warming as I realised all eyes at our table were now on me.

"Umm." I abruptly stood, the chair scraping awkwardly as I struggled to ignore the chuckles and gentle teasing from my colleagues. I picked up the plate, muttering, "Be right back."

I worked for a private security company. Elliot Securities was fast becoming one of the biggest names in the business. They did everything from private security for the rich and famous through to investigations and software checks. If it involved security, Elliot Securities was involved.

A computer geek, my job involved uncovering weaknesses in a company's cyber security, including information about people who may be doing the wrong thing.

The second-best part of my job, besides doing cool sometimes questionably legal activities, was working with some of the best minds in the industry. The Nucleus, as we referred to ourselves, were a bunch of guys who, like me, were good with computers. We knew how to work technology to our advantage. We even had badges. And a theme song.

Which brought me back to Luc – my direct boss. We'd first been introduced during my interview for the Nucleus. By that stage, I'd been at Elliot Securities for two years but working in tech support. My skills had been woefully underutilised until I'd assisted my boss in building a customised firewall and backup solution. The interview offer had come as a surprise. I'd attended it completely unprepared for the sheer beauty of Luc.

"You can come in now." The elderly receptionist had ushered me into the meeting room. I'd stepped through, thanking her, and promptly stumbled, fumbling my resume and note pad papers scattered across the floor.

I dropped to the floor, face flaming as I scrambled for my papers. His tall body moved with perfect grace as he stood, rounding the table to help . I could tell he worked out because, while lean, he was solidly built. He stood a few inches taller than my five feet eleven but moved with power and deliberation, all of him in perfect balance.

He'd crouched, reaching out to assist. He'd kept his thick chestnut hair cut but not cropped. He had stubble, the dark scruff framed the edge of his face and mouth, drawing attention to his lips.

His eyes were blue. Not green or grey-blue but piercing clear blue. Long, impossibly perfect dark lashes framed his amazing eyes. Strong eyebrows and nose, a smile on his lips - no dimples. My flush deepened.

"Hi." He'd held out a few sheets of paper which I quickly accepted and shoved into my folder, hair falling over my face. Still crouched on the floor, he'd offered a hand. "I'm Lucien Falco. Luc."

"Emmie Franklin." We shook, remaining crouched.

"Should I leave?" I'd whispered, my eyes finally meeting his.

"Do you want to leave?" He'd whispered back, a small smile tugging his lips.

"No. I want the job."

"Then" – he'd straightened to stand, reaching his hand down to help me up – "let's do the interview."

I'd talked through my experience and been invited back to complete online testing. The tests were straight forward, checking to see if my skills matched my words. At the end of the day, the job was mine.

Elliot Securities used the Nucleus by assigning each member to a case leader. The case leader then utilised your skills for anything they had on the books. Could be a security assessment, physical security advice, inside threat assessment, or information security testing. These days something as basic as physical security still had a technical element – stalkers often started their obsessions online. I'd pinpointed a few threats through a simple internet search.

I'd been assigned to Lucien Falco. I'd now worked for Elliot Securities for three and a bit years, the last eighteen months directly under Lucien. We were a great team, our case-closure rate was excellent, and we got along well.

The only downside? I wasn't sticking around for much longer. And I had no idea how to tell him.

Heading to the kitchen, I weaved in and out of the crowded line waiting at the bar. As I shifted around a group of girls, hands clutched at my back dragging me down. I lost the grip on the plate, sending it spiralling. My plate shattered as our bodies hit the floor with a loud thud. The bar briefly quietened as heads turned to me and the woman who'd desperately clasped me to her.

"Oh my God! I'm so sorry! These damn heels. There's a wet patch, I just couldn't stop–"

I disentangled myself from the woman gushing apologies at me.

"No worries." I waved off offers of assistance from the

crowd, then offered her a smile and a hand, helping her stand.

"What the fuck, Mel!"

My limp salad dripped from the jean leg of the angry voice's owner. Over six foot, built like a line-backer, his neck and cheeks were a mottled purple-red as he glared at the tiny woman beside me. She cowered, arms curling around her middle as her shoulders hunched, her eyes on his feet. I could smell the alcohol on his breath as he weaved unsteadily.

"I'm so sorry, I didn't–"

The man swept his hand back, moving to strike her. Years of training kicked in. As he swung to backhand her face, I stepped forward, deflecting the blow with my forearm, following it up with a hard jab to his collarbone, knocking him back. I shifted in front of the woman, hands raised. He came back, taking a wild swing, roaring as he tried to punch me.

I ducked his arm, stepping forward to knee him in the balls. Taking his other arm, I used the momentum of his body to twist his arm up and around, pegging it behind him as he crashed to the floor, his free hand moving to cup his balls.

Dimly aware of yelling and screams, I tried to calm my racing heart while the man squirmed under me. I dug a knee in his back, pushing harder on his arm to keep him subdued.

"I got him." Luc pulled the guy's free arm back, pinning the arm while taking over from me. "You can let go, Emmie."

I dropped my hands, stepping back, eyes immediately searching for the best exit.

"Okay, guys, that's enough. Everyone back to your seat." Security entered the fray, assessing the situation with a glance. His eyes hit me before skittering off to the sobbing woman on my left.

"You need me to call the cops? You wanna make a report?"

I hesitated, glancing at the woman. She nodded, mascara running.

"He's my boyfriend. Was. Is. I don't... he hits... I can't..." She broke down, crying harder.

The gathered crowd slowly dissipated as the bar attempted to start the next round of trivia, distracting them from our small group.

Addie pushed her way through to pull the sobbing woman into a tight hug. "Don't you worry, honey. You're safe now."

An hour later, the grumbling in my stomach had intensified, but the police had taken my statement.

"You okay?"

I nodded.

"So." Addie shook her long wavy auburn hair as one of her perfectly sculpted eyebrows raised in my direction. "Where have you been hiding your kung fu fighting moves, little miss karate?"

A chuckle came from behind me.

I turned, a blush warming my face. Luc had been joined by the owner of Elliot Securities, Paxton Elliot. Both laughed quietly.

"Hey." I gave them a nod. "Thanks for helping."

Luc grinned. "I would say any time, but you seemed to have it under control."

I chuckled nervously. "Still, thanks."

"Plan now?"

I rubbed a hand over my face. "I'm grabbing a burger and heading home."

They stayed with me, waiting for my food. As I tucked the paper bag filled with deliciousness into my backpack, Luc offered me a ride.

"Nah, I'm good. My car's just out front." The last hour had allowed me to brush off my latest bad memory; my hands were steady now the adrenaline had worn off.

Luc shrugged. "I'll follow you home, then."

"I'm okay. You don't have to."

"Humour me."

I ducked my head, fighting another blush. "Okay."

Luc trailed me to my car. I waited while he got on his Ducati.

My apartment was in the city but not exactly in the most vibrant place to live. A set of four buildings, each only two storeys high, I lived on the second floor of the third building. All the buildings were red brick, cracked concrete, and in various states of disrepair. The general sense of abandonment and the fact they attracted people of questionable habits lent them their nickname – the drug flats.

I peeled off at my driveway, waving a hand out the window in thanks. I expected Luc to keep going, instead he turned in to my complex, following.

I pulled into my allocated space in the open park, expecting Luc to circle, then leave. Instead, he parked beside my car. He didn't say anything as I led him up the stairs to my apartment. The hallway sensor light stayed off as we headed to my door. I made a mental note to drag another fluorescent bulb from my supply. Maintenance never did anything.

I hit the locks on my door, there were three, and opened it up. I paused, uncertain. I'd never invited anyone here. I'd always claimed it was much too small, which wasn't exactly a lie.

"Want to come in for a coffee or something?"

Luc glanced down the hall, frowning, his gaze sharp. Down the corridor, my neighbours' door had opened, their TV blasting into the hall.

"Yeah." A muscle in his jaw ticked as he watched their door slowly close.

My small one-bedroom unit had a tiny bathroom, minus the bath. The shower felt more like a standing coffin, but the bathroom had a small mirror, a basin, and a toilet. I'd painted the unit, trying to create my own little oasis. Plants overflowed pots in every corner and on every bookshelf. On my kitchen windowsill sat two small rows of assorted teacups full of fresh herbs ready for cooking. My eye-bleed of a couch was a horrific explosion of florals from the early nineties. Used but comfortable, I'd picked it up at the Salvation Army store for a bargain.

The most expensive thing in my apartment was my TV. There was no other word for it except massive. Huge. A monstrosity. It had taken the delivery guys forty minutes to work out how to navigate it up the narrow staircase and through my door.

Luc looked around as I moved to the kitchen.

"I've got instant, is that okay?"

He shrugged off his jacket while moving to straddle one of my bar stools.

"Sounds good."

I set the kettle to boil and opened my dinner bag, munching on a still warm chip.

As the water heated, I turned, leaning back against the kitchen bench opposite Luc. I picked up my burger, taking a big bite. He watched me, a slight wrinkle between his eyes.

"What?" I asked, swallowing.

Luc raised an eyebrow. "Why this place?"

The kettle whistled, and I set about making our drinks.

"You know." I shrugged, back to him. "It's cheap and close to everything." I splashed one sugar and a dash of milk into his coffee.

"Cheap? I do your evaluations. I know how much I pay you." He said it teasingly, but there was an undercurrent.

I handed him the mug, then retreated to the other side of my kitchen, blowing a little on the tea as I avoided his eyes.

"Everyone needs money, Luc. Even me." I dodged his actual question.

After a long silence, he shrugged, changing the subject. "You've got a freaking huge TV."

I grinned. It had taken me two years to decide to buy it.

"All the better to get my geek on," I teased back.

Luc stood, moving to look over my DVD collection. I chewed another few chips, watching.

My collection took up half of one wall. The other half held my book collection alphabetised by author and series. Comic books were the bottom half of the bookshelf, novels the top.

"Got anything I'd like?"

I had to think. "Depends. I do action, I don't do horror."

"I do action."

I sat the remains of my burger on the counter, dusting my hands on my jean leg as I moved to the wall of epic DVD-ness and started sifting through my series.

"Hmm... animated sci-fi?" I glanced over, and he shook his head.

"I do Saturday morning cartoons, that's as far as I go."

"Right," I murmured, looking back through my collection. "What about Saturday night cartoons?"

"So long as it's not some Star Trek shit, I'm open to it."

I laughed. "You'd like it if you tried it! Here, it's an adult cartoon. Archer. Heard of it?"

He shook his head.

"It's one of my favourite series. It's hilarious and action and reminds me of our workplace sometimes. Short and sweet, only a few seasons so far. You may like it."

Luc laughed as he looked at the cover. "Boobs, guns, and explosions? I'm in."

"Speaking of explosions. Thanks again for tonight. Sorry you had to get involved."

His face darkened. "I hope that woman leaves the dick. Shit like that, it pisses me off."

Warmth pooled in my belly. "Me too."

"You did good, Emmie. Handled yourself real well."

The warmth expanded.

You need to tell him.

Tomorrow. I'll tell him tomorrow. I promised myself.

"Anyways." I fluttered my hands about, suddenly flustered. "It's getting late. I'm sure you have places to go, people to see, women to kiss." The last bit accidentally popped out. I immediately blushed.

Smooth. Real smooth there, Emmie.

A grin stole across his lips, and his brilliant blue eyes darkened just a hint. He leaned in slowly. "No to the first two, maybe to–"

His phone interrupted him. I jumped away, unsuccessfully trying to hide the blush burning up my neck, colouring my cheeks. Swearing, Luc pulled the mobile out and pressed the screen.

"Luc."

He jerked upright, body shifting to alert.

"You are fucking *kidding* me." He paused, listening. "Shit. Who do you need?" His head swung to me. "I've got her here." Another pause. "No, I followed her home after some jerk grabbed her in the bar." His eyes raked me up and down, and a small smile played at the corners of his mouth. "Yeah, she does. Okay. We'll be there in thirty." He hit the end button and slipped it back into his pocket. "Declan."

Declan had the night shift at Elliot Securities.

"That dick Rueben, from Grosford and Sons?"

I had to think for a moment. "The one we're tracking for embezzlement?"

"That's him. Grosford just got the call. His money is gone. Declan's calling us in."

"Damn!" I headed for my purse. "Goddamn it! I wanted to sleep tonight."

I moved to grab my keys, but Luc stopped me.

"No time. You ride with me."

"But–"

"I'll drop you home. Let's go."

EMMIE

"**G**oddamn, Rueben!" It had quickly become the phrase of the day.

Grosford and Sons was a small company who assisted older Australians with their savings. They looked after people's financial situation when they got too old and had no family to assist them. Grosford and Sons were known for their honesty and integrity.

Mr Grosford, a man now in his early sixties, had started the company thirty years earlier after watching a close friend of his mother lose her savings. She'd had dementia, and with no family and not wanting to burden her friends with her affairs, she'd trusted a "financial expert." They'd taken her money and disappeared. Mr Grosford had spent his own money looking after the friend until her death.

During our investigation, I'd found other accounts Mr Grosford had topped up. The accounts were all of people without family, who without his generous support, would be turned out of their care facilities. There were times when working on a case you met some real horrible people. Mr Grosford and his sons were sincere. When I'd reported my findings to Luc, he'd agreed. This case was personal.

Rueben had been an employee for twenty years and skimming money for fifteen. We'd been called in because the idiot had gotten greedy. I'd put a bug on the Grosford accounts. I'd tracked the money to a foreign bank two months ago. We'd known Rueben was planning a big move, but thought he'd have another week. The idiot had gotten wind of our involvement, freaked, and moved early. The bug had done its job, alerting Grosford and us to Rueben's sudden change of plans.

I'd been up all night, powered by 3:00 a.m. chocolate and copious amounts of soda. It was now after midday, and I'd tracked the bastard to a small airport where he'd attempted to use some of the many millions to buy a one-way ticket to Fiji. God knows where he'd jump off to next if he managed to get there. I hit my headphone. "Luc?"

"Yo."

"Looks like he's hiring a private jet at St Paul's. I've contacted the airport. They're delaying the flight due to 'mechanical issues.' Is an hour long enough to get the police involved?"

"We're on it." He disconnected the call, and I sat back, rubbing my eyes. In another hour or two, I'd be handing my research over to the police. Fingers crossed, by then the scum-of-the-earth dickwad would be in custody, and eventually these people would get their money back. Job well done.

I headed to the bathroom. I splashed water on my face, glancing at the mirror. It didn't reflect a pretty picture. By this stage, I'd been awake for close to thirty hours. Greasy limp ash-blond hair, bloodshot eyes circled by angry dark smudges.

I patted my face dry and headed back to my desk. The Nucleus had the second floor to ourselves. There were only eight of us, but we liked space. A physical manifestation of our introversion perhaps? We'd turned our space into a shrine to geek. A Lego town sat under construction in the middle of the room, Nerf guns lined the walls, and a life-sized Dalek took up one of the corners. Posters of various memes with "All the baddies!" or "I can haz cheezburger?" hung on the walls.

While the company was an equal opportunity employer, currently only three women worked at head office - Addie, me, and another woman, Kel, who worked for the investigation side of the business. A slim red-head, Kel made Miranda Kerr look like the plain stepsister.

I stood swaying in the door to my floor. Foam suction-tipped bullets flew as my colleagues ducked under tables, hid behind desks, and barrel-rolled while firing Nerf guns, shouting taunts. I'd normally be up for a match, but right now I wanted sleep. *All* the sleeps.

I turned and headed for the down room. Located on the fourth floor, the large room was a mish-mash of gym equipment and a lounge area complete with massive TV and couches. An Xbox, PlayStation, and DVDs sat on a massive entertainment unit and ready for a moment's notice. I found it, thankfully, empty.

Flopping face down on one of the couches, I grunted as my body bounced slightly on impact. Still face down, I blindly reached for the coffee table, feeling around for the stereo remote. I hit the play button, shifted to Emmie's relaxation mix, and promptly fell asleep.

I woke to the boys from One Direction singing about hearts, and a hand gently turning me on my side. The chorus thumped out as Luc crouched beside the couch, smiling down at me while gently rubbing my shoulder.

"I don't know why these 1D boys are singing about carrying anyone."

I blinked up at him, confused by both his statement and appearance.

"They wouldn't be able to carry a bag of flour, let alone another human. They do not even lift, bro."

I laughed a little, reaching up to rub my dry eyes.

"You've been holding out on me." He sounded amused.

"Hmm?" I struggled to sit, stretching and yawning as I valiantly tried to shake the drowsy cloud of my nap.

"You're a romantic."

I shrugged, stifling another yawn. "Isn't everyone?"

"Come on you. Let's go." He tugged my hands, pulling me up and off the couch. I stumbled into his chest, and he absorbed me, hands settling briefly on my hips. I looked up at him. He grinned, reaching a hand up to brush a chunk of my hair behind my ear. I flushed, quickly stepping back.

Luc dropped his hand. "I swung by home and picked up the Alfa. You can sleep on the way."

We headed outside to a sky painted in deep pinks and purple as the sun set. "Crap. How long did I sleep?"

Luc smirked. "About five hours. The boys were about to kill you if they heard another prepubescent song about love."

I shrugged, getting in the car. "I like happy endings. Love songs make me happy. They're relaxing and have great melody."

"Next time? Fall asleep to a mix longer than an hour."

I shrugged again and snuggled into the side of the door. "Did you get him?"

Luc barked out a laugh, short, sharp, and unamused. "Yeah, we got him. The cops are questioning him now. I grabbed the stuff you sent through and provided the file notes. The Grosfords should recover their money soon enough."

"Good. I like it when we get the bad guys."

He chuckled. "Same."

EMMIE

A reasonably uneventful week followed the closure of the Grosford case. Lots of paperwork and interviews with the police, a few written testimonies and walking through my evidence-collection methods. The usual things I did following a case closure. The only abnormal occurrence was the introduction of one Ms Jetta Oliver.

As in, Jetta Oliver, daughter of rock legends who'd tragically died, sister to Courtney Oliver the current top-of-the-charts pop princess. Jetta Oliver, lyricist to the stars. *That* Jetta Oliver.

Addie had been purposefully vague about why Ms Oliver was at Elliot Securities. Despite our best efforts, she'd only dropped enough hints for us to piece together that Jetta and Paxton Elliot - owner of Elliot Securities- had romantic history and Jetta had gotten into trouble. Pax considered the situation serious enough that he'd moved her into his house. The gossip mill was going crazy chewing over the mystery.

Saturday night saw me sliding onto a seat at Eighty-six.

Diners chatted, orders were called from the open kitchen which ran along one wall, and people chatted while watching the chefs work. Big blackboards took up the other walls with large white letters proclaiming the specials. The place had great share food and drinks alcoholic enough to make you tipsy with one sip.

I volunteered as designated driver, having stopped to pick up Jarrett, one of my closest friends at Elliot Securities, Kel, and Addie before heading in. We were all seated and waiting when Luc walked in with Pax's blast from the past. Cute tight skirt, silk top with just a hint of cleavage, ankle boot heels, and styled hair, Jetta Oliver looked like a curvier, edgier Taylor Swift. As Jetta introduced herself, the hair on the back of my neck lifted. Automatically my hand curled into a fist under the table as I slowly shifted, casually checking my exit pathways as I searched for the danger. I found only Luc's eyes on me. I relaxed, unclenching my fist and wiping my sweaty palm against my jeans.

"Are you staying for the gossip?" I teased, watching a smile play at the corners of his mouth.

Luc shook his head. "I'll be at the bar." We all watched as he walked off, his butt looking phenomenal in his jeans. Kel sighed heavily. "If I didn't work with that boy…"

She turned back to the table, winking at Jetta as she held out a hand. "I'm Kel."

Addie scoffed, rolling her eyes. "That's a shitty greeting. Here."

She waved a hand at me. "That's Emmie, she's a hacker. Emmie is our go-to, she can do pretty much anything with computers. You need IT support? This girl is it! She's responsible for background checking all my boyfriends." I blushed and look down at the table. I couldn't deny her claims because, alas, I'd screened the last three of Addie's boyfriends and vetoed all of them. She had truly atrocious taste in men.

"This," Addie continued, sweeping a hand towards Kel, "is Kel. Kel is our undercover sis-ta. Pax hired her for her looks, but also her kick arse-ness. Complete bad arse."

Kel chuckled. "I just like the pay. It keeps me in designer cars."

I watched as Jetta laughed along with the table.

Addie gestured to the lone guy in our group. "And this, my darling, is Jarrett Shannon McKinnon the third. He's half Maori, half Scottish."

Jarrett reached over and clasped one of Jetta's hands, drawing it to his lips and pressing a kiss against her knuckles. "Absolutely charmed."

We kept the conversation light, sounding each other out. We chatted, savouring delicious food, and I watched as they drank, getting loose and laughing a lot. I found myself relaxing, warming to this new person. Despite her intimidating background, Jetta shunned the spotlight in favour of normality.

"I mean, it helps that I'm petrified of performing. Stage fright barely describes what I suffer." Jetta chuckled.

I stole glances at Luc throughout the night, watching as he laughed with the waitresses at the bar where he ate his meal, one eye on the door the other on Jetta.

I hadn't had a chance to talk to Luc. Despite my best promises, I hadn't handed in my notice.

You're only delaying the inevitable. Time's ticking.

Over dinner Jetta revealed her everlasting love for Paxton Elliot and solved the mystery of her sudden appearance. It involved her sister, Courtney, who'd amassed a significant drug debt (now in rehab thanks to Pax), their dead parents, and a mob boss looking for his money.

The whole thing sounded like something out of a Tarantino film or a soap opera. It definitely put my problems into perspective.

Monday. You're telling him Monday.

We were debating dessert when the first bullet punched through the glass panelling at the front of the restaurant. I heard the gunshot, and without thinking, started to move. I clocked Luc at the bar, our eyes meeting as the second shot shattered the glass frontage. The restaurant's jovial atmosphere splintered as Luc yelled, "GET DOWN!"

Panicked customers screamed and bolted, others ducked as the bullets kept coming. Luc crouched, hand going to the pistol at his hip as he moved towards us. I spun, throwing myself at Jetta, pushing her to the floor. I pulled my hands up to cover my head as I spread my body protectively over her.

I couldn't hear past the deafening sound of the guns and the crack of wood, glass, and plaster as bullets hit walls, floor, and furniture. To cover Jetta, I'd twisted away from Jarrett, Kel, and Addie. I couldn't see if they were hurt. I screwed my eyes shut and prayed.

"Emmie." Jetta's hands clutched at my shirt as something hot and brutal tore through my body. A red haze clouded my vision as pain in my side radiated outwards, immeasurable in its agony.

I swore, as a second bullet arched across my thigh. I felt the gush of wetness from both areas as utter agony exploded across my left side. The shots abruptly halted as the getaway car screeched away, leaving behind an eerie silence.

A woman to our left began screaming. It broke the strange stillness, sending customers scrambling for the door, screaming, shouting, shoving each other in their haste. Feet stomped on me, people tripped over my prone body as they heedlessly raced to safety. I heard Luc yell but I didn't look up until Addie and Luc crouched beside me, Kel and Jarrett standing protectively above.

Addie rolled me, and I groaned, barely registering her questions. The excruciating pain in my side radiated out from my hip and down my leg. I bit my cheek, tasting blood, desperately trying to stem the urge to scream.

I fell on my back, my breathing ragged as I blinked rapidly, trying to clear the tears from my eyes and struggling against panic. I turned my head, watching as Jetta scrambled to her knees. "Jetta?"

"I'm okay. I'm, I'm fine. You protected me." She sat up, running shaking hands down her body. She reached out clasping her fingers in mine. "I'm fine."

"Good." The world spun slightly as I tried to breathe through the pain. My eyelids lowered. "I'm gonna sleep now." My voice sounded off, heavy.

A strong hand gripped my wrist, checking my pulse as another started roaming my body.

"Don't you *fucking dare*! Emmie, open your eyes and look at me!"

Unable to resist his demands I met Luc's gaze. "When did you get here?"

Where was I? What happened?

"Luc!" Addie squealed, her voice high and panicked. I glanced down to see her raise a blood-covered hand.

"Fuck. Put pressure on it."

My eyelids fluttered, and I fought to keep them open. Dimly, I heard calls for an ambulance, sirens sounding distantly in the background. Luc shifted to my side and pressed against the wound.

"Solid. Like a fucking rock." Luc looked down at me with

a smile, but his warm blue eyes worried, a hint of ill-concealed panic swimming in their depth.

"You're a pain in my side right now," I panted, wanting to offer reassurance. I dimly registered moments of lucidity even as my brain fogged, pain overriding my ability to process events in a rational manner.

Luc huffed out a strained laugh. "This isn't a time for puns, Emmie."

I shifted slightly and gasped as my thigh immediately protested the movement. "Guess I should tell you that's not the only bullet, right?" I felt everyone's eyes on me.

"Da fuck!"

I was losing the battle to stay conscious.

"You have got to be shitting me."

My lids closed as I slurred. "My leg got hit too. I think it's my thigh."

I felt a hand run over my leg and then heard Addie swear softly as she pressed against it.

Hands turned me, as someone pulled my right arm straight, administering an IV. The paramedics asked me questions I barely registered.

"What?" My voice heavy and muted. I felt woozy, my head spun uncontrollably.

"It's okay, Emmie. You're okay, baby. We're gonna get you to a hospital," Luc promised. "Stay awake for me and I promise, I'll watch any of those cartoon things you like. I don't care which one. Your choice," Luc reassured me.

"Liar," I muttered. My eyelids closed again. An unexpected movement caused my stomach to drop as they lifted me onto what I assumed was a stretcher. Someone kept pressure on my wounds while they moved me. I could hear people around us, sirens. Lights flashed on the fronts of my eyelids, but I couldn't find the strength to open them. A door slammed followed quickly by the grumble and shake of the ambulance under me. The paramedic spoke, I could barely hear him through the rushing sound in my ears. One thought overrode my need for unconsciousness.

"Luc?"

"Yeah, baby?" His voice sounded far away.

"You're..."

"What?"

I tried to answer, but darkness rushed in, pulling me under.

LUC

Hospitals always felt like death. Cold, sterile, and entirely devoid of comforting smells like grass, sunshine, or decent food. I'd been in too many hospitals in the last ten years to not immediately think of death when I walked through those doors.

The emergency doctors had taken one look at her injuries and immediately taken her to surgery. A nurse directed me to the bathroom to clean while I waited for a change of clothes. Blood soaked my shirt and jeans, drying on my hands.

I washed, gritting my teeth as I struggled against the adrenaline coursing through my veins. The muscles in my body were tense, readying for another attack.

Breathe. Calm. Find your centre.

Years of training, therapy, and discipline kicked in. I prioritised what I needed to know.

I drew my phone, hitting speed dial. Jarrett answered.

"Who's Emmie's next of kin?" I didn't bother with pleasantries, knowing Jarrett would have already called this in to the office.

"You and Addie."

Fuck. I knew it.

"Her family?"

A pause, the sound of a phone being passed, then Kel's voice.

"We don't know."

"She never told you?"

"She barely speaks about her day, let alone her past."

I ran wet hands through my hair, sucking in a breath between clenched teeth.

"Luc?"

"Allergies?" I asked, knowing it would be in her personnel file.

"Nothing. Her file said she had a broken arm in '96 and that's it."

I dropped my arm. "Okay. Got it."

A nurse hovered by the toilet as I exited. "Mr Falco? I need you to fill out the admittance form. Is there anything I need to let the surgeons know about Ms Franklin? Allergies, illnesses?"

"No. Emmie's in perfect health."

She nodded. "I know this is hard, but is there anyone we should notify?"

"No. Emmie's–" I choked on the words. I didn't know if she was an orphan, estranged from her family. I didn't know jackshit about the woman I worked with.

"No," I finally said. "It's just me."

She nodded again, stepping close to place a comforting hand on my arm. "I need to get in and let the surgeons know. There's a waiting room just down the hall. You're probably in shock. I'd really recommend calling someone."

"They're on their way."

"Do you need–"

"No," I interrupted her. "Sorry. Just, go look after my girl."

She hesitated, then nodded. "I'll be back with news as soon as I can."

I walked to the waiting room, taking a seat on the hard plastic.

"Fuck." I blew out a breath. "Who the fuck are you, Emmie Franklin?"

EMMIE

Dreams interspersed with memories came like whispers of smoke, small scenes brushing across my mind before disappearing back into the black.

"Rise daughter of God." A hand pressed to my head, heavy and warm. *"You shall be set apart from your sisters. You are blessed."* The memory faded.

An eyeless doll chased me down a hallway, calling my name. I opened a door, stepping inside, plunging into darkness.

I sat in a chair, a computer screen in front of me. The text cursor blinked awaiting my input. I tried to lift my hands, but they were weighted down. I struggled against the heaviness pulling at my arms, my shoulders aching as I strained. A familiar voice spoke from behind me, taunting, the hairs on the back of my neck standing to attention. His breath brushed the shell of my ear, fear shivering down my spine.

"You killed him."

"No."

Black pulled me under.

LUC

True to form, Elliot Securities had turned out in full force. Colleagues and friends spilled out of the hospital waiting room, all anxious for news.

When Pax and I took over Elliot Securities, we wanted to create an environment where the people who worked for us were loyal because they felt valued and appreciated. Ross, Pax's father, had started that legacy. This show of force for Emmie proved we were maintaining it.

I alternated between pacing, sitting, or leaning against the wall beside Jarrett.

"This is fucking hard," Jarrett murmured, eyes on the clock.

I rubbed a hand over my face. "Waiting always is."

"You did this with Paxton, yeah?"

I offered one quick nod of affirmation, ignoring the memories the question stirred up.

A doctor entered the room, distracting me from my morbid thoughts.

"Mr Falco?"

I stepped forward with a nod. "She okay?"

"If you could follow me?" The doctor gestured outside the room.

Fuck that.

I crossed my arms, planting my feet, head shaking. "We're all here for Emmie. Is she okay?" The doctor hesitated. I rumbled out a growl. "Hurry the fuck up, man. Is she okay?"

"Yes."

Thank Christ.

"But she's still in a serious condition. She's lost a lot of blood. There was extensive internal bleeding, but we've managed to stop that. I'm afraid both bullets tore roughly through her. It took us quite a while to repair the muscles and remove all the debris. The wound to her side fractured part of her ilium and resulted in a damage to her femoral shaft."

"English?"

"Her hip bone has been injured quite severely. Our priority was wound treatment, minimising blood loss and stabilisation of the fracture. As a result, we've externally pinned the hip at this stage, but will need to move to an internal solution once Ms Franklin is stabilised. We've examined Ms Franklin, and she doesn't appear to have suffered any bowel injuries, which"– the surgeon shook his head– "frankly is a miracle. She'll be in ICU for another few hours, perhaps another day, before we move her to a ward for further recovery." He looked around the room.

"I do warn you, it's not pretty. Her wounds are extensive and will take a long time to heal. There is also the risk of lead toxicity from the bullet itself, as well as infections."

"Can I see her?"

The surgeon nodded. "She's sleeping now, but you can come in and sit with her. You'll have to wear some scrubs. I can get a nurse to show you to her." He paused and glanced at the other people in the room.

"You can peek through the ICU windows if you want. I'd prefer to keep visitors to an absolute minimum at the moment. Ms Franklin needs her rest."

I followed him out, brain racing. "You said more surgery?"

"We've put external pins in place to brace the fracture while we worked on the bleeding. We'll reassess in the next two days. Recovery will be four to twelve weeks. She'll be able to walk but will need to keep weight off her hips while the ilium repairs. The ilium will be fine, it's the femur that we'll need to keep an eye on"

He opened a set of double doors, leading me down another hallway.

"That's your thigh bone?"

"Yes. The bullet went up, tearing muscles. It hit the bone fracturing the shaft. It's why the surgery took so long. There was haemorrhaging into the abdomen."

I blew out a breath. He stopped in front a door, turning to look at me. "It's only a hairline fracture and the damage should take about the same time to heal, but we'll need to keep an eye on her to ensure the wound remains stabilised."

He pulled the door open. "My nurses are inside. They'll show you what you need to do."

I held out a hand. "Thanks, doctor."

He shook it, nodding. "I'll refer her to a specialist tomorrow. They'll take over."

"Appreciate it."

I walked through the door, changing into the scrubs the nurses handed me. They led me through a room, settling me in a chair beside Emmie's bed. The nurse patted me on the shoulder. "She'll be asleep for quite a while. We keep them sedated. Don't worry. It's just to keep her as pain-free and comfortable as possible."

I swallowed around the lump in my throat. "Gotcha."

She checked Emmie's vitals, then drifted away.

I watched Emmie's chest rise and fall with each breath, falling into rhythm with her. Her cheeks were pale, her body limp on the bed. I ran through what I knew of this woman and came to a decision.

"Just FYI," I whispered, leaning close to her, my pinkie grazing the top of her hand. "You're in big trouble, missy." I watched her chest rise again.

"Don't worry. I got your back. But when you wake up?" I shook my head. "You've got some explaining to do."

EMMIE

Black. Black with little pinpricks of swirling light.

I wanted to stay here. Here in the dark with the pretty dancing specks. Here where it was warm and safe, and there was no pain.

"Emmie?"

My eyelids fluttered, valiantly struggling against the rough edge of unconsciousness. I felt groggy, sore, disconnected from my body. My head spun, nausea overwhelming.

My eyelids, I decided, were much too heavy to lift.

"Mr Falco? She's resting. It's doubtful she'll wake until tomorrow."

Luc's here?

I struggled and won the battle to open my eyes, immediately shutting them tight against the dim lights of the room. I huffed out a pain-filled breath.

"Em?"

I grunted, my throat bone dry.

"Emmie? Come on, beautiful," he coaxed.

I opened my eyes again and rapidly blinked as everything slowly came into focus. I squinted, absently taking in the space.

White walls and roof. Tubes, switches, and cords decorated my bedding. I shivered uncontrollably, distantly registering that everything hurt.

Cold. Why am I so cold? Why do I hurt so much?

"Hey." Luc reached out a hand and brushed my hair off my cheek. "It's good to see those green eyes." He smiled.

I croaked out a word. "Water."

He looked to the nurse standing on the other side of my bed. She'd placed a pressure cuff on my bicep, watching as it tracked my blood pressure. "Can she have some water?"

The nurse made a note on my chart before removing the cuff. "I'll ask her doctor after I finish checking Ms Franklin."

She looked down at me, pulling a small pen light from her tool belt and using it to shine in my eyes. "Emmie, my name is Sylvia. Do you remember what happened?"

I grimaced. "Some bastard shot me."

Luc barked out a laugh.

"Do you know what day it is?"

I answered questions finding myself both lucid and confused in equal measures.

The nurse made a final note on my chart before sliding it back into the pigeon hole at the end of my bed. "I'll just check with the doctor and be right back."

"Are you staying?" I clung to Luc's hand, my grip weak and clammy.

He nodded, his eyes warm. "Of course."

I closed my eyes. "Good."

As I drifted back to unconsciousness, I heard him mutter, "What are boyfriends for?"

EMMIE

I woke throughout the day, pain overruling my body's need to sleep. I had external screws stabilising my leg to prevent further stress. They alternately elevated or lowered my leg depending on the hour and level of swelling. Stitches criss-crossed my thigh. It felt as if daggers were grinding into the bone. Morphine became my saviour.

Luc stayed. Anytime I woke crying in pain, he was there, stroking my hair, wiping away my tears.

The doctor came later that day. Words like internal bleeding, operation, infection, and fractures were uttered as I struggled against the seductive pull of sleep. I was too drugged and in too much pain to comprehend much of what was agreed. Still, Luc stayed.

Pax and Jetta arrived mid-morning, their visit over before I could properly wake.

And so, the day went, sleep, pain meds, nurses and doctors and bandages. And always there was Luc.

Early evening Jarrett arrived. He took one look at me, burst into tears, then spent ten minutes convincing Luc to go home and rest.

Luc finally gave in. He'd bent, pressing a kiss to my forehead. "Two hours. I'll just grab a shower and some clothes."

"Go sleep," I whispered, blinking slowly my eyelids heavy.

As soon as he'd walked out the door Jarrett turned, sending me a look.

"Em." Raised eyebrows punctuated his statement.

"What?" I mumbled, lifting a hand to rub my nose. The tubes for my IV caught on the bed frame. Jarrett tutted, reaching over to untangle them.

"This is a simple question, baby girl. Where's your family?"

I lifted one shoulder in a shrug, groaning as my side protested. My face screwed up as I fought for breath, focussing on breathing through the pain.

His hand brushed across my forehead, stroking my hair as he murmured comfortingly. The pain subsiding, I looked up meeting his warm, brown gaze.

"Okay?"

I nodded.

"Do you have family?"

"Yes."

"Where are they?"

I squeezed his hand. "You're right here."

He blinked rapidly, his eyes watery. He sniffed twice, abruptly standing and shifting around the bed. He fussed with my blankets, pulling them about to tuck me in tighter.

"That's right, baby girl. We're right here." He finished with the blanket, returning to the seat by the bed. He reached over, pulling my hand into his, a thumb gently stroking my palm. "We'll be right here while you get better."

Something inside me loosened. A little part of me warmed.

"I love you, Jarrett."
"Love you too. Sleep now. We've got you."
The nightmares closed in.
"Time to prove your worth, daughter of God."

LUC

"She has an infection."

I rubbed a hand over my face. Emmie had spent the last three hours vomiting. Her cheeks were flushed with fever, and her blood pressure had dropped. I felt like a useless prick as I held her vomit bag and rubbed her back while she retched painfully.

Three days. Three fucking days and she'd been through two surgeries, had pins holding her bones together, and now this?

Emmie slumped back, eyes closed, swallowing rapidly as she tried breathing through her nose.

"The last surgery was a success, but we did warn infection was a risk." I didn't trust this doctor. For one, he looked like a hipster. He should be serving lattes down at the café, not looking after a human being.

"What are our options?" I asked, handing the used vomit bag to a nurse. She handed me a new one, whisking it off to God knew where.

"We've already removed all the debris. This is just one of those pump the antibiotics, then wait and see moments."

"Is it dangerous?" I asked, brushing a hand over Emmie's clammy face, tucking loose hair behind her ears. She didn't move, just lay there, eyes closed, breathing shallow pants.

"The infection doesn't present an unreasonable risk at this time."

"Then why the fuck is she so sick?" I couldn't keep the frustration from my voice.

"Antibiotics need time to work."

"Can't you do something?"

"We've already given her anti-nausea medication. Until that works or the antibiotics kick in, we just have to ride it out."

"Fuck." I resumed rubbing circles across Emmie's back

Dr. CJ checked his watch. "I have a surgery I need to prep for. Did you have any other questions or concerns?"

"Emmie?" I brushed a hand over her cheek. She shook her head, eyes still closed.

"We're good," I told him, pushing down the frustration. "Thanks."

"My nurses will check on Ms Franklin. See you shortly, Emmie." He patted her good leg, then turned, leaving the room.

I shook my head. "Kids shouldn't be allowed to–"

Emmie let out a strangled choke, hands frantically reaching for the vomit bag. I thrust it in her face and she clutched the bag, retching painfully.

"The anti-nausea should kick in shortly," the nurse told me, moving around the bed to assist. "She didn't respond to our normal medication, but this one is stronger."

Emmie slumped back, tears running down her face.

"I want to go home," she whispered, sobs silently shaking her shoulders.

"I know." I couldn't do anything. I had nothing to offer. Impotent rage boiled in my veins.

"I'm just going to swap this bag out." The nurse interrupted our moment. I stepped back, letting her work.

Emmie's nausea appeared to subside as she flushed her IV.

"You'll stay?" Emmie asked, her fingers clinging weakly to my wrist. I placed a hand over hers, soothing the tight muscles.

"Of course."

She relaxed, letting go of my hand. "Thank you."

It took an hour, but slowly she drifted, eventually falling into a restless sleep.

"Yo."

I lifted a finger to my lips, hushing Jarrett.

He made a sorry face, nodding as he stepped quietly into the room.

"She's a fighter," he whispered, squeezing my shoulder as he dropped into the chair beside mine. I slumped back, rubbing tired eyes. I'd spent the last hour hunched over a laptop attempting to get some work done while she slept.

"No question," I agreed, frowning at my emails. I'd typed the same sentence three times. I sighed, hitting the delete button marginally harder than required.

"The case is ramping up," Jarrett offered.

"Mm?" I gave up, closing the screen. "Tell me."

"It's definitely related to Jetta."

"It's been confirmed?"

"Not outright. But one of the bullets has the exact markings of one found at a drug shootout. The shootout was likened to Esso's operation."

"What's Pax think?"

"Nothing yet. He's not holding his breath."

"But you think it's the missing link."

"It's awfully coincidental."

I rubbed my chin, beard catching on the rough skin of my thumb.

"This may be related to Jetta, but I'm not chancing it. We keep up the protection for Emmie." When I wasn't in the room, Jack or Jarrett were. There was no way in hell I'd leave her vulnerable.

"Agreed. Has she clued in yet?"

"No. Let's keep it that way."

Jarrett nodded. He rolled a paper coffee cup between his big hands, staring at it for a long moment.

"Her family..." he started.

"I'm on it." I nodded, meeting his questioning look. "After we get her settled and Jetta safe. First priority."

Jarrett nodded. "Good."

LUC

My arse was at work, trying to get on top of emails. As much as I wanted to be there for Emmie, our work didn't stop.

Pax knocked on my open office door. "Hey, can you take Jetta to the hospital?"

I tensed, immediately on alert. "What's wrong?"

"Nothing. Jetta just wants to see Emmie. I'd take her, but I got an emergency meeting with the people from White Dog Pictures. Ben's covering Jetta, but White Dog is his client, so I want him back in the office to field the new bullshit these people are bound to throw up." Pax frowned. "Why would you assume...?"

"The infection."

"Jack's with her now."

I resisted the urge to roll my eyes. "Dude, just because someone's there doesn't mean my responsibility ends."

Pax's mouth twisted down. "You're not her keeper."

I stood, reaching for my phone and wallet. "True. But I'm her friend."

Pax watched me, his eyes entirely too knowing. "We have a policy."

"No dating the employees." I rolled my eyes. "Yeah. I know."

And I'm trying to figure a way around that.

He scratched his chin. "She's our best analyst, bar Sawyer."

"She's our best analyst period." I corrected. "Sawyer's a flake. Sure, he gets the job done, but Emmie's solid as a fucking rock. Her completion rates are–"

Pax shoved a hand in my face, pushing me away. "Just get Jetta to the fucking hospital."

I shoved him back, chuckling. "I don't know if I want her there."

Pax tensed. "Why?"

"Dude, the woman took a blow torch to your safe room."

"I'm going to fucking kill Jack." But the man chuckled.

"You're laughing?"

"She's a nut. But I can't but be impressed with her blow-torch skills."

Jesus. He had it bad.

Jack had spilled the beans. Jetta had experienced an emotional meltdown, taking a blowtorch to a locked room in his house. While impressed, I was also a little concerned.

I knit my fingers together in what I imagined was a stereotypical psych pose. "We gonna talk about your relationship? It's been a long time coming."

Pax turned away, calling over his shoulder. "Sure. I'll bring the tea, you bring the crumpets. We'll both hand our balls in at the door."

"It's called Toxic Masculinity, Paxton!" I yelled after him. "A real man learns to embrace his emotions!"

He flicked me the bird over his shoulder.

It took me less than twenty minutes to swing by and pick up Jetta from Pax's. She chatted nervously in the car, rubbing her palms repeatedly on her thighs, tracing a thumb over the tattoo on her other wrist.

"You good?"

"Yeah." Her thumb flicked over the tattoo again. "You and Paxton are close, right?"

"Mm."

"I..." She stopped, biting her lip.

"You?" I prompted.

She blew out a long breath. "Nothing."

My shoulders tensed. I had sisters. I knew what nothing said in that tone meant.

"You sure?"

"Yeah. I'm fine."

Ah, fuck.

At the hospital, we got out of the car, heading to Emmie's room. I let Jetta lead, my hand slipping into my back pocket to pull out my phone.

Luc: Code 501

Addie: Really? Who this time?

Luc: Jetta. We're visiting Emmie.

Addie: On my way. You OWE me.

As soon as we hit Emmie's room the wall broke. Jetta cracked, big crazy tears breaking free as she sobbed. I ushered her into a chair, then went to the nurses' station for tissues. By the time I returned, Emmie had also begun to cry uncontrollably.

Hurry up, Addie!

I handed out tissues, made soothing sounds, and was generally useless in the face of the sobbing.

Just as I reached breaking point, Addie appeared,

handing me her purse, and quickly setting the room to rights. And throwing me under a bus.

"I cannot believe you used a five-oh-one on us!"

"Emmie–"

"No." She held a hand up, halting my excuses. "You can go and sit in that chair." She pointed to one in the far corner of the room.

"You sit, you read the newspaper, and you pretend you cannot hear a word we're saying." She narrowed her eyes menacingly. "And if you say one word from today's–"

"I get it." I grinned, struggling not to laugh. "Calm ya tits."

Her back went ramrod straight. "Calm my–"

"Would you prefer soothe your breasts?" I asked, blinking innocently.

"I'll soothe your–" She threw back the covers, struggling to move.

"Fine." I made a settle motion with my hands. "I'll sit quietly–"

"Silently!"

"Silently," I agreed, "in the corner and let you girls chat."

Now I listened with half an ear, flicking through a trashy magazine while Emmie let rip on her frustrations. Personally, I thought she had every reason to be pissed with the world. The woman had taken a bullet for God's sake.

They moved on to Jetta and Paxton's relationship, and I felt like a voyeur listening to my best friend's girlfriend spill her deepest hopes and fears for their relationship.

I finally had to interrupt when they started celebrating Jetta and Paxton's successful coitus.

"No. Nope. I don't want to hear about the sexual prowess of my best friend and boss." I shook my head, lips curling.

"So, don't listen." Addie threw a pen at me. I caught it

mid-air, tucking it behind my ear. I shot her a grin, then shuddered as they immediately went back to relationship dissection.

Jesus. Women really overthink shit.

I gave up fake listening right around the point Jetta declared she may love Paxton, but she couldn't trust him. Apparently when a man leaves you just a few days after your parents' funeral to join the army and you don't hear from him for ten years, there is some unresolved shit.

"I need to sort my head and sort my issues with him so we can move onto a path where we have an actual partner-ship." She carried on for another moment and I sighed. As much as I liked Jetta, I couldn't let my brother hang. I dropped the magazine, standing.

"Having this conversation with him, not your girls would be a good start."

I shouldn't have bothered to try and drop my truth bombs on these undeserving cretins. Emmie and Addie both glared daggers while Jetta looked at me with all the pain in the world in her eyes. I stretched, trying to be the best wingman.

Dude, you owe me.

"Look, Pax has shit he still has to deal with. Shit he hasn't." I folded my arms over my chest, rubbing absently at the patch of puckered skin where the bullet had torn through my bicep.

"We're men. We don't do emotion and stuff on a good day. But worse, we're army– we don't do crying and emotions and bullshit like that because that's not what gets you through tours of duty. I came home to a mother and sisters who wouldn't leave me alone. They basically moved in with me and made me talk. You ever met my mother? She makes Leigh Anne Tuohy look like a lamb."

Emmie snorted. "Is that a *Blind Side* reference?"

I shook my head. "I thought it was a football movie. It is *not*." I turned back to Jetta. "Look, I get you have Pax issues. But he has Jetta issues. And those hens just came home to roost. The motherfucker is so tied up in you that he laughed about you trashing his house. Laughed!" I tossed up my hands.

Addie, for once in her life, didn't give me shit. Colour me rainbow, the woman backed me up. "And that's before you even throw both of you bumping naughties into the mix."

"Addie!"

"What?" Addie grinned, shrugging delicately. "I'm just saying sex, especially as the guy is your first love, complicates things."

The woman spoke truth.

Jetta sighed, shoulders slumping as she curled into herself. "You're right. We need to abstain."

I choked. For a beat the room remained silent as we all stared at Jetta. Then I tipped back my head, letting the laughter burst free. Emmie and Addie joined me, all of us roaring at the hilarity of this situation.

"Good luck," Emmie chocked out. She grimaced, hands raising to flutter above the bandage at her injured side. I sobered, moving to the bed.

A nurse bustled in at that moment, likely drawn by our noise. She took one look at Emmie's pinched, pale face and frowned.

"Out! Now! Ms Franklin is meant to have taken her painkillers and be sleeping right now."

Emmie shrugged sheepishly. "Hashtag sorry, not sorry."

"Out!" The nurse ordered.

I followed the girls, throwing a glance over my shoulder. Emmie gave a finger wave.

"Luc?"

"Yo?" I turned back to the two women in front of me.

"Can you take me to the office?"

"Sure."

Jack rounded the corner, a sandwich in hand.

"Stay with Jack for a minute. I left something in the room."

I jerked my head at Jack. He nodded. I turned, jogging back.

The nurse had left, but Emmie was awake, fat tears rolling down her cheek.

"Hey," I called, coming back into the room. "You okay?"

She wiped frantically at her face. "Of course, yes. I mean, of course." She cleared her throat.

"You know you don't have to lie to me." I sank into the chair beside the bed, reaching out a hand for hers. "You're entitled to tears."

She chewed her lip, looking anywhere but at me, her green eyes shimmering. "I don't like feeling helpless," she admitted in a whisper. "And I really hate the painkillers."

"Why?" I brushed my thumb over her knuckles.

She shrugged, her eyes on our hands.

"Emmie?"

"The medication gives me nightmares." Her voice cracked on her whispered confession.

"You need me to stay?"

She shook her head, withdrawing her hand.

I hesitated. "You want me to stay until you fall asleep?"

"I'm okay. I'm used to it."

"What do you dream about?"

"Monsters." She shuddered.

I frowned. "The real or imagined type?"

She jerked, head swinging my way, staring at me with wide eyes. "How did you...?"

"We all have bones that rattle." I tapped the side of my head. "Memories writher and morph in my dreams until I can't tell what is real and what my brain created."

She blew out a long breath, her eyelids growing heavy. "I really hate being weak."

"You're weak in body at the moment, true. But soon you'll be strong and kicking all our arses again."

She chuckled, her lashes fluttering down to dust the bruised shadows under her eyes. "Yeah, I will," she mumbled. "I just hate the nightmares."

I reached over, pressing a kiss to her forehead.

She blinked up at me, "What was that for?"

"To hurry the sweet dreams."

She grinned, her eyelids once again lowering. I watched, waiting. A moment later her breathing eased as she fell into unconsciousness.

"Luc? You ready?" Jetta asked from the door. Addie propped a hand on her hip, glancing from Emmie to me and back. Jack entered, settling in my seat in the corner.

I hesitated, watching Emmie's chest rise and fall peacefully.

"Yeah. Let's go."

EMMIE

This dream always started the same.

A room with rows of desks, computers positioned just so. Children arranged by age, youngest at the front, eldest at the back. Girls on one side of the room, boys on the other.

I sat three rows from the back, the room silent bar the click of fingers on keyboards.

Sweat dripped down my spine as I hunched over, jabbing fingers against the keys. My eyes were dry, blurring. My stomach clenched with hunger, my tongue thick as I wished for water.

We had a choice. Complete the challenge or accept the punishment.

No one willingly chose the punishment.

The clock ticked on the wall. The little ones completing their tasks. The older students continued through the night, struggling to achieve our individual taskings.

I'd been told to investigate a local police officer. His financials, his history, anything I could find.

And then I was to create a destruction plan.

My fingers were silent on the keyboard. Around me, one-by-

one the students completed their tasks until only me and the teacher remained.

"Punishment or nourishment?" She asked, glancing pointedly at the clock.

I looked down at the text cursor. It blinked menacingly on the screen.

No. The word danced on the tip of my tongue even as my stomach clenched and my throat begged for water. If I refused, I'd be whipped.

My fingers flexed over the keys.

A paddle slapped down on the desk. "Decide!"

I pressed a key. Then another. Letters formed words, words formed sentences and sentences formed the demise of a person.

I submitted the pages, waiting for approval.

The teacher scanned the document, pursing her lips.

"This is good work. You may go."

I turned to the door.

"But fifteen lashes tomorrow."

I spun back around. "What!"

"God's work should not be questioned. Your hesitation brings shame to him."

I bit my tongue, clenching fists together. "I understand, sister." I forced the words out between clenched teeth.

The dream faded, leaving behind only the fear and guilt.

EMMIE

As much as I liked Dr. CJ, and I really did, right at this moment it took all I had not to hit him over the head with a bedpan. Preferably a used one.

"Ms Franklin?" Dr. CJ asked.

"I reject your diagnosis."

He blinked at my statement. "Ms Franklin–"

I'd spent the ten days recovering. I'd battled an infection. I'd vomited more in one day than I had in my entire life. I wore a bandage that itched like crazy. But this?

Ridiculous.

"Sixteen weeks to full recovery? It's too long." I sounded like a petulant child, and I didn't give a flying toot.

"Emmie–"

I shoved my hand up in Luc's face, halting whatever nonsense he was about to spout. The man may have spent the last few weeks working out of my hospital room, but I had no time for him right now.

"No. No words from you." I looked back at the doctor. "Tell me what I need to do to be out of here, home and healed."

The doctor blew out a slow breath.

"Your bones are still healing, and we can't start rehab until that infection is completely gone. We push this too quickly and we could damage the healing we've achieved. We're going as fast we can, but your body speaks for itself. It's telling us it needs more time." He tapped a pen against the clipboard in emphasis. "At this stage, another two days in hospital."

"And then I can go home?"

"And then, if you pass all the tests, you can go home."

I sat back on the bed with a smile.

"With a walker."

My smile twisted down.

"That's impossible. Her apartment's a walk-up."

I glared daggers at Luc. He ignored me.

Dr. CJ frowned. "Is Mr Falco correct? Does your apartment have stairs?"

I continued to scowl at Luc. "Yes, but it's *fine*."

The doctor shook his head. "No stairs. The injury alone makes you unstable, even with the walker. We need alternative arrangements until you're well enough to manage on your own."

"But–"

"She can stay with me."

"I'm not staying with you," I snapped, narrowing my eyes at Luc before switching my gaze back to the doctor, offering a breezy smile. "Seriously, I'm *fine*."

I can't afford not to be.

"I'm not discharging you unless someone is available to assist. You'll require a wheelchair, a walker, and eventually a walking stick. We haven't even got you up yet."

"But–"

"Emmie, I told you, you can stay with me," Luc interjected.

No way in hell, buddy.

I let out a frustrated grunt. "No. One." I held up a finger, ticking off the reasons. "You have work during the days. Two, I refuse to impose on you. Three, your house is under renovations, four–"

"You're not–"

Dr. CJ interrupted our bickering. "Another option would be our respite care suites. They're pricey, but have live in nurses, easy access to medical staff and facilities, and our gymnasium has an indoor pool to assist with your rehabilitation." The doctor cleared his throat, looking at Luc. "It's also a secure building."

I shook my head. "I don't think–"

"She'll take it."

"Luc!"

"Emmie." He ran a hand through his hair, looking exhausted. "Work is covering all this. If you won't stay with me, then that's your only option."

"I–"

"Just hush up and let Pax cover it. Without you, Jetta would be dead and he'd be living a half life."

Ugh.

"Fine." I crossed my arms over my chest, turning my nose up to the ceiling. "But don't expect me to like it."

He grinned, blue eyes dancing. "I would never dare presume."

The doctor cleared his throat. "I'll organise the paperwork."

He exited, leaving Luc and I locked in a stare battle. He looked away first.

"Ha! I win." I crowed, grinning.

"True. But I won the true battle." He tapped my leg, settling into the seat beside my bed.

I narrowed my eyes on him, taking in his familiar shape.

"You're a bully. You know that? You wrangle people into doing what you want."

"I prefer the term conscientious objector."

I rolled my eyes. "You're incorrigible."

"More compliments? Anyone would think you have a crush." He grinned.

My heart squeezed, butterflies taking flight in my stomach.

"They obviously don't know me then." I held up a hand, tapping my chest. "This heart is dead."

He rolled his eyes. "Puh-lease. You're a big softie." Luc reached across, running a thumb over my knuckles. "It's why I like you."

I looked down at our hands, feeling things I had no business feeling. I pushed down the emotions, ignoring the wistful regret for things I wanted but could never have.

"You should go." I whispered, gaze still locked on our hands. His thumb paused, then started its slow path once again.

"Nah," He drawled softly. "I'm good. Besides, I like the way you're looking at me."

I glanced up, blinking at him. "How I'm...? How am I looking at you?"

His lips quirked. "Like I'm full of awesome."

My lips lifted in an answering smile. "Sometimes you are."

"Only sometimes?" He shifted, lacing our fingers together.

"Don't push your luck, Falco."

He grinned. "Anyone ever told you, you're adorable when riled?"

I rolled my eyes, desperately fighting a blush. "If you're staying at least make yourself useful. Get me a cup of tea."

"Your wish, as ever, is my command." He rose, turning my hand over. He leaned down, bowing, pressing a kiss to the inside of my wrist. I watched, eyes wide.

He grinned, straightening. "Be right back."

As he left the room, I cradled the wrist in my other hand, running my thumb across the spot his lips had been.

"You're leaving." I whispered. "You can't do this."

Regret remained.

EMMIE

Two weeks after being admitted, they cleared me to move to the private respite facility located about fifty yards from the hospital. The rooms were equipped with accessibility items like push-open drawers and cupboards, assistance bars, a seat in the shower, and emergency call buttons in every room.

It felt like living in a really nice nursing home. Judging by the average age of my neighbours... I didn't want to know how much this cost.

"I want to go home." My bottom lip stuck out in a full pout. I knew I was being petulant, but damn it, I wanted my bed and my things. Not a duffel bag filled with whatever item of clothing Addie or Kel or whoever my maid of the day had thought to pack.

"I know. But think of this as a really nice holiday. Like a health clinic."

I laughed, tilting my head back to look up at Luc pushing my wheelchair. "Health clinic?"

"Would you have preferred something else?"

"Nursing home?"

"You know, nursing is the profession of providing care for the sick and infirm. Technically you wouldn't be incorrect for calling it that." He ruffled my hair playfully.

I leaned away from his hand, rolling my eyes. "Well done, Captain Definition."

"Do I get a cape?"

"Not that kind of captain."

"Well that's disappointing."

I laughed. "Suck it up, princess."

"Ugh." He made an exaggerated shudder. "Don't. Pax calls Jetta that, it's sickly sweet."

"Really?"

"Uh-huh."

"I think it's cute."

"My woman's not getting a cutesy nickname. She's gonna be Spitfire, or Hottie, or Karen."

"Karen?" I raised an eyebrow.

He shrugged. "Karen was my eighth-grade teacher. Every boy's wet dream."

I wrinkled my nose. "Right. Good luck with that. Every chick's secret wish is to be called by another's name."

"Hush, Minx."

"Nope. Not a thing."

"Totally our thing... Keys?"

"What?"

He let go of the chair, pretending to type. "Keys, get it?"

I rolled my eyes so hard I worried I'd pulled a muscle. "Just keep pushing."

"As you wish, Ms Keys!"

"Say it one more time and I'll–"

"We're here!" He stopped the wheelchair.

My physiotherapist, Amy, stood in the kitchen, waving as Luc rolled me through the entry.

"Hey! I'm just putting away your groceries." She closed a lower cabinet door, offering me a smile.

"Let me show you around."

Amy walked or, in my case, rolled us through the small space. The apartment itself was compact, but still bigger than my current flat. I guess it had to be, to accommodate wheelchairs and walkers.

"Remember, it's important to stand as much as you can and keep moving using the techniques we discussed. We'll work on gaining back your strength and mobility over the next few weeks, but as long as you can stand, you can walk." She handed me a bunch of papers. "These are my initial thoughts regarding your rehab regime and a suggested diet. At least until we get the all clear. We'll talk more about this at the first session. If there's nothing else, I'll see you tomorrow. Fair warning, it'll be brutal. We'll be getting you walking. We need to rebuild your motion and muscle strength in your other leg while we wait for the fractures to heal."

I nodded and, after goodbyes, she left Luc and I alone.

"What do you need?"

I blushed, avoiding his eyes as I muttered, "A bathroom."

"Right." He turned the chair, wheeling me down the hall to the room.

I'd started serious PT earlier that morning. I was used to being active. I held a black belt in karate. I tried to run at least five kilometres each day. I did both to stay fit and ensure that, when the time came, I'd be able to protect myself. Being weak was never an option.

Yet, here I was. Shaking like a new lamb, weak as a baby, relying on Luc to assist me to the bathroom. He helped me up, shifting me in a practiced motion.

"This is embarrassing." I tucked my head into his neck.

Even the act of simply standing had robbed me of my strength.

"Nah." He grinned down at me. "Makes me look gentlemanly. I get to imagine I'm a ye olden knight, sent to help the damsel in distress."

"Oh great." I rolled my eyes. "I'm the flake in this story."

"The damsel who fought a dragon and won but got hurt doing it?"

"Slightly better."

"The damsel who fought a dragon and won and now gets the whole pot of gold?"

"Better."

"The damsel who fought a dragon, won, and gets the gold and the guy?"

"I'd prefer the dragon. I want to be Khaleesi, riding my giant fire-breathing pet through the skies."

"Naked."

"What?" I laughed, swatting at his forearm. "Luc!"

"Hush. My fantasy." He positioned my hands onto the bar next to the toilet. "Okay?"

"Yeah good. Go." I waved him off with one hand.

"Call if you need, I'll be right outside." He walked out, leaving me to silently die of embarrassment.

The mirror and sink were opposite the toilet, about six feet away. As I sat doing my business, I examined my face in the mirror. It didn't paint a pretty picture. Pale cheeks, hair limp and greasy from lack of washing and sunlight, dark rings circling both eyes.

You don't have time for this.

I finished, heaving myself up. Standing, I realised I couldn't make the short distance to the sink unassisted. Feeling useless, I called out. The door immediately opened, Luc coming to help.

"And to think, I told all the girls you weren't a pervert," I joked to hide my mortification.

He held an arm out, bracing as I leant against him.

"Don't worry. The affidavit is only valid in Queensland." We both smiled as he easily assisted me the five steps to the sink. I washed my hands, leaning heavily against the basin before collapsing into the chair. He pushed me out and down to a bedroom.

He'd turned down the bed. A TV sat on the large dresser on the wall at the foot of the bed. A sitcom played on mute.

Slowly, Luc helped me to rise and pivot to sit on the bed. The small effort of moving caught up with me. I settled in as he shuffled around the room, unpacking my clothes, and putting items I may need within arm reach of the bed.

He exited and returned a moment later, a glass of water and some pills in hand. I made a face but took them, forcing it down.

As I started to drift off, the bed dipped.

"What are you...?"

"Ssh. Go back to sleep." He settled on the other side of the mattress.

"Luc..." I didn't know what to say. "Thank you."

He pressed a kiss to my forehead, whispering, "For good dreams."

I settled, sinking deeper into the bed while he gently stroked my hair as I fell asleep.

EMMIE

"**G**od, Luc." I panted his name, breathless.

"That's it. A little more. You're so close." He encouraged.

"It's too much."

"Fuck, Em. You're so close. Come–"

"Oh my God..." I groaned and collapsed into Luc's arms. My legs were jelly, my arms aching. I looked up at him, flushed, sweaty, and deliriously proud. "I did it!"

"Yeah, you did! Ten whole minutes! You're killing it today!" He grinned back.

"Ten-minute rest, then round two, Emmie." We both looked over at my physical therapist. Or Satan as I now called her.

"Computer says no, Amy."

"Computer says get your arse up and keep going." She turned away to assist another client.

I poked my tongue out.

"I saw that," she called over her shoulder.

Recovering from a bullet wound hurt. It hurt so bad. It hurt and took forever. Every little movement sent pain shooting up and down my thigh; it all hurt. Sometimes it even hurt to breathe.

The muscles on the left side of my body screamed in protest as my leg trembled. Despite my joy at today's achievement, I felt helpless, weak, frustrated, angry, and depressed.

Two weeks post-hospital and I'd finally started shuffle-walking during physiotherapy. And, glory be, I could stand for a whole three minutes unassisted.

Not good enough. You're vulnerable. You need to–

"Ten minutes are done. Round two, Ding!" Luc pretended to hit a gong. "Begin."

I groaned, struggling to push off the chair. My fingers death gripped the arm rests.

"If you make it ten minutes – just ten, Emmie– then I'll buy you some chocolate." Luc dangled that delicious temptation in front of me.

Gritting my teeth, I shuffle-walked those ten minutes, using the balance bars to stubbornly hold myself up as I paced on the treadmill.

One, two, five, eight, ten! Thank God!

Grunting in frustration and pain, Luc caught me as I dropped back into the wheelchair. Tears burned, threatening to overflow as he pulled my head against his stomach and rubbed my back soothingly.

"White, dark, or milk?"

"Frozen bananas rolled in dark chocolate with nuts," I muttered fighting for control.

"There's always money in the banana stand."

I huffed out a tired but surprised laugh. "I didn't know you watched Arrested Development." His hand slipped under my jaw, tilting my head back.

"There's a lot you don't know about me." Our eyes held.

Luc opened his mouth about to speak when Amy interrupted.

"Time for round three, Emmie!"

I swore softly as Luc chuckled.

"What do I get this time?" I asked as I slowly braced myself, readying to stand.

"I'll break you out of this heap next Saturday and take you to karaoke."

"Not exactly a bribe."

"Let me finish." He tapped my nose with his finger in admonishment. "And I'll sing any song you want."

"I pick One Direction." I flashed a smile as I struggled to push myself up off the wheelchair.

"The fuck you do!" Luc stepped back as I took a step forward, my hands braced in a death lock on the beams.

"Never thought I'd say this, but fail. Just give up!"

I wanted to laugh but could barely breathe as I panted through the pain and exhaustion. I stumbled forward, taking two steps as the treadmill slowly rolled under my feet. I gasped, bracing as my leg muscles began to spasm.

"Come on, Emmie!" I glanced over to see Addie, Kel, and Jetta all standing at the door to the gym, cheering. Luc straightened from his crouch before me and glared at them. "Don't encourage her!"

"If you're trying to sabotage her, it must be good!" Kel laughed, punching a fist in the air. "You go girl!"

I took another step, pushing through the pain.

Four minutes down, six to go.

"For the love of the Rolling Stones, don't do this to me!" Luc begged as I hit five minutes.

Half way.

Pleas for mercy, cheers from the girls, and my own determination to see Luc suffer pushed me over the threshold. As

I slumped into his arms, gasping for breath, I grinned up at him.

"Damn, Keys." He smiled down at me, blue eyes twinkling. "Guess I better brush off my boy band moves."

I huffed out a quiet chuckle, feeling hands on me. The girls were right there, helping Luc rearrange my body into the wheelchair.

"She done?" Jetta asked.

Amy came over, hands moving to her hips. "Em?"

I sighed, closing my eyes, knowing this was her way of asking me to push my limits.

"One more. Then stretches."

Amy nodded, grinning in approval. "Good girl. Finish on a high note."

My final attempt took me twice as long, the treadmill slow. My leg shook uncontrollably, my body felt a limp noodle while my hip burned. I fought the pain, gritting my teeth as I finally reached the end.

Thank you, God.

I lay on the mats, Amy stretching out my joints, listening to her and Luc banter, too tired and broken to make small talk. I wanted a bottle of painkillers and silence. I wanted my bed.

"You're good." Amy stood, holding a hand out to help me to a sitting position. "Shower, then rest. Take two painkillers, no more. I want to see how you go after. Make sure you stand and do those stretches tonight. Tomorrow we'll get you into the pool."

I nodded, no energy left.

"She's all yours. Put her in the chair to get back. She's not going to make it on the walker." Amy slapped a hand on my shoulder, squeezing, before turning to another patient.

He helped me up and began to wheel me towards the bathroom area. A nurse stood waiting.

"Good workout?"

I nodded too exhausted to speak.

"She's wrecked. Doubt she'll be able to stand today." This came from Luc.

"Don't worry," the nurse said cheerfully, "We'll get her cleaned up."

Twenty minutes later, showered and dressed in stretchy pyjamas, my wheelchair handed off to Luc with a happy goodbye from the nurse.

Back in the apartment, the girls bustled about, dropping grocery bags and setting about cooking dinner. Addie ordered me to take a nap while they entertained themselves. I let Luc wheel me down the corridor and into the bedroom.

"Do you need a hand?"

I shook my head, bracing. It took me an agonizingly long time to stand, turn, then sit on the bed. I slowly swung my legs up and in, reaching for the blanket. Once settled, I looked up at Luc. In the time it had taken for me to get into bed, he'd returned with water and pills.

We didn't speak as I reached for them. Tossing my head back I swallowed with a gulp of water. He whisked the glass from my hand setting it on the bedside table.

I closed my eyes, every part of me throbbing in pain.

The bed dipped, a hand on my hair, gently brushing it away from my cheek.

"You did good today," he whispered, tracing the apple of my cheek.

I nodded, eyes still closed.

"It's gonna take time, Em. Don't beat yourself up."

I don't have time.

Tears I'd been fighting burned my eyelids.

"Dr. CJ said–"

"I know," I interrupted him quietly, curling into myself slightly. "I know, Luc. I get it. It's a matter of time." I blew out a shaky breath before looking up at him. "I have to tell you something."

"After you nap. I'll be in the lounge room chilling till you wake."

I fought back the warm feeling that settled in my belly every time he tried to take care of me.

"No." I shook my head firmly. "Now." I pulled in a breath. "I'm leaving."

His lips tugged up into a smile. "We've already been through this. In a few weeks you can–"

"I mean after this. Once I'm recovered. Consider this my notice. I'm leaving Canberra."

He turned to stone.

I struggled up, sitting on the edge of the bed beside him. "Luc–"

"Why?"

"It's time."

He turned, pinning me with a glare. "Is this because of the shooting?"

"No. Yes. No. I planned to resign before this."

"Why?"

"Because it's time."

He pushed off the bed, standing to pace. "What does that even mean?"

"I just need a change."

"I didn't know you were unhappy." He ran a hand through his hair. "You never said anything."

I'm not.

I shrugged.

"Where are you going?"

The lie fell easily from my lips. "London. I got a job offer and–"

"A job offer? Who?"

"A start-up. No one you know."

"So that's it. You're just leaving?" For a moment his blue eyes raked my face, searching for... something.

"Yes."

"Right." He turned abruptly. "Sleep well."

I waited, listening to him speak to the girls briefly before I heard the apartment door open and close.

It didn't reopen.

I let the tears come.

EMMIE

Luc hadn't come around for a week. I had no idea where he was, what he was doing, or if he would return.

Dr. CJ had told me I'd made good progress and agreed to sign off on me trying more complex physio. We'd started therapy on my bad leg, and I'd progressed to ten minutes of walking (though still stop-start). Amy had agreed I'd be able to upgrade to a walking stick soon. But for now, I zoomed about with my walker.

I miss Luc.

I shushed the voice, knowing that path led to poor choices. Once healed, I'd work my month while they found a replacement and then take off.

I was the queen of the quick getaway, getting closer to Luc would be a mistake.

He was a stayer. I ran.

Luc was a keeper. I was disposable.

This option kept us both safe.

The reminders didn't stop the pain I pretended didn't exist.

"Emmie?"

I blinked, looking at Jarrett. "Sorry?"

His gaze sharp, his wise eyes knowing, he sighed. "I said I've got an update, if you're interested."

I nodded. "Sure. I mean, of course."

I got what Jarrett dished out. This was his way of giving me an update on the investigation.

Following my release from hospital, I'd finally been briefed. The investigation into the shooting had ramped up. We suspected it related to Jetta, but the link wasn't yet clear. The local police were sharing info thanks to our contract with the Australian Federal Police.

The story went like this: Jetta's sister, Courtney, had become hooked on drugs. She'd gone in deep and now owed a large debt to a dealer by the name of Simon Esso. Esso had also been Jetta's dad's dealer back in the day. Turned out Esso had been sitting on the fact Jetta's dad also owed him money. Jetta's parents had tragically died in a car accident before the debt had been settled. Esso wanted his money.

These days, Esso operated out of four states. We knew about him as we knew about most crime figures in Australia, via our connections. When you worked in our line of business, you grew to know the big players. We'd had one or two run-ins with the guy previously, and each time Paxton had swiftly dealt with it. We were a good business, above board. We didn't deal with shady creeps.

The current working theory was the shooting had been a warning, a reminder of the stakes. But so far, the evidence didn't necessarily reflect a direct tie back to Jetta.

The cops had found the SUV abandoned and burnt out in bushland outside of Canberra. It'd been stolen. The occupants of the car were masked and covered, no identities. A dead end.

The bullet casings were from black-market firearms. One had matched a gun used in a previous drug-related shooting that'd been linked back to Esso. But it was weak. We were at a loss, the pieces of the puzzle hidden from us.

For the guys I worked with, this was an unacceptable outcome. They were working on the case 24/7 trying to come up with answers to all the questions.

And trying to protect Jetta.

Me? I wasn't of value to anyone. A dispensable pawn in the broader game, I'd quickly been ruled out as an innocent bystander caught in the crossfire.

"Our friend got in contact. He's ready to come home. Plans are in place, and our friends are organising the welcome."

I nodded. I got it. We could only say so much in an insecure environment.

Translation? Brean O'Malley, one of our agents working undercover in Esso's organisation wanted out. He'd been under for over a year. If he was calling, it meant the situation wasn't good. Not good at all.

"When's the party?"

"This weekend. After Jetta's concert."

With Courtney in rehab, Jetta had been forced to take her place in a reunion tour headed by the former band of Jetta's parents'. It was all very sudden and seemed a bit strange to me. But all power to Jetta for facing her fears.

It's more than you've ever done.

I squashed the little voice, turning back to Jarrett.

"Maybe I could–"

"It's okay. People understand you're unavailable." Jarrett's face hardened, his eyes telling me to not even think about it.

"Right." I slumped back in my chair, playing with my teaspoon. "Does Jetta know?"

"She didn't. She does now."

I nodded. Paxton had told the guys to keep things on the down-low with Jetta. Apparently, he didn't want her to worry. Personally, I thought it was a dick move. Paxton handled her with kid gloves, intentionally keeping her in the dark. Jetta was the victim here, she had every right to know about progress on the case.

"Explain to me how this concert came about?"

Jarrett shifted his weight, settling back in the chair. "Apparently her uncle, Paul White, was drummer for her dad's band."

"He's a producer now, right?"

"Yeah. And he manages Courtney."

"This was meant to be Courtney's concert?"

"Yeah. But with her in rehab, and Paul trying to keep that on the down-low, he went back to the sponsors and pitched an alternative."

"Jetta and her parents' band reuniting?" I scratched absently at the healing scar on my thigh. Jarrett reached out, swatting my hand away.

"Stop scratching. But yes. It's the ten-year anniversary of the Olivers' deaths. White proposed a reunion tour instead of cancellation."

"But the tickets would have already been sold to teenagers. Courtney's not exactly targeting her parents' demographic."

"The tickets were refunded. But the venues are the big cash. Even with insurance, they would have lost out."

"So, Jetta's agreed to sing?"

"She's headlining."

"She any good?"

Jarrett shrugged. "No idea."

"Well let me know how it goes."

"Will do." Jarrett stood, collecting our plates and cups, placing them in the dishwasher. I lifted, standing with the help of the walker.

"Thanks for coming over. I miss you guys."

Jarrett paused by the door. "He come yet?"

I hesitated, then shook my head. "Not yet."

"Right." Jarrett's face tightened.

"I'm leaving, Jarrett. He has every right to be upset. He's losing a star employee."

"If you think that's the only reason he's upset, then you're either an idiot or he's an ass who's letting you think that." Jarrett shook his head. "I've seen you two together. You have more chemistry than me and Ricky Martin."

I ignored the pleasant shiver that sparked down my spine at his words. "You've never met Ricky Martin."

"And if I ever did, we would make sweet explosions together."

We both chuckled. "Go." I shoved his arm with one hand. "Get back to work."

He winked. "On it. Bye, baby girl." He pressed a kiss to my forehead.

The door clicked shut leaving me with the walker and a room full of sadness.

"It's better this way," I reminded myself. "It'll be easier in the long run."

If only I could convince myself.

LUC

The lights outside Pax's office blinked off. I glanced at the clock, registering the late hour. The office was empty but for Pax, Jarrett, and myself. We were in Pax's office, nursing beers, pondering the woes of the world.

"She's driving me crazy." Pax muttered, thumb wearing at the label of his bottle.

"Emmie?" I asked.

"No, Jetta." He looked up, giving me a frown. "Why... no. I don't want to know."

"I do." Jarrett pointed at me. "First, we'll deal with Mister Grumpypants, then we'll get to you."

He tipped his bottle towards Pax. "Time to spill, Elliot."

Pax sighed, slumping back in his chair. "Jetta is..."

"Awesome? Talented? Gorgeous? Funny? Intelligent?" Jarrett prompted.

"Yes. And confusing, difficult, fearful, different."

"Mate." I rolled my eyes. "It's been ten years. Of course, the woman is going to be different. She's grown. You've changed."

Pax tapped a finger on the desk. "She's difficult."

"How?"

I watched him search for the words. "She... challenges me. Wants me to be someone I'm not."

I frowned, exchanging a glance with Jarrett. "What? You mean a show pony or something?"

"No. She wants everything. No secrets, no half-truths. She wants shit I'm not sure I can give her. I'm not even sure I can be true to myself. The only way I survived the shit we went through overseas is by building walls."

Afghanistan. Death of men I'd called brothers.

I took a long gulp of my beer.

"Do you love her?"

Pax blew out a breath, running a hand through his hair. "Don't think I ever really stopped. And it's fucking terrifying."

We were all quiet for a few moments.

"Do you want a future with her?" I asked.

Pax took a long moment. "For as long as I'm here, yes."

"Well, shit." Jarrett huffed. "Go home and get your house in order. The girl isn't asking a lot."

"I don't know how to give her the trust she's asking for. I don't know how to build that between us."

"Well, having this fucking conversation with *her* would be a good start." Jarrett pointed out.

Pax shoved up from the desk, heading for the door. "Shit. I gotta get home."

I sniggered, taking a sip of my beer.

"Oh no." Jarrett turned to me, waggling a finger in my face. "You're next, buddy."

"What did I do?"

"When was the last time you saw Em?"

I crossed my arms, staring Jarrett down. "When she last invited me."

"That girl is crazy about you."

"Bullshit. She's leaving. She's not interested in a–"

Jarrett held up a hand, sighing. "Goddamn straight people. Oprah, give me strength." He focussed back on me. "Swallow your damn pride, get in your fucking car, and go speak to her. She *says* she's leaving. Bitch, she hasn't left yet. Make her want to stay."

"She's just been shot. The last thing she wants is me hitting on her."

"Ru Paul, Diane Sawyer, and Freddie Fucking Mercury, give me strength!" Jarrett cursed, crossing himself. "I'm not asking you to bang her. I'm telling you to be her friend. Emmie is a woman who needs to be handled gently. Not because she's weak or a woman, but because she's got trust issues. She needs to be *wooed.*" Jarrett pointed the neck of his beer at me. "Woo her."

I sat back, considering his words. "You're a dick, you know that?"

"The truth always hurts." Jarrett stood, stretching. "And now Jarrett's relationship counselling session is over. I'm off to my tinder date. If I'm not in tomorrow, don't call me." He walked out, leaving me nursing a beer in Pax's empty office.

Woo her. Be her friend. Make her want to stay.

Jarrett was right.

Fuck, I'm a prick.

I couldn't just lay shit out the way I would with other women in my life.

Woo her. I can do that.

EMMIE

The loud knocking on my door was obnoxiously persistent.

I hauled myself out of bed, clutching at the walker and shuffling through the apartment as quickly as I could manage.

"I'm coming!" I yelled as I hit the lounge room entrance. I wrenched open the door and backed up the walker as Luc brushed past.

"Luc?" The door snicked shut behind me, closing us in.

He came to a stop in the middle of my living room, turning to face me, a frown creasing his brow.

"I'm sorry." He tucked hands into his jean pockets, gaze firmly on me. "I was a prick."

"Okay..." I drank in his appearance. Hair dishevelled, scruff slightly raggedy, tight royal blue T-shirt, dark wash jeans, and black Converse. Even at stupid o'clock in the morning, he looked like a model.

"I'm still pissed at you." His lips quirked up at the sides. "But I miss you too much to stay away."

I gripped my walker and counted to ten, waiting for my heart to stop hurting.

"Luc..."

"If you won't stay for–" His hands scrubbed rapidly over his face and hair. "Look. I just want you to be happy. If this London job is it, then so be it. But at least promise you'll visit."

It was deceptively easy to love Luc. And that's what made it hard to lie.

"Of course."

When I left, I wouldn't be able to visit. I'd be the kind of gone where they put your picture on the back of a milk carton.

But I couldn't tell Luc that.

Why not?

My gut twisted, memories and fear shadowing my rationale.

Luc's lips twisted up into a shadow of a smile. "Gives me an excuse to visit Europe."

Perhaps I wanted to pretend normality. Perhaps I'd embraced denial. Either way, I gave into my selfish desire for acceptance.

"I'll make sure to keep my diary free."

We stood in the middle of the room, staring at each other for a long moment. Finally, he broke eye contact, looking down at my leg.

"You're moving better."

"Yeah. I've been working hard."

He rubbed his chin. "It feel okay?"

"Aches but definitely improving."

We both stared at each other awkwardly, at a loss for words. Our easy friendship felt strained.

Finally, Luc asked, "There's a Studio Ghibli marathon on tonight. Wanna watch with me?"

"Are you joking? Yes! How did I not know about this?"

We went to the bedroom. I still had trouble sitting for long periods of time, and the bed was much more comfortable. Luc stretched out beside me, one arm tucked under his head, the other lazily draped across his stomach.

The credits rolled on *My Neighbour Totoro* when Luc rolled over, propping a hand on the side of his head.

"Can I come here? After the... party on Saturday?"

"Part– oh." Luc meant after they took down Simon Esso. I bit my lip.

After an operation you were jazzed, needed to talk it out. If you didn't have a long-term partner you reached out to a friend. Esso's operation was going down on Saturday. It would be over late Saturday night.

And Luc wanted to come and wind down with me.

Say no.

"What about Paxton?"

"Pax is busy with Jetta."

"Right." The blush warmed my cheeks.

"Saturday?"

Say no. It'll only make it harder to leave.

"Saturday night." I agreed.

EMMIE

I looked at the clock for what felt like the millionth time. The evil red numbers told me the truth.

Luc wasn't coming.

I wheeled my chair around, rolling into the kitchen.

Today had been a hard session. I'd tried a walking stick for the first time and fallen twice –thankfully landing on my good side. Amy had told me I'd pushed myself too hard and ordered me to rest for the next two days. No walker or stick.

I picked up the apartment's phone and hit Luc's digits, listening to the dial tone.

"This is Luc, leave a message." The beep sounded, waiting for me to speak.

"Luc, it's Emmie. I guess things didn't go to plan. I'm off to bed. Call me tomorrow. Hope nothing went wrong." I hit the end button, hesitating at putting the phone down.

Should I call Addie or Jarrett or one of the others and check if they're okay?

Tonight was Jetta's big concert. Tonight, we were meant to be taking down Simon Esso and his entire operation. Tonight, I would have an answer. Tonight, I would know if the men who shot me were the same men that were after Jetta.

And if they weren't...

I shut that thinking down.

You can't do anything right now. Not while you could barely hold your own body weight.

But what if...

"They'll call. You can't be distracting them just because you're feeling paranoid."

I placed the phone back on the counter and wheeled myself to the door. For the fifth time that night, I checked the locks, moving around the apartment to check the windows as well. Nightmares, paranoia, and fear.

What if...

In the bedroom, I hauled myself out of the wheelchair and onto the bed. I lay staring at the ceiling wishing I knew what had happened, wishing someone would call.

Finally, hours later, I fell asleep.

LUC

"We'll find her," I assured Pax as he sped down the dark road.

The concert was over. Jetta had rocked out, and we'd taken down Simon Esso exactly as planned. But in the chaos Jetta had disappeared.

Pax hunched over the steering wheel, his eyes on the dark road as we drove towards Fairburn. I texted Sawyer, trying to get an update on Jetta's mobile.

"I should have seen it," Pax muttered. "I knew the uncle was shifty as fuck."

Jetta's uncle, Paul White had kidnapped her. This whole time we'd been chasing Simon Esso when it was Paul White who had planned this shit.

A call lit the screen of Pax's phone.

"Why is Dylan calling you?" I asked, hitting accept and putting Dylan on loud speaker.

"His facility is where we put Courtney."

Dylan was an ex-colleague. He'd retired from the forces a year after us and set up a rehab clinic with his wife.

"Pax?" Dylan asked.

"Yo."

"Courtney's gone."

Pax pulled the SUV off to the side of the road. "She's what?"

"She's gone. Disappeared. We've looked everywhere. She went out for her meditation walk and never came back. Jeanette is beside herself."

"Motherfucker!"

I looked down at my phone, thumbs typing out the new information for Sawyer.

"'I'm sorry, Pax. I've let you—"

"No." He cut off Dylan's apology, swearing again. "No, Dylan. She's been kidnapped. Jetta's missing too. Shit is going off down here. It's not your fault. We dropped the ball. I underestimated our opponent."

Silence met this declaration. Finally, Dylan coughed, clearing his throat. "What can I do?"

"Look after Jeanette. We'll call you as soon as we know."

"Good luck."

Pax hit the end button, muttering, "Fuck."

"Fuck about covers it," I agreed.

"This is escalating."

"We're on it," Brean assured from the backseat.

"It was meant to be me."

"What?" I twisted to look at my best friend.

"This whole thing. It's meant to be me," he muttered, fingers drumming on the steering wheel.

"What are you on about?" Brean leaned between the seats, frowning.

Pax turned the car, merging back into traffic. "Nothing, forget it."

Forget it?

"Seriously, Pax?" I shook my head. "After this is said and

done, we're sitting down for a beer and you're talking that dark shit out."

We arrived at the office to a packed room. AFP and our guys were frantic as news trickled in. Our lead said it was likely Jetta and Courtney would be held at White's Thredbo property. Sawyer had sent through a schematic of the building. A large property with three wine cellars scattered across the grounds, the place was heavily fortified.

"Who the fuck needs three wine cellars?" I asked, frowning at the damn map.

Rich fuckers.

Swat arrived, readying for the extraction. They planned to squeeze us out, push us to the back.

Fuck that.

I pulled Pax aside.

"Plan?"

"I'm going in. Fuck what they say."

I nodded. "I got you. Whatever you need."

Pax clasped my forearm. "You'll take care of her, yeah?" His eyes were dead.

"Yeah. But, dude, you'll be here to take care of her yourself."

He looked away. "Let's go."

LUC

Wind whipped through the helicopter. Paul White, kingpin of a fucking drug cartel. He'd had Jetta and Courtney under his thumb for years. Simon Esso had been nothing but a figure head, a pawn used by Paul for his ultimate purpose. What that was? We had no idea.

The helicopter banked, starting to descend.

I adjusted my grip on my gun, jerking my head up at Pax. He nodded.

Let's do this.

We bounded out, racing down the hill towards the cellars.

I hesitated, slowing as a figure appeared in the doorway of one. Paul White held a gun to Jetta's head.

"Fall back!"

Paxton powered forward, ignoring the directions.

Jesus fuck.

I shook off my unease, following Pax, trusting his instincts.

Paul had a gun pressed to Jetta's forehead. His eyes were wide, crazed. I breathed, stopping, lining up my shot.

Breathe. Look for the gap.

Years of training took over, I tuned out Paul's rants, my eyes sharp as I watched the scene play out. Body language told me more than a person's words.

He ranted, Paxton watching. Jetta's eyes were firmly trained on Pax, hope and fear warring.

Paul pressed the gun harder to Jetta's temple, his body language changing. I raised my pistol, squeezing.

Paul's gun stalled in the chamber, jumping. My bullet grazed his cheek as he flinched.

Fuck.

Pax's bullet hit Paul's shoulder, another his arm, while my second embedded in his chest. He stumbled backwards, Jetta still clutched to him.

I moved, watching as they struggled, Jetta desperately squirming to get away. Paul tripped, pulling them both down into the cellar.

"Fuck!"

I chased Pax down the stairs, finding him at the bottom, blood decorating his body, Jetta moved into the recovery position.

"It was meant to be me. It was meant to be me," Pax chanted as Jetta spluttered. I moved immediately to Paul, taking their back against the potential danger.

I dragged Paul away, pressing a hand to stem the bleeding at his chest. The man gasped, his eyes wide with fear.

A woman crouched behind me while the tactical team swarmed the cellar, securing the room.

"You the sister?" I barked.

She nodded, eyes narrowed on Paul. "Courtney."

A man dropped beside me, pulling out a first aid kit.

I raised up, letting the medic work. Moved to the younger Oliver.

"You good?"

She nodded, eyes still on her uncle.

"Courtney?"

She finally turned, blinking up at me. "Sorry?"

I frowned. "You hit your head?"

"I..." She swallowed. "I don't think so?"

I shrugged off my jacket, wrapping her in its warmth.

"Let's get you above ground and in a chopper. They'll be dropping Jetta at a hospital. Let's make sure you're there too."

She allowed me to escort her up the stairs, her teeth chattering. The shock kicking in.

Pax had tucked Jetta into a seat, the pilot turning to watch. I strapped Courtney in, jumping into the seat next to her. Pax looked at me, his arms around his girl.

"You good?" I asked.

He nodded, giving Jetta a tight squeeze. "Solid, mate."

I nodded at the pilot. "Ready when you are, chief."

The helicopter lifted, starting the journey back to Canberra.

Jetta leaned against Pax, her eyes drifting closed. I watched as Pax leaned down, pressing kisses to her hair. The relief on his face was painful. It was as if a burden had been lifted.

At the hospital, they rushed Jetta and Courtney off for testing. Pax stood outside the theatre while they were in getting X-rayed. Jetta had injured her wrist in the fall down the cellar stairs.

I leaned against the wall next to him, hands in pockets as I watched his face.

"You wanna talk about it?"

He sighed, running a hand over his face. "I should have told you."

"Of course."

He shoved my arm. "You don't even know what I'm talking about."

"Doesn't matter. You should have told me anyway." I bumped his shoulder. "We're in this."

Pax blew out a breath. "I need therapy."

I nodded, biting my tongue. He glanced at me, then huffed out a laugh. "Yeah, yeah. You told me so."

I shrugged. "We can't all be perfect."

He snorted before sobering. "It's fucked up, but after the incident... I thought I was on a countdown."

I raised an eyebrow. The incident. Two words to describe the event that changed our lives. Two of our best friends ripped from this world. The trajectory of our life changed as Pax suffered a life changing injury, and we were both left to deal with memories that in war were all too familiar.

"PTSD?"

"I guess." He rubbed his chest. "You ever think about it?"

"All the time." I swallowed. "But I also think about Brick and Limo. I try to be and live the life they didn't get. Do them proud and all that shit. You know?"

Pax sighed, slumping into the wall. "I was prepared to die. I'm not sure I know how to live."

"We all gotta go sometime, bro." I jerked my head towards the theatre. "You ask Jetta for help?"

"No. But I'm gonna get her to go to therapy with me." He pushed off the wall. "Gotta get mine and her heads right if this thing is gonna last."

I chuckled. "Bro, you've been hung up on her for ten years. If it wasn't going to last you wouldn't be here right now."

He rolled his eyes. The doors behind us opened, a bed rolling out. Jetta smiled from under a pile of blankets.

"You good to look after them if I take off?" I asked.

"Yeah. Come over tomorrow. They're gonna need the love."

"Of course." I clasped my forearm to his, squeezing tight. "One day at a time, Paxton. That's how we get through this."

He nodded, lips thinning.

I squeezed once more, dropping his hand to slap him on his back.

I turned, waving to Jetta as I headed for the exit. "No more adventures, Missy!"

She laughed, offering me a wave.

I walked out of the hospital, heading for my car. The adrenaline had worn off, leaving only guilt and anger in its wake.

"Fuck." I glanced at my watch. Late.

As I started my car, I debated the merits of visiting Emmie. My stomach clenched as I remembered Pax's face, his mutters as he positioned Jetta's body.

"Fuck it." I turned left, heading for Em's respite centre.

EMMIE

The bed dipped, ripping me from a deep sleep as I rolled into a hard body. I hit out, my hands automatically trying to fend off the intruder.

"Oof." The body let out an expletive before hands came up to restrain my struggles. "Emmie! Stop! It's me!"

I froze. My heart thumped uncontrollably in my chest. In the soft light of the bedside lamp, there he was.

Luc.

He looked horrible. Exhausted. A quick glance at the clock said it was close to 5:00 a.m.

"What are you...?" I choked out the words, my voice strangled, still tight with panic.

"We just got back." He let my hands drop. "Everyone's okay."

"But if you just...?" I pushed to sitting.

He pulled me in, avoiding my hip as he tucked his face in my hair, shuddering.

"It all went south. We got Esso and his whole operation. Turns out the AFP were right, Esso was a puppet. The master was Paul White, Jetta's uncle."

I brushed hands over his back, frowning at the rigidity of his muscles. "Fuck. Just, fuck." His arms flexed around me. I pulled him tighter.

"I've never seen Pax like that. Not since... he was... I couldn't do anything." He pulled back, shaking his head. "We nearly lost her, Em. Paul, he kidnapped Jetta while we were busy with Esso."

"How?" They'd had people on her. We weren't some half-bit operation.

"Her guard got caught in a distraction. It was like Paul was three steps ahead of us, pulling all our strings. It was..." He didn't say anything for a long moment, letting me stroke his back.

"He took Courtney too. Wanted them dead."

"I don't understand. Why?"

"It's fucked. The whole thing is fucked. A twisted, fucked-up revenge ploy. The guy's deranged. Jetta's mum left Paul for her dad. Paul and the dad were band mates. Paul stayed with the band but came up with this plan to get her back. It involved drugs and shit. I don't fully understand. When they died, Paul had nothing. He transferred all those years of hate and loathing to Jetta and Courtney. None of it makes sense to anyone but Paul White. There's no logic or reason or..." His voice trailed off.

"Sick people do evil things," I whispered.

"Esso's people talked. Paul organised the shooting. It was a warning for Jetta."

I closed my eyes.

Safe.

That doesn't mean you get to stay.

"He pulled a gun on her."

"Jetta?"

"She's fine. The bullet stalled in the chamber. Pax shot

him. One in the shoulder, one in the arm. I got him in the chest. The bastard isn't even dead. He's in surgery. ICU. Fucker will probably live."

His bloodshot eyes looked weary.

"I wanted to kill him. I was second down into the cellar, saw Pax freaking out over Jetta. Her covered in blood, seeing my best friend getting blood all over himself, crying, rocking. I–" He turned away, fists clenching.

"It's okay, Luc, it's okay." I lifted a hand to cup his jaw. "Let it out."

"I haven't fucking seen him like that since Afghanistan. He lost it tonight. Fucking broke down. The shit he was saying. He thought he was going to die. PTSD. PT-fucking-SD. Jesus. Do you know how many friends I've lost from that? From the fucking voices in their heads? And here I am, my best fucking friend, and I didn't know. I didn't even fucking know. If Jetta–"

"She didn't. They're fine. You said they were. All of them. If White lives or if he dies, it doesn't matter. What matters is it's over and they're good. Pax and Jetta will work it out. They will, because they deserve a beautiful life. We all do." I tried to soothe him.

Luc's eyes searched my face once, twice, three times. Like he was memorising it. Unable to bear the intensity I settled into the bed, pulling him down beside me.

"Sleep. We'll see them when you're rested."

"Emmie..." He fell silent. His hands roamed my body, brushing my side, back, and face while he fidgeted, shifting about. Eventually his hands slowed and his breathing evened out. I lay like that, Luc wrapped tight around me, my fingers gently combing his hair, keeping watch as he slept.

This was what friends did. Right?

You keep telling yourself that.

EMMIE

I was bored. Bored out of my brain.

The respite facility had a recreation centre. The centre was a gathering place for those who stayed here. The room consisted of faded vinyl floors, baby-blue walls, a TV, and some old couches. Scattered here and there were a few tables and chairs for coffee or tea, reading or playing board games.

I'd waged war against Zac, a sassy fourteen-year-old stuck here while undergoing treatment for leukemia. I don't want to brag, but I was whooping his arse in chess. Granted, his eyes kept wandering to fifteen-year-old Sonya. I'd noticed her eyes wandering his way occasionally.

A text lit up my phone.

Luc: What you doing?

Me: Beating children...

Luc: Are you stealing their candy too?

Me: Only when the nurses aren't around

Me: Truthfully? I'm bored. Tell me something fun

Luc: You want me to break you out?

Me: Can't, Physio at 7am. Need to be in bed early

Luc: I'll be there in 30
Me: ??
Me: Luc?
Me: Hello?

All hope of a decent game of chess was lost as Zac gave into the allure of the pretty Sonya, and I continued to glance at my phone awaiting a reply.

A commotion at the door to the rec centre interrupted my pack up. Luc walked in, carrying a guitar and small amp. He winked at me, before heading to the stage area. Normally reserved for school choirs or the yearly Christmas play, today it was apparently playing host to Luc's band.

King, Dom, and Mark, Luc's band mates, followed, waving and calling greetings. Jetta strolled in, hand in hand with Paxton ten minutes later. She threw a smile my way, heading for the stage.

Paxton claimed the seat beside me. The residents watched, murmuring. I saw the resident gossip head for the doors. We'd be joined by the rest of the patients soon enough.

"What is even happening right now?" I asked, gesturing to the stage.

Pax smirked. "I'd say he's trying to impress you."

I opened my mouth to respond only to be interrupted by Luc.

"Yo, yo, yo." His voice pitched and he nodded after a moment at the sound level. His head came up, his eyes twinkled and he looked right at me.

"We're Behind Utopia, and I hope you don't mind that we've hijacked your Sunday afternoon."

The residents laughed.

"Take your shirt off!" This came from Shirley, who punctuated her excitement with a clap of her hands. The woman had to be at least ninety and still rocked it.

#GrandmaGoals

"Maybe later." Luc winked at her, then turned back to the rest of the gathering. "Tonight, we also have a special guest, Ms Jetta Oliver." He nodded to Jetta who stood beside him, microphone in hand. She grinned shyly at the squeals that followed Luc's introduction.

"I thought the concert was her first and final with the tour now cancelled?" I asked, turning to Pax.

"Decided to face her fear. She's too good for the shadows. Fucking proud of her." Pax's eyes remained firmly on his woman.

I hid my smile.

"We're here to entertain and amaze you – we hope. So, without further ado..."

The band started and launched straight into a rousing rendition of Sam Hunt's "House Party."

The majority of the residents were unable to dance due to injury or sickness. Instead we clapped, stamped, and chair boogied. I think I fell a little in love with Luc for giving the residents a unique and unexpected way to break the monotony of illness.

The band crossed genres, launching into "Classic" by MKTO, "Dear Future Husband" by Meghan Trainor, then into "Timber" by Pitbull. Jetta killed it. She owned the stage, moving into the crowd, dancing with little old women, laughing at the old men, living it up with the teens.

Luc left the stage, coming to undulate over Shirley, who reciprocated by trying to feel his crotch. Pax and I both laughed until tears ran down our face.

The young kids loved it. They called out requests and

filmed the band on their phones, most of them focussing in on Jetta.

They flowed through old classics, Luc rocking out, his growly voice sending pleasant shivers curling down my body as he belted out Stevie Wright's, Evie, only he changed the lyric to 'Emmie'.

I rolled my eyes, ignoring the slight flutter in my stomach as he pointed at me, grinning.

Finally, after an hour of music and fun, people started flagging, and they wrapped it up with a rousing rendition of Journey's "Don't Stop Believing." Perfect.

Once the crowd dissipated, I pulled myself to standing, using the walking stick to cross to where they were packing up. Luc watched me slowly shuffle across the linoleum floor, his eyes on my legs.

"Well, that was some surprise." I smiled, reaching him.

"We had practice anyway, just moved venue."

"Thank you." I reached out, touching his arm. "Seriously, thank you."

"What are friends for?" He ruffled my hair before turning to finish packing.

EMMIE

On my seventh week, Dr. CJ finally allowed me to go home. It took me thirty minutes to walk up to my apartment. Luc had time to go up, open my door, dump my bags, put the kettle on, and walk back down to help me up.

He never complained as I huffed and puffed my way up, determined to do it myself.

When we finally walked through that door, I collapsed on the couch face down, loathed to move.

A mug of tea and a glass of water appeared on the coffee table. Luc's arms snaked around my torso, and he gently shifted me up, positioning a pillow on my bad side.

As I settled, he moved to sit at the foot of my couch, scowling and shaking his head.

I glanced over as I reached for the meds and water. "What?"

"Don't know if I should leave you. Maybe you should stay with me. At least I don't have stairs."

"You do too!"

"Only to the extra rooms downstairs. You don't need to use them. My dungeon is still under construction."

I laughed throwing the painkillers and antibiotics in my mouth, tilting my head back, downing the water.

I'd developed another unfortunate infection in my thigh two days ago. They'd let me come home on the condition I returned every second day to outpatients for checking until it cleared. Either way, it sucked balls. At least I was on the tail end of the recovery period. Another few days and I would be off the meds.

I grimaced at the taste of the medication before stretching forward to dump the cup and pick up the mug. My side protested the movement, but I didn't comment. Luc sipped his coffee, giving me a side eye.

I raised an eyebrow at him in question.

"You haven't answered my question."

"What question?"

"Moving in with me."

I blinked. "You can't be serious."

"As a bullet wound."

"Ha. Soooo funny." I shook my head. "No. I need to get back into a routine. I need to be home with my things and my clothes and water my plants. Look at my herbs, they're–"

"Perfectly fine. I watered them." I blinked at him, looked at the herbs and then back to him. Luc rubbed a hand over his face, rasping fingers across his stubble.

"I'm not comfortable with you being here alone, Em. What happens if you fall in the shower or something?"

"I would die before letting you see me naked."

Luc grinned, the corners of his eyes crinkling. "I guess I shouldn't mention the ambulance ride then?"

I paused, tea halfway to my mouth. "Wait, what?"

He threw his head back, laughter sending his shaggy hair bouncing. "Gotcha!"

"Dear lord. I... You need to leave. Now!" I shoved him with my good foot and then groaned as my body protested the movement. He grinned, reaching over to rub my left calf.

I turned away, face flaming, but not withdrawing. His fingers were hitting the tight muscles just right.

Luc changed subject. "Pass the remote."

We settled in, finding a *Die Hard* marathon.

Three hours later, I woke in bed, pain meds and water on my bedside table, a note tucked under the glass.

Apartment's locked. Sleep well, Beautiful.

IT TOOK me an age to shuffle down the stairs the next morning. My pits were damp, and I couldn't quite catch my breath by the time I reached the ground. Leaning heavily against the brick wall of the staircase, I raised the arm that wasn't clutching my cane in limp celebration.

"Yay...!"

"Hey."

My head shot up as Luc filled my vision. Leaning casually against the outer wall of the apartment building, a coffee cup in one hand, aviator sunglasses protecting him from the glare of the early morning sun, a black and blue collared, long-sleeved shirt open at the neck. He'd left his black jacket open over the long shirt. His spare hand held a second cup of steaming brew.

Luc tilted the first to his mouth for a sip as I struggled to focus.

"What are you doing here?"

"Good morning to you too." He pushed off the wall, coming to stand in front of me.

"Tea?" He held out the spare cup, as I continued panting and leaning against the brick wall of the stairwell entrance. I ignored the cup.

"Seriously, Luc. What are you doing here?"

He shrugged, still holding out the tea. "I was in the area."

I looked around the deserted car park. A bike on bricks, my little shitbox car–Rudolph–and Luc's Alfa Romeo were the only cars in the empty lot.

"You were in the area... Okay, Pinocchio."

He grinned, eyes crinkling. "You know I love these pet names, Keys."

I pushed off the wall, not wanting to look weak. He took another sip before pushing his sunglasses up his nose with his thumb.

Birds chirped in the distance, cars passed the empty lot, and I struggled to supress my annoyance.

I was unsuccessful. "Seriously, what are you doing here?"

He ignored the question.

"Never seen that dress before."

My dress was an old gift from Addie. Knee length, I'd paired the robin's-egg blue patterned sundress with a long coat Kel had gifted me last year, thick tights to ward against the cold, and flats.

I flipped him off, pissed at his lack of answers. I turned, moving towards my car, gritting my teeth against the pain, cane making an angry clicking noise on the pavement as I shuffled forward.

Luc fell into line beside me as we crept towards the car.

"I'm just saying. You look nice. Healthy."

"Yeah. Sure." I rolled my eyes. "I'm sure the general public will assume the cane is a fashion statement."

"We could take my car, you know." He talked down to his coffee cup, ignoring my sarcastic statement. I halted, twisting my neck to look up at him.

"I have a car." I pointed at my little red machine. "See? It even runs." I sarcastically jingled the keys clutched in my free hand.

"And I have a better one."

I couldn't argue with that. His Alfa Romeo was gorgeous.

"Mine is also higher than yours. And you get to sit there and look pretty." His eyes met mine, a slight smirk on his lips. "And you don't need to move your foot for the clutch."

My little Rudolph was a manual. I hadn't been looking forward to the pain.

"Besides, she needs a good rev. I've left her rusting in the garage too long since I got the bike."

I sighed heavily, shifted to my left, and aimed for his car. I didn't ask questions, grateful to not have to freaking drive anywhere with this bloody injury. But he didn't need to know that.

He clicked the locks, and in I slid, taking the cup of tea from him and letting him close the door behind me. As he walked around the car, I released a small groan and breathed deeply against the pain.

We didn't speak as Luc got in. I took another sip of tea, then glanced over, catching him watching me. "What?"

"You're not ready to do this."

I frowned at his tone. "I am doing this. I need this, Luc."

His eyes raked over my face. Whatever he saw there made him sigh.

"Fuck." A hand pushed through his hair. "Fuck me." He

turned to the wheel, hand going to the ignition. "Drink your fucking tea before I change my mind."

I hid a grin, lifting the cup to my lips. "*Sailor Moon* tonight?"

"No." His eyes met mine. "The last time we watched that I dreamt I was Tuxedo."

"Hot. I'd totally date him." I sipped my beverage as Luc backed out of the lot.

"Oh really? Is it the mask or the tux that makes you hot?"

"Neither." I watched his strong hand move the gear stick, trying to ignore the warm feeling pooling deep in my belly as we spoke.

"Have you ever read *Fifty Shades of Grey*?"

Luc gave me a look.

"Okay... seen the movie?"

He rolled his eyes and looked back at the road.

"So, no on the *Fifty*. Okay. Got it. As the story goes, in *Fifty Shades* the lead male character says to the lead female character–" I deepen my voice imitating Mr Grey, "–I don't *do* romance."

Luc sputtered out a laugh. "What the fuck?"

I nodded emphatically. "Right? It's okay he redeems himself later, but yeah. Jerk."

We both lapsed into comfortable silence as he concentrated on negotiating out of my apartment complex.

"Continue," he directed as he eased the car into traffic.

"Well, I like the fact Tux is a guy who appreciates romance. He doesn't see it as sissy or silly. He gets that making his woman feel appreciated is a big thing. That's the kind of guy I'd like to date." God knew it would never happen.

He laughed. "You're such a romantic."

"I know." I grinned unrepentantly.

"Sooo..." He drew out the word.

"So?" I mimicked, balancing the now empty cup on my knee.

"You like music."

After a long pause, I laughed. "Well, yeah. And...?"

"You've never come to one of my gigs." True. The first time I'd seen him perform was at the rehabilitation centre.

"And...?" I asked.

We cruised to a stop at the traffic lights. Luc's blue eyes met mine.

"And I want you to come to my house party next weekend. We'll be playing. You should at least see us once more before you jet off to London."

Luc's house was old, decrepit, and badly in need of a complete renovation. The only thing that didn't need improvement was the outdoor area. The old owners had created their own little piece of perfection. Luc planned to slowly renovate it himself.

"Okay." The word flew out of my mouth before I could reel it back.

"Good." He refocused on the road. We sat in companionable silence for another few minutes.

"Will you drink?"

I blinked over at him. "What?"

"Will you drink? Have a beer? Or a wine. Let yourself have fun."

"I don't drink." The automatic response fell with ease.

"Why?" I watched his profile, the strong jaw with its hot dusting of scruff. His slightly too long dark hair.

"I'm on medication." The excuse rolled easily off my tongue.

His eyes flicked over to me, then back to the road.

"You won't be next weekend."

True. I shouldn't have asked him to come to my last check-up.

"I... I like to be in control." I tried to put a seed of truth into my answer.

"And?"

I shrugged. "I just do. End of story."

We didn't talk as he drove the rest of the way to the office.

EMMIE

"I love this song!" I yelled at Jetta and Addie, struggling to be heard over the music as we all shimmy-danced on our pool chairs.

We were at Luc's house party on one of the last good days of warmth. The sun had set an hour ago, and Luc's house now teemed with people.

My leg ached, and I felt bone weary after a long week back at work, but damn was I glad I'd womaned up and came tonight.

Jarrett arrived back to our little spot, dumping our drinks on a small table someone had dug up for me.

Pax handed over a giant bowl of chips, as Luc and his band flowed straight from a Led Zeppelin classic into a smooth Nirvana jam. I grinned and stole a chip.

"Come on." Pax led Jetta onto the makeshift dance floor. He pulled her close as they slow danced to "Smells Like Teen Spirit." Addie and I giggled as Jetta and Pax ignored everything, swaying to their own tune as people rocked out around them.

"I want that," Jarrett sighed, resting his head on my shoulder.

"Me too." Addie snuggled into my other side. "If only life would give me a love like theirs."

Me three.

I lifted my gaze from the sweet couple and rested on Luc yell-singing into the microphone.

He offered me a wink as he strummed his guitar, a heart-stealing grin lighting his face. My heart dipped and my stomach warmed as I grinned back.

Just friends. You're leaving. Remember?

I was in so much trouble.

"Did you meet Luc's sisters?" This came from Addie.

"Yeah. They're lovely."

"Yeah."

From the corner of my eye, I saw her squint in my direction. She opened her mouth as if to continue, then snapped it shut pursing her lips, then turning to watch the band.

"Has anyone seen Courtney?" Kel asked after a few moments, looking around for Jetta's pop-princess sister.

"I haven't seen Sawyer either." Addie commented, referring to another of our hackers.

We all grinned. To everyone's surprise, Sawyer and Courtney had hit it off following her and Jetta's rescue. When Courtney had returned to rehab, they'd kept in touch, writing postcards and letters to each other. Sawyer now regularly danced around the office singing Courtney's pop hits, planting earworms. Her attendance tonight had been a surprise planned especially for Jetta.

"We're going to take a break," Luc said as the song came to an end. "Feel free to hit up the karaoke!"

He placed his guitar on the stand, then moved to leave the makeshift stage. A cute brunette hovering off to the side caught his hand. He grinned at her and stopped for a chat.

"Who's that?" Jarrett asked, nodding towards the attractive twosome.

"Sienna," I murmured, watching them interact. She'd arrived with one of Luc's sisters. Beautiful, intelligent, and friendly, she seemed into Luc, and he seemed friendly towards her.

Personally, I hated her with the heat of a thousand suns. Though, she was so nice she made it hard not to like her.

But still. Heat of a thousand suns.

I looked away. Jarrett, head still on my shoulder, squeezed my hand.

"You could have him. And by him I mean Luc. And by have I mean in both the relationship and biblical sense."

I extracted my hand and slowly pulled away, reaching for my cane. "I don't want him like that."

"Liar."

Yep. My pants were burning.

I struggled to a stand. "Anyone need anything?"

A negative response left me free to make my way inside. After visiting the bathroom, I found myself in the kitchen conversing with Sophia, one of Luc's sisters. It hurt to hear her gushing praise of Sienna, but I nodded and smiled, calculating how long it would be before I could politely escape.

"Hey."

We both turned, Luc stood in the entrance of the kitchen, smiling. "Having fun?"

"Good to see you, brother." Sophia wrestled him into a hug. "Your house is a dump, and mum is currently measuring your bathroom for a refit. I wish I was joking." They exchanged a knowing smile.

"It'll keep her off your back about the babies for a while."

Sophia rolled her eyes. "Thank God." She looked over, inviting me to share the joke. "She's been on my case ever since Phil and I got married. There is nothing like a French mother wanting grandbabies. She got me a crib for my birthday with a note telling me my eggs were frying."

I laughed. "Sounds awful."

Sophia shook her head. "She acts like she doesn't already have five with another on the way."

Sienna entered the kitchen interrupting our party of three. She zeroed in on Luc, her hand immediately finding his arm.

"Hey, you disappeared." Her eyes were soft and dewy as she blinked up at Luc.

"Just grabbing a drink." He shifted out of her grasp, moving to the fridge.

As Sophia engaged us in conversation, I watched as Sienna teased Luc, bringing forth a belly laugh. The bittersweet knot of regret settled in my stomach.

This was his future. Family, friends, laughter, and a woman who gave him joy.

I slowly backed out of the kitchen, moving down the hallway to the front study/ impromptu coat room. Collecting my things, I took one final look around the sparse interior of the home. Faded floral wall paper, scuffed uncared for floor boards, dirty chandelier in the entrance. This house would be an amazing home one day.

I took out the small wrapped present from my handbag and left it on the entry side table. With a final glance at the chandelier, I pulled the door closed behind me.

LUC

"Have you seen Emmie?" I asked, glancing around the party.

"She headed towards the hallway last I saw," Jarrett said as he brushed past me on the way to the kitchen.

"Thanks." I headed down, glancing in each of the empty rooms. No luck.

The glint of gold on my side table caught my eye. The tag read *To Luc from Emmie.*

I slid my finger through the sticky tape, carefully peeling back the gold wrapping paper.

"Captain Dictionary." I barked out a laugh.

A framed drawing, she'd captured me in superhero pose, a giant D on my chest, a cape fluttering behind me, a red rose between my clenched teeth. The tag line; *Captain Dictionary, giving life meaning.*

I rubbed a hand over my chest. "Well. Game on."

EMMIE
THE PAST

"Sister, come in. Sit, sit! We have blessed news for you." Sister Anna beamed at me from across the desk. In the corner of the room stood the Prophet Edward and his brother David. They both watched me settle.

Anna handed me an envelope.

"What is it?" I asked, taking it but not opening.

"God's work in action," Edward told me, folding his arms over his chest. "God has blessed your efforts."

I opened the envelope, pulling from it a series of thick papers. On them were pictures, no. Photos.

A man's lifeless eyes stared out at me from the paper, his body resting in a pool of blood.

I dropped the pictures, hands pressing against my mouth as bile burned up the back of my throat.

"Do you know who this is?" David prompted.

"It's the policeman," I whispered, unable to tear my gaze from the pictures on the floor.

"Yes." Edward came forward, scooping up the papers, depositing them in my lap. "Your plan worked. He did as bid, then killed himself. Another successful mission for God."

I lifted my head, tears burning as I stared at him, unable to find my voice.

"This is number five by my count. Truly, you are blessed, my child." Edward pressed a kiss to my forehead. He withdrew, standing and moving to Sister Anna's side. "God has shown us a vision."

"Oh yes," Anna cried, clapping her hands. "You're to lead us."

Edward nodded. "You're going to design the end."

"The end?" I whispered, my blood freezing in my veins.

"The final coming."

LUC

THE PRESENT

"You have a minute?" Paxton asked, leaning against my office door. I sat back, opening my arms in a welcoming gesture.

"Only if you're bringing me donuts."

He entered, shutting the door. He sat, tossing a folder on my desk.

"We have a situation." He nodded at the folder.

Photos of mutilated dolls and letters with threats in thick black ink.

I sobered, frowning. "Who is the client?"

"It's not a client. They were sent to Emmie."

"What the fuck?" I re-examined the letters. "What's our plan?"

"Mailroom reported it. They've been coming for the last week."

"Shit. These are –" I tossed the photos on the desk. "She know?"

"No."

"Fuck." I leaned back, pinching the bridge of my nose.

"Sawyer's been digging up her past. There's nothing. Literally nothing."

Pax crossed his arms, pegging me with a glare. "And why is one of my analysts doing that without my permission?"

"I'm her next of kin. Not an actual fucking family member. You ever hear about her past? No. She deflects. All the fucking time. She pushes you away. She keeps people at arm's length, she–"

"No, it's because you're into her."

"Fuck off."

"*You* fuck off, douchebag." Pax leaned forward. "You're into her. I've been distracted, but I'm not blind. Don't bullshit a bullshitter. If you try to tell me you're not into her, then you're a fucking idiot and I'll take you outside."

"Well, fuck." I offered a wry smile. "Can't pull one over you."

"You idiot." He tossed a pen at me. I caught it, spinning it with one hand.

"What are we doing about this?" I tapped the photos.

"We need to find the threat."

"Stalker?"

"Maybe." Pax reached for one of the photos. "This is disturbing." He held it up. The dolls genitals were melted, its mouth covered by duct tape.

"It's personal. And angry. There's a lot of rage in this picture. That's dangerous."

"She needs protection."

"She's leaving. Got her official resignation letter today." The words tasted like sawdust. "London."

"What's the new job?"

"Some start-up."

"You didn't do the referee check?"

I frowned. "No. I assumed you did."

Pax leaned forward, tapping a hand against his knee. "Do you know the name of the company?"

I shook my head. "Let me call Sawyer." I hit the digits on my handset, leaving it on loudspeaker.

"Yel-low?" Sawyer answered.

"Sawyer, I'm here with Pax. Which start-up is Emmie working for in London."

Sawyer paused. "I... I don't think she's said."

I exchanged a look with Pax. "Can you find out? Quietly?"

"Give me five."

We waited, hearing his keys as he typed, muttering to himself.

"Umm, this is unexpected." He murmured down the phoneline.

"What is?" I prompted.

"She doesn't have a passport. Or any flights booked. There are no visa applications either."

"She's meant to be leaving at the end of the month."

"Dude. She may be leaving us, but there is no evidence that she's leaving the country."

"Thanks." I hung up, looking over at Pax. "She's hiding."

Pax nodded. "This." He tapped a picture on the table. "And her leaving? Too coincidental."

"Fuck." I ran a hand through my hair. "Just... fuck."

"You're gonna need to get the full story."

"If she's been planning this, I highly doubt she's going to do anything but run."

"Way I see it, you have two options. One, you tell her and she runs. Or two, you tell her and she stays. Either way, you need to tell her. Learn from my mistakes. Don't keep her in the dark."

"You dick." I threw the pen back at him. He caught it mid-air, sending me a shit-eating grin.

"Am I wrong?"

I rubbed a hand over my mouth, frowning. "Fine. But I'll handle it."

"And if she runs?"

"We'll find her."

Pax grinned. "Finally. You have your balls back."

"Fucker."

EMMIE

Tuesday saw me working on a patch for a customer's database. They liked us to double check any of their work, make sure the vulnerabilities were shored up.

"Em."

I looked up to see Luc and two guys I'd never met walking towards me. The older man wore a smart suit and tie, I placed him at maybe mid-fifties, with grey-brown hair, brown eyes, and a friendly smile.

I held out a hand. "Hi, I'm Emmie."

"Grant Stoltz, CEO West Investment." We shook hands.

The younger had to be early thirties, dressed in an equally sharp suit with blond hair and extremely light blue eyes. I held out a hand and for a moment he hesitated, then easily slipped his hand in mine, offering a smile.

"Eric Flowers. I'm the COO."

"What can I do for you?"

"Conference room six is open, I'll explain there." We headed downstairs to the wood and tile room.

Luc helped me sit, leaning down to whisper, "Sorry,

would have put it in your calendar, but Addie scheduled this last minute. Apparently, it's an emergency."

I offered him a smile, putting my hand on his. "Honestly, it's no problem."

After we'd taken seats and Addie had set up coffee and tea, Luc and Grant got down to business.

"Emmie, Grant's had some issues with money transfers. Eric caught it. They're concerned that someone, or many someones, are taking advantage of the business. His company only recently acquired West Investments so he wants an overhaul. Full vulnerability testing, surveillance, physical security, employee background checks- the works." I nodded, jotting down notes.

"Em and I will pull together a workplan this week. Can you tell us a bit about the issue?"

Grant explained his concerns and the reason he'd come to our agency. It seemed to be in line with what had happened at the Grosford's, only more covert.

Charges disguised as interest were charged each month but never from the same account. It seemed random, like a small unintentional computer glitch appearing as an unexpected fee. But when Eric had started an investigation the trail had become twisted. Realising something or someone was skimming cash, he and Grant started looking around for outside assistance. This was where we stepped in.

"You've been there the whole time?" I asked Eric, making notes.

He nodded. "But not as COO. I've only been in the role since Grant took over in February."

"And the merger?" Luc asked.

"Completely above board. The old business had the big money coming in from long-term clients. But they were lagging in terms of upgrades of technology and so on. We were a newer company without the solid reputation or big numbers, but we have the best investment software. We just weren't expecting the issues on the security side."

"Investment software?"

"Software that predicts market trends to get the best outcomes for our clients. We've been developing it for years."

"Right. And the fraud was only just reported?" Luc asked.

"It's subtle." Eric shrugged. "If I hadn't picked it up as a result of one of my new clients asking about additional fees, I wouldn't have noticed."

"How far along are you in terms of updates to systems?" I asked.

"We're not. The roll out isn't scheduled until next year. We've been focused on building the back end to ensure the transition doesn't result in any issues for our customers." Grant huffed out a laugh. "This has thrown that timeline right out. We can't integrate our secure systems or upgrade our existing platform until we know the extent of the problem and if we can mitigate."

Sitting down after they left, Luc and I mapped out a plan of attack for the immediate and a time frame with pretty open endings.

As these things went, they could take us five minutes or five months. Our longest job still going – just under two years and lots of money and we were only in the beginning stages of the job. Time, in this industry, is everything.

We finished an hour later with a rough plan of attack. I started to pack up my pens and papers as Luc leaned back in his chair, hands hooked behind his head, watching me with a blank expression.

I glanced over frowning at him. "Everything okay?"

"Emmie, you need to tell me what's going on."

I blinked and sat down. "Going on? We're looking into a skimming case."

Luc tapped a hand against the table, eyes narrowing on me. "When are you leaving for London?"

"Twenty-first." The lie fell easily.

He leaned back in his chair. "What's the company called?"

I blanked.

Oh, damn.

"It's a research and development arm of a parent company. I'm not sure they have a name just yet."

Idiot! Basic cover 101. How did I not anticipate this?

Because you don't want to leave...

I ruthlessly blocked the subversive voice.

He raised an eyebrow. "And you're comfortable with that?"

"Sure." I shrugged, playing with the lid of one of my pens. "I've always wanted to visit Europe. Now's a good time to go. Nothing holding me here."

"Nothing?"

I shrugged again, eyes on my hands.

"You'd tell me if something was wrong?"

I glanced up, immediately glancing away. "Yeah."

"Emmie."

He waited till I finally looked up.

"Just tell me."

I stood abruptly, pushing up, reaching for my cane with one hand as I scrambled to pull my papers together with my other. "You're crazy. There's nothing to... I have–" I sucked in a breath, forcing calm. "There's nothing to tell. I need to get back to work."

Luc watched me walk to the door. "Em, one chance. I'll give you till tonight."

I took a deep breath forcing a smile on my face, turning back to reassure him. "I'm not sure why you think anything's wrong, but I'm good. I'm excited. Everything's good. Thanks though."

Luc's eyes narrowed. "You're sticking with that?"

I forced a laugh. "You're funny. I'll catch you later."

Shit.

EMMIE

My plan for tonight had been to start packing. Instead, I'd made dinner and crashed in front of the TV. Turned out life threatening injuries took time to recover. Go figure.

A knock interrupted my viewing. I shuffled to the door, finding a grim-faced Luc on the other side. My heart leapt. I forced a casual smile.

"Hey, what are you doing here?"

A muscle jumped in his cheek. "Let me in."

I pushed a thick lock of hair behind my ear and leant against the door, blocking his entrance. "Did we have plans?"

He placed a hand on my belly and gently pushed, moving into my apartment and dropping a bag on my small coffee table.

"Sit."

I blinked, still beside the door. "What?"

"Keys, sit down."

Door closed, we sat on my couch. I tucked a soft pullover around me and curled my legs up on one side, as he opened the backpack and started laying out thick manila files. My tongue felt too big for my mouth, my pulse thumping as I struggled against the anxious clamp of my stomach.

His blue eyes met mine. "You know what these are?"

I shook my head.

"These are examples of our employee files. You work for Pax, you get a file. We have to know who we're working with. Our reputation is too important to jack it up by hiring an unknown."

"Okay...?"

He pointed at the thickest two. "Those are mine and Brean's." Luc pulled out a slim file less than a quarter of their size. "This is yours."

He leaned back, all charcoal long-sleeved Henley rippling over dark jeans, and looked directly at me, blue eyes stormy.

"You ready to tell me what's going on?"

I avoided his gaze. "I'm not very interesting."

"Bullshit." My eyes flew to him. He glowered at me, every muscle in his body alert. "Don't make me search. You know I won't play fair. Not after the last few months."

I swallowed nervously and shuffled on the couch, plucking at the blanket with sweaty palms. "Seriously, Luc, I'm boring."

"I don't work with people I don't trust. My gut, the last few months, the last year? I trust you. Everything says you're a good person." He ran a hand through his thick hair, causing the unruly ends to stick up, and shook his head. "But my info says you've got shit to hide. Just tell me what it is."

Little bubbles of anger and resentment burst. I looked him dead in the eye, my voice tight. "You got this from what exactly? My small folder?"

"Jesus, Emmie. Stop fucking with me. I got this from the

way you dress, the way you drive a piece-of-shit disposable car, the apartment that's a throwaway. Fuck. The last three months I've been here" –he waved a hand around gesturing to the apartment, then stabbed a finger down at the couch– "I've practically been living in your apartment and have you taken a chance? No."

"If you didn't want to be here–"

"This is not about me!"

"Then why do you care about the way I dress?!"

He rolled his eyes and gestured to me. "Jesus. You wear camouflage. You're hot. You flaunt that shit? No. You hide. And that isn't right."

"Fuck you, Lucien. I didn't ask for this."

"I do not have time for this shit. You wanna tell me what's going on, or am I going to have to lay it out?"

I huffed out an angry breath. "I don't even understand what is going on right now! Why are you doing this? Bring up all this shit?"

He looked me dead in the eye. "Because I want you to be happy. That night..."

We were both silent remembering the shooting. He reached across the couch, tucking a chunk of hair behind my ear, eyes serious.

"I need to know if you've got problems. Tell me what's causing you to live like this."

Shit.

I changed the subject, desperate to distract him from the real issue. "What's wrong with the way I live?"

"Keys." He looked at me. It's *The Look*. The one which said, *Seriously? I gotta point this out to you?* My fear ticked over into anger as I jerked towards him, a finger in his face.

"I'm serious. What's wrong with the way I live? I like my

apartment, I like my car, I even like my motherfucking clothes you piece of–"

He cut me off. "Exactly. You *like*. You don't love." He leaned forward, cupping one hand around my ankle. "That's your problem, Emmie, everything you have is disposable. How old is this couch? I know what you earn, you should be living large, being happy. Instead you work, you crash here, you sometimes go out, and this..." He retrieved another file from his bag.

"What's this?" I took it resting it on my lap.

"You tell me. The mailroom picked it up." His eyes were hard.

I opened the folder, slowly flicking through. Bile burned the back of my throat.

Photos and notes. All of me.

The photos showed me laughing, talking, eating, driving. Behind the pictures were notes. Scarily detailed notes. Scarily graphic notes. Scrawled in the big, bold handwriting I sometimes wondered if I'd ever forget.

My throat and chest constricted. I began hyperventilating.

Run.

"When did these start?" I whispered, my body shaking.

"Emmie–"

Run.

I threw the papers down, scattering them across the floor, shattering the peace and safety of my apartment. I reached over to grab Luc's shirt, hands fisting the material.

"WHEN DID THESE START?"

"Fuck. Emmie–"

"WHEN!"

His hands wrapped around my wrists, trying to hold me still. "Calm down–"

"WHEN!?" I pushed my fists against his chest, attempting to force him to speak.

Run.

"About a week ago."

RUN!

"You know everything is screened." His eyes swept my face as he attempted to read my emotions. "We thought maybe a stalker, but I'm guessing you know who this–"

Overwhelming nausea had me surging to my feet, stumbling for the bathroom. I vomited, violent retching followed. A warm hand brushed my hair back as tears streamed down my face.

"Emmie…"

I closed my eyes and slumped back, immediately pulling myself away from his touch.

He crouched beside me.

"Tell me."

I shook my head, curling into myself. "I have to leave."

"Why?"

"He'll find me."

"Who?"

"My husband."

EMMIE
THE PAST

I slowly slid from beneath the covers of the bed, painfully careful not to disturb the sleeping occupant.

I turned, tripping on the ripped wedding dress bundled on the floor. I landed on my hands with a soft thump. My head twisted frantically back towards the bed, my heart pounded loudly in my ears as I bit my tongue. He grunted then, rolled over, away from me, still asleep.

Thank God.

My cheek ached. My shoulder throbbed. The area between my thighs felt raw, aching painfully every time I moved. My hand hit something wet. My underwear. He'd shoved it in my mouth to muffle my screams.

I snatched them in a fist, gingerly pushing up from the rough carpet. Silently, painfully, I slipped from the room.

It was after 2:00 a.m.; everyone in the house was tucked away, sleeping peacefully.

I moved to the third bedroom, leaving the door partially open. Nothing had been unpacked. The sum total of my possessions was a small duffel bag of clothes. I pulled on a shirt and jeans, covering the bruises that dotted my skin, wishing I could so easily hide the memories of the last few hours, wishing I had time to wash away the sweat and blood. Quietly, I cracked open the old window, inching it up slowly to avoid the frame scraping. I dropped the bags outside, climbing down behind them. I clutched the duffle handles tightly in my hand. Keeping low, I ran through the silent commune, heading towards the entrance of the property. I'd stashed a bicycle down the end of the property's long driveway. It would be a twenty-kilometre ride to town, but I was confident I could make it before anyone awoke.

You don't have any other options.

I'd fleeced the old rusted bike from town. It had panniers on either side of the seat and a lopsided basket at the front. I dropped the bag, falling to my knees to dig under the bikes' front tire. A few inches down I hit the plastic zip-lock bag. A thousand dollars in crisp, rolled notes and a fake license were stored safely inside. It was enough to buy the shitty car I'd lined up and fuel it to Perth.

I hope.

I'd emptied my clothes into the panniers when the snap of a stick caught my attention, freezing me in place.

"What are you doing?"

I whirled, picking out the familiar shape of my brother against the dark brush.

"Abel?" *Dread settled in my stomach, my shoulder drooped as he stepped closer.*

Caught.

"Why are you here, sis? Did he bring you here?" *His gaze dropped to my bag.* "You're running."

A denial burned the tip of my tongue. Despair crept in, the bike was right here, the cash clutched in my hand.

"Yes." *I closed my eyes, the tears burning.*

So close...

"Good."

My head jerked up at his vicious whisper. "Good?"

"He's a rapist. A goddamned rapist. I'm gonna kill him."

"Abel, you—"

"Hush. You need to go." He lent over, helping me pack the remaining items in the pannier. "Don't come back. You run, you hide. They'll try to find you. Don't use your real name. You got that sorted?"

I nodded.

"Good. They'll be looking. More so after tonight. All of them will. Don't get comfortable, don't trust anyone." His eyes bore into mine. "I'll try and find you."

"Come with me."

"I can't." He shook his head. "I need to protect the others."

"They're not like us, Abel." I spoke truth. Our siblings saw no issue with the way we lived.

"I know. But I have to try."

A sob broke free. Abel hesitated, his hand coming out, hovering for a moment before he snatched at my arm, crushing me to his chest. He smelt of soap, sweat, and grease. His proximity, his smell, his feel drove home my decision. I was leaving my only family, my only friend. My heart clenched, panic crushing me.

"Maybe I should—"

"No." He released me, shaking my shoulders. "You're doing this. Now. Run, sis." Whispered fiercely as his fingers dug into my shoulders, his eyes bright with unshed tears. Gently, Abel helped me onto the bike. I gasped, pain spiralling out as I settled on the seat. I immediately pushed to stand. Abel's face darkened.

"Go."

He pushed, holding me steady until I got a rhythm, his hands slipping back allowing me to pedal away.

I glanced back. There he stood, Abel, a boy-man trapped in between duty and desire. He raised a hand, then turned, pushing back into the thick bush.

I turned, watching the road ahead.

My virginity had been brutally taken from me. A sham wedding where my sister-wives stood, eyes downcast, baring silent witness as the meanest man in the commune promised to cherish me. He hadn't waited for the reception before breaking that promise. Taking me, kicking and screaming, back to his house. A house I would share with him, his two wives and their children. My father had watched, laughing and calling encouragement. My siblings shook their heads in disappointment as I fought my husband. My protest meant nothing when God and the commune had supposedly blessed the marriage. Only Abel had tried to intervene. For that, he'd received a black eye and been banished for the night.

Virginity had been sacrificed to achieve my ultimate goal –freedom.

Into the dark night I rode, pushing my aching body to pedal faster, the small light on the handle bars flickered in the darkness, illuminating rock and plant, lighting the dirt road.

As dawn broke over the horizon, mother nature painted her promise of a new day in pink and orange glory.

The outskirts of town came into view. A man leaned against a car parked at the sign post welcoming people into town. Just as I'd planned. Just as he'd agreed. Four in the morning and he'd delivered.

Relief, pure relief.

LUC
THE PRESENT

I'd fought tooth and nail to get Emmie to my place. I'd pointed out that running would make more sense tomorrow, once she had time to prepare. I'd pointed out it was safer to travel when there were multiple people on the road, more witnesses in case she had a tail. I'd used every weak, stupid, outrageous excuse to get her in my car. In the end, Emmie had only given in because I'd refused to leave her.

Her face pale, her body trembling, she burrowed into the corner of the couch, jumping at every little noise. It'd been a long while since I'd seen such bone-deep terror. There was no way in hell I'd let her leave. There was no fucking way she was leaving period.

Over my fucking dead body.

EMMIE

The adrenaline faded leaving behind a fine tremor and sweaty palms.

I'd forgotten the fear.

I'd stayed in Canberra for six years. Six years is a long time when you're on the run. More than long enough for me to become complacent. To forget.

I sat in Lucien's house, on his dark grey couch, watching him watch me drink tea. He leaned against the far wall, a mug in his hand.

"So." He drew out the short word.

I took a sip not answering.

He sighed. "Don't make me spell it out."

I ignored him and looked into my tea cup, wondering if it held the answers to the mysteries of life. I attempted to ignore the fine tremble of my hands.

"Keys, come on. Tell me about the letters."

"No." I immediately retreated, pulling my foot away. I turned to curve into the arm of the couch.

"Emmie–"

"No." I held out a hand, blocking him.

"Beautiful, you gotta tell me."

"No."

Luc watched me for a minute, his stormy blue eyes taking in my legs curled up to my chest, the blanket tucked tight around me, arms wrapped around my legs holding the cup. He pulled the cup from my hands, setting it on the coffee table before reaching over to gently haul me into his arms and across his lap. I opened my mouth, then immediately shut it, halting the protest. It felt so freaking good to be held.

"Okay. You don't have to tell me."

I relaxed against him.

"But here's what I see."

I tensed.

"You've got next to no background. You're friendly, a good listener and generous." I stayed silent, eyes fixed determinedly on the far wall.

"You're quiet, you don't let people in. You keep your head down, cruising under the radar. Even after the last few months, I know next to nothing about Emmie Franklin. Tonight, I come to you with information, you freak. I haven't seen you react like that to anything. Not even when you got shot. Twice."

I cringed but didn't comment.

"You react bad, so bad it makes you physically ill. You say it's your husband, then give me nothing, simply get up, brush your teeth and start throwing shit in a bag while I'm trying to get information out of you."

I cringed again, this time because I know he saw too much. I'd panicked. I'd let him in without thinking. Even that small detail revealed more than anyone had gotten before.

"The lack of information I can accept. What I can't

accept is as you're racing around throwing shit in a bag, you walk across to your dick of a neighbour, hand him a bundle of cash, and he comes back with a safe in which you've stashed even more cash, fake IDs, and shit which tells me you've done this before. Now, that. That is the one thing I can't leave alone." His hand slipped under my chin, tilting my head, forcing me to look him in the eye.

"Are you going to tell me what's going on, or do I need to start digging?"

I took him in. He had that serious glint in his eye, the one I saw when we were on a case and he'd gotten really pissed off. He was readying to go all in.

Damn.

I pulled away, shifting on his lap as I sighed heavily.

"You're a terrible person."

"Emmie."

"Shut up, I'm getting there." I pulled in a shaky breath and paused to collect my thoughts.

Don't do it.

Just give in. He wants to help. Let him.

You can't rely on anyone but yourself.

"Beautiful, I'm right here." His arms tightened around me for a second and then loosened, reminding me that, for the first time in a long time, I wasn't alone.

I climbed out of his arms and moved to the far corner of the lounge. I wouldn't get through this if he touched me. Those arms weren't mine to have.

Luc watched me move and settle. I breathed deep.

"Do you know how ISIS recruit their members?"

His eyes narrowed, lips drawing tight. "They mobilise people through social media."

"Yeah. They use propaganda to build their base. People can be radicalised in extremely compressed timelines. Some they encouraged to stay in country and become martyrs or physical recruiters. Others they would ask to join them in Syria."

"You were a member of ISIS?"

"Ha, not quite. There's a group in Australia called the God's Patriot. They operate using a similar technique but have different fundamental beliefs. You know a few years back, maybe five? When that guy drove a car filled with explosives into Parliament house? It didn't go off, but they made all those changes to security and stuff?"

Luc nodded, his eyes narrowing.

"A lone wolf martyr, the God's Patriots encouraged him to do it. The police never tied it back." It felt good to admit.

"Jesus, Emmie." He reached for me, but I held up a hand.

"The God's Patriots believe their leader, Edward, is Christ. He's the second coming. They recruit people online using soft and hard techniques."

"Soft and hard?"

"They have a soft evangelical approach. Just preaching the good word. They look, on the surface, like any other legit religious group. They have a website, social media profiles, are a registered charity." I ran a hand over my face. "They suck people in slowly but surely. Then there's the hard approach. Hacking of websites to spread the good word. If they identify someone of high value, someone of power who they can bring into the fold, they will research them until they know everything about their lives. Then they'll target their message. Ruthlessly dogging that person until they are either radicalised into a dogmatic disciple, blackmailed into joining, or disappear."

"Disappear?"

"I've witnessed two people who killed themselves rather than put up with the threats."

Luc's lips frown deepened. "How did you end up there?"

"They told us my mum ran off. I don't remember her. It could be true, but I don't know. My dad was someone they needed. They targeted him, sending him a young, pretty thing to help with the kids and house. Offering a job and a way out. Eventually he married the nanny, Mary, and they took us to join the commune in the middle of whoop-whoop, Western Australia." I let out a breath as memories flooded in. "I can't remember my name from before, but when you enter the cult, they baptise you and assign you a new name." My throat tightened as the name echoed in my ears, ghosts whispering memories I'd sooner forget. I rubbed the back of my neck, soothing the raised hairs.

"At first they didn't have the infrastructure to school us. To avoid attention from Child Protective Services, they sent us to a proper school until they finished building the commune. That was their mistake. The brainwashing that worked so well on my siblings just didn't take with me." I shrugged.

Luc pinched the bridge of his nose, looking away. After a long moment, he turned back. "You said the leader is Edward?"

"Yeah. A Hack-tivist. I don't know his background, but he's convinced he's God's son. He'd have to be, maybe late fifties by now? He's charismatic, intelligent, handsome. Edward railed against capitalism, greed, and the government. He preached that we were the chosen and our actions were only dictated by God's Law. He taught us how to manipulate computers for our own benefit."

"That's where you got your skills?"

I nodded. "Edward referred to me as his 'protégée.' He

predicted that one day I would use my skills to set in motion the apocalypse. A rapture that would bring down the governments, break the banks, bringing with it the end of times. He would lead us into the new era, the second era where only the chosen would be spared."

I recited the lines that were forever etched in my conscious. "The nations were angry, and your wrath has come. The time has come for judging the dead, and for rewarding your servants, the prophets, and your people who revere your name, both great and small— and for destroying those who destroy the earth. Revelation eleven, eighteen."

"How did you escape?"

I huffed out a bitter laugh. "I was the chosen one right up until I hit puberty. A late bloomer. When my..." I hesitated, glancing at him, then away, blushing. "When my breasts grew, I went from nothing to a C-cup in about six months. I kept getting punished by the elders for tempting the men, so I started wearing baggy clothing. It became automatic."

Luc reached over, gently cupping my chin, moving my head until our eyes met. His were blue fire.

"What do you mean by 'tempt'?" His eyes narrowed on mine. "You were a teenager, Emmie. A child."

I ignored him, pulling my head away, determined to get it all out. "Let me finish. By the time I was fifteen, I was a D-cup, and that shit is hard to hide when you're wearing hand-me-downs. They decided I was too tempting for the boys in the commune and needed to be married off. I was to be wife number three to Edward's brother. David was forty-something at the time."

"Fuck. Fuck." Luc pushed off the couch, pacing to the wall. He ran a hand through his thick hair. I watched as he took three deep breaths, calming. He turned back. "Emmie, you don't–"

I held up a hand again, absently noting it trembled.

"I'm okay." I breathed deep, continuing. "David already had two wives, which wasn't uncommon in the commune. He beat his wives, and rumours were, he had sex with his daughters. Fifteen with no money or transport, but I knew there was no way in hell I'd marry that monster. I'd been counting down the days until I was eighteen and could legally escape. I had an exit strategy. But at fifteen, I wasn't nearly ready. So, I... I did what I had to do." I looked away, feeling my cheeks burn with shame. "I hacked their accounts. I set up an automatic program, ready to wire myself fifty thousand into a series of elaborate dummy accounts for when I finally escaped." I huffed out a breath. "David decided to up the wedding date. Instead of escaping the night before, I ended up married."

"Fuck, Emmie–"

"Let me finish. After he fell asleep, I crept out. I'd hidden away cash prior to the wedding. Bumping up the wedding meant I was limited in what I could take without getting caught. The night I bailed, I got on a bike and cycled to the nearest town. I'd arranged to meet a guy who sold me a car at four in the morning. I still have no idea how I lucked out with him. I used it to drive to Perth. Once there, I ditched the car and caught the first plane to Adelaide." I closed my eyes, remembering the fear and pain.

"I could forge documents that looked legit. I didn't have a driver's license, but on the commune, we were taught to drive from a young age. I forged all that before leaving, including my name change. I had about a week in which to do it and not get caught. They were the last items on my list, it was too risky to do them earlier. Room inspections were conducted to ensure we didn't have contraband. After I left, I knew they couldn't report me for the thefts."

"Why didn't you go to the police? Report them?"

I looked at Luc, pleading for understanding. "It would never have gotten to trial. And even if they'd put one guy away, or shut down the commune, there are others all over the world doing Edward's bidding. I was a young kid with few options. My best seemed to be to run."

"Where'd you go?"

"When I got to Adelaide, I found a share house, told them I was working, but actually attended a technical college to get my high school certificate. I moved to Melbourne and stated working for an IT firm after forging a degree. I got complacent. I grew used to the bustle of Melbourne. I felt like they wouldn't find me in a big city. They did."

I swallowed and reached for the folder Luc had placed on his coffee table. I drew the pictures I wanted from the pile, handing them to Luc as I spoke. "I got the postcards to begin with. Then photos and dolls with their boobs burnt off or their genitals melted. It scared the hell out of me. I got up the guts to report it. The police couldn't do much. These guys cover their tracks, and state police weren't equipped at the time to deal with cyber incidents. I moved three times, but somehow, they kept tracking me down. So, I backpacked around Australia for six months, scared they'd find me if I stayed in one place too long."

"Why not try overseas?"

"I didn't have the tools or connections for a fake passport. Visas are required to stay too long overseas. That requires identification I can't replicate in a way that would pass any decent scrutiny. Anyway, I changed my name a few times, kept moving, and after a while they didn't find me.

This last time, I went from Brisbane across to Darwin, then bought a cheap car and drove to Canberra. I figured the state had a high transient population, so there'd be plenty of people wanting someone who was happy to share for short leases. It was as good a place as any to hide." I reached for my tea, took a sip and continued.

"I moved into my current apartment. I'd done my home-work, knew the guy had no online records, and he accepts cash. I didn't want an online employee presence so I worked for cash for a guy Pax's dad knew. I got a job with Elliot Securities, built a profile. I figured I was safer looking like everyone else on the grid than being an anomaly off it."

I stopped, watching as Luc's face darkened. I quickly stammered out the rest. "I'm sorry I lied, but this" –I gestured at the folder– "means they've found me again."

Luc remained silent and still for a long moment. I bit my lip, waiting.

"There's a lot in that story, but I'll start with Pax and his dad. Even if Ross had taken you at face value, Pax never does. That guy is thorough. The fact you're still working for Elliot Securities tells me you're fucking good at your job."

A ghost of a smile flirted with my lips. "I've had to be. My name changes. My moves. The only reason these guys found me is because Edward is the best. He knows what to look for."

Luc shook his head, "We'll deal with that later. But let's start with your name."

"Hey now, I love Emmie. I feel I am more of an Emmie."

He didn't laugh. "Keys, what was your name?"

"You don't need to know that."

"Keys, I think I do."

"No, you don't. That's information you don't need."

"You want me to deal with these pricks or not?"

I froze. Fear striking me deep.

"No." My blood turned to ice, shivers racing down my spine.

"What?" He frowned. "You don't want me to–"

"No!" I surged forward to cup his face, ignoring the twinge of pain as my side protested the sudden movement. "Jesus, Lucien, no! You can't go near them! Fuck, fuck!" I started shaking, fear ripping through me. He wrapped his arms around me, holding me tight against him.

"Em–"

"No, Lucien! No. These guys cease to exist for you. Tomorrow I'm leaving. You don't look for me, you don't look for them. They will hurt you. I've seen them kill people. They destroyed some guy's life by exposing everything online. The private pictures of his wife, his bank account, they got him fired for things he didn't do. It was awful. I won't have any of you tarred by that."

"Emmie, if that's happened, then you have to report it. We can help you."

"Luc, the guy it happened to reported it, and he died!"

"Did the guy have a whole team of hackers and investigators in his arsenal?"

"Luc, I can't ask–" He pulled me closer, halting my protests.

"Shut up, Emmie, this is happening. This is what friends do."

I shook my head. "No, it's not."

"Emmie, please. Let your friends help."

"I said no."

"Keys–"

"Fuck, no." I reared back, pointing a finger in his face. "Don't you nickname me, you jackarse! Let me go."

"Emmie–"

I pulled out of his arms and threw myself off the couch. Whirling I struck the universal I-am-pissed-at-you pose. One hand cocked on my hip, the other stretched out, finger directly in his face.

"You don't get it, Luc. I am walking out of this door, and I'm gone." I whirled to go do just that, but Luc stopped me with a hand around my arm. He gently swung me back.

"I thought we were past this. We've got your back. We're not letting you go. I'm not letting you go. The last three months have been torture for all of us. You, me, our friends. I get that you're scared. I get you got hurt. But seriously? It's time to fight."

I blinked.

"Life should be lived to the fullest, not in fear. You have people who care about you, and not one of us is letting you just disappear from our lives."

I felt myself waver, my body sway slightly towards him. "I can't keep you safe if you don't let me go."

"And I'm telling you, Keys, I'm here to keep you, *you*, safe."

Fear flooded my system. "Please, Luc, let me disappear."

"Can't do that, Keys. You know I can't. Pax would kill me, Addie would chop off my balls, Jetta would give me that sad little face she has, Kel would wear my dick like a goddamn necklace, and Jarrett would be holding me down to let them do it. And that doesn't even cover Ben, Jack, Sawyer, or Brean. You have to trust someone, Emmie. You have to trust we can protect you."

Something in me shattered. I wanted to. I badly wanted to trust that they could do this. But experience, years of experience, had taught me to never hope. To only rely on myself.

"I don't want anyone to get hurt."

"Trust me, Emmie."

Tears burned. "Please, Luc. Please don't get hurt. I couldn't handle it."

He pulled me into his arms as I sniffled against his chest. "Are you going to stay?"

I drew in a shuddering breath. "Yes."

For now.

EMMIE

We'd named our secure meeting room, The War Room. Located in the basement of Elliot Securities, reinforced by titanium steel doors and inches of sound-proof padding, we used it for the big jobs. Jobs that required utmost discretion and hours of planning.

Today, that's me. Me, the one they're planning for. Me, the one who is standing awkwardly at the front of the room while Addie shuffled the coffee cart about. Me, the one who people were reading about in the briefing material.

Me.

A throat cleared. Someone sniffled. One of the guys swore softly under his breath.

Me.

My history. All I knew about the group named God's Patriots filled the background brief. All the information I'd kept locked in my brain for years.

The brief provided a rundown of my part in their group. Where my skills came from, my age, my date of birth, my family history, my siblings, my knowledge of Edward and David, my experience with the group.

My sham marriage.

My husband.

My rape.

My crimes.

All of it in black and white print. Words I'd written on a page. I'd spent the night diligently writing my history out, line by cursed line. With the slash of a pen, I'd relived every moment. Every sentence felt like I'd bled evil onto the page.

Me.

Not Emmie Franklin. Not the woman who people admired and respected. I'd once been good and pure and worthy of their regard.

The words on the page were the real me. I'd been cut open, flayed, exposed, one line at a time by my own hand.

Anxiety and fear waged with an almost overwhelming need to retreat to numbness.

It never paid to care. Caring gave people the power to destroy you. If I felt nothing, no one could hurt me.

"Emmie?" Paxton's soft voice drew me back to the room. All eyes were on me. No one showed any emotion. Shame caused my cheeks to flush and my eyes to burn.

"I'm ready. I'm good," I reassured him, before speaking to the room at large. "Last night Luc brought a file to my apartment." I hit the power point remote, brought up an image of a letter I'd received via Elliot Securities.

"Letters and photos, postcards and images were sent to our mailroom addressed to me under my current name." I ignored the soft murmurs that followed. "Dolls with burned genitals and breasts were also received." I clicked to the next slide, a composite of images, all with dolls showing damage. "All together over one hundred articles have been received in the last week and a half." I clicked again, bringing up a still from a video.

"It looks like a YouTube video was posted back in February. I happen to appear in the background."

A quick search last night uncovered the video of Jetta and Luc performing at the nursing home. It must have been how they'd found me.

"They must have tracked Jetta and Paxton down, then figured out my connection to them." I shook my head.

I missed it. They didn't.

I clicked to the next slide, turning the screen to black. I took a breath and turned back to the table at large. These were the cream of Elliot Securities, the men and women who worked hard and got shit done. I tightened my grip on my cane, nervously pressing a hand to my stomach.

"At fifteen, I ran from the God's Patriots. The group is an extreme variation of Christianity. Their leader is the final coming of God. Think Scientology, only less welcoming." That got a few smiles around the table.

"Their leader is Edward. No known last name. He has one known relative, a brother, David, also in the church. Together, they form the religious hierarchy. The church believes they are ordained by God to bring forth the final coming. They're prepared to do anything to protect and grow their flock. Edward's a hacker. His skill with computers is unparalleled. I don't know his background, but I do know he's one of the best I've ever seen. He uses these skills to reach out to others, to convince them he is God reincarnate." I gestured at the briefing pack before them. "As outlined, child marriages, sexual abuse, physical abuse, and psychological trauma are some of the crimes the group perpetrates. Fraud, blackmail, and cybercrime are highly encouraged." I pinched the bridge of my nose with two fingers.

"Their last known location is WA. I've described the compound as I knew it. They have their own servers, own solar panels, live off the grid as much as possible." I dropped my hand. "The only times they went to town were when they needed something they couldn't make or grow. Fuel, spare parts, that kind of thing. The children went to school to ensure they weren't flagged in any child service systems." I shrugged. "At least until they built their own."

I looked at the group. "These people are well-trained and dangerous. Anything you have online they will get to. Bank accounts, medical files, pictures, anything. If you have an online presence, they'll get to it." I let that sink in. "They will use blackmail, threats, and have the skills to do horrific acts. I watched them trial bomb making. I've watched them hack into webcams and set up a surveillance on people in order to blackmail them. I've watched them ruin a man to the point he committed suicide." I swallowed, my mouth dry. "These are not nice people. They teach you blind loyalty from the moment you enter to the moment you die. You leave? You're still their property, and they'll hunt you down."

I reached for the glass of water on the table, taking my time. Replacing the glass, I kept my eyes on the back wall.

"When I was... younger... I was married to David. After the wedding night, I escaped while he slept. I took with me fifty thousand dollars I stole from their accounts. I remain the property of the church. My father and siblings are still there, as far as I know. I stole from their church, and I'm married to one of their leaders – as much as I hate that fact. That's three strikes. They won't stop until I'm back." I finally looked at the group. "You want out? That's okay. I understand and encourage it. They'll do whatever they need to get their property back. Threaten you, lie, steal, kill. I can't guarantee your safety. I can't guarantee anything." I stopped, unsure of how to finish. "I just don't want anyone to get hurt."

I waited in silence as the group pondered my words. Jack spoke first.

"So, we start with last known location?" He looked around the table.

Kel nodded. "I say we fly someone up to WA to have a chat to the local police, see if we can't get someone over there on some kind of 'business meeting.'" She used fingers for emphasis. "That way if they're watching any of us, we don't tip them off."

"AFP need to be brought in." This came from Brean. "They have a cyber unit for a reason. Chances are, these guys will be known to them."

"Let's map this." Jack stood, walking to the giant whiteboard, which took up a whole wall and began to write names and places.

I looked around the table, men and women who were ignoring the danger.

"Em?" Addie wrapped soft fingers around my arm, squeezing reassuringly.

"I don't... I don't understand..." I shook my head. Watching as Pax stood, talking to Jack, before taking another marker and writing some information on the board.

"They love you, Em. Can't you see that?"

I shook my head again. "But why?"

She looked at me a long time. People moved around us, conversations loud and animated as they brainstormed my problem.

"If you don't know, then we haven't done our job properly." With that she pulled me in for a hug.

I clutched at her.

"Emmie?" Pax stared intently at the whiteboard, tapping a marker against the palm of one hand.

"Boss?" I moved beside him.

"We need your father's name. Don't care if it's an alias. He had a history before this cult, chances are he's got information we can dig up. Associates. We can see if any of that gives us an entry."

I nodded, taking the offered whiteboard marker.

"Siblings as well. Who knows? One of them may have gotten out, they could be looking for you, have left breadcrumbs somewhere along the way."

I hesitated. "Right." I doubted any had managed after me.

"We need the names of anyone who was around, the school you went to, the cars you drove, the place you bought fuel, etcetera. Anything we can use to track back to them."

Pax rubbed his chin. "We need the IT guys down here. Someone get me..." He paused, "Someone get me Sawyer and Max. I want them in on this." His gaze whipped around the room. "Everything we discuss stays in here. This is not on a computer, this is not mentioned in an email, this is kept in this room. Clear?"

Everyone nodded.

"Good." His gaze came to me. "You get a choice. You can move in with Jetta and me, or with Luc. Your choice."

I blinked. "Um, neither?"

"You're the one who emphasised the danger. You need protection. I can't guarantee your apartment. Luc and I have gated, high-fenced properties. We've got the best security systems. We can have eyes on the property 24/7. Further, both properties have their own generators. They try to fuck with us, they're going to find it difficult. Those are your choices."

I hesitated, feeling Luc approach from behind. "I don't want to put you and Jetta out."

"Good. It's settled." Luc clapped a hand on my shoulder. "You're staying with me."

"I didn't–"

"Get her stuff this afternoon, take one of the company trucks if necessary. I want her out today." With that Pax turned his back on me, moving to where Brean and Kel were huddled, discussing their options in Western Australia.

I looked over at Luc. "I'm not moving in."

"I'm not having this argument." He shook his head. "This is happening, Em. Either accept that we're now part of it, or we'll drag you along for the ride." He dropped his hand and turned on his heel, heading for the door.

I sunk into a nearby chair, nervously tapping the marker against my leg. I watched as the men and women around me drew lines, discussed links, and did what they did best – look for solutions.

With a tired sigh, I pushed up from the chair and turned to the whiteboard. I pulled the lid off with my teeth and began to write.

Father - John Gwynn - Deacon

Mother - Helen Gwynn, nee Pye - Whereabouts unknown

And so it went. Line after line I drew my family tree. Abel, my eldest brother. Cain my second. Moses my third. Me. Esther, Charity, Mary and Beth, my younger sisters.

My father's second wife. My half-siblings.

My husband. His brother, the Prophet Edward.

Their wives.

Their children.

The elders of the church.

Their families.

And so on and so on and so on. All of it, line after line, as much information as I could remember in the ten years it had been since I'd escaped.

A hand touched the small of my back. "Em?"

I jumped, shying away, turning. "What?" I blinked at Luc, realising we were alone.

"Where is everyone?"

He frowned. "Working upstairs. They need to clear their cases to make this their priority."

"Right." I nodded, lifting a shaky hand to my hair. "Of course." I tucked a strand behind my ear, catching Luc's eye. "What?"

He hesitated, then shook his head, taking a step back and moving to face the whiteboard. I looked at my progress.

It was horrifying. Details I'd suppressed for years filled on the board. Dates, times, places, my aliases.

He whistled. "If nothing else, we know you've got a good memory."

We both stood silent for a long moment, my eyes reading over the family trees, trying to remember if I'd missed anything.

"What was your real name?"

"Hmm?" I looked over at Luc. He pointed to where I'd written Emmie Franklin into the hierarchy. "You need to put your name in."

"Uh. No."

"Uh. Yes."

"No."

"Yes."

"Luc–"

"Emmie."

I glared at him. "I said no."

His hands went to cross over his chest, legs hip width apart. I knew that pose. It was his I'm-a-stubborn-jackarse pose. "I said yes, Em. This is need-to-know time."

I knew that. I did. I just didn't want it to be that time.

"Maybe tomorrow."

"Maybe today. Maybe now."

I sighed. "Please…" I kept my voice soft, pleading.

"We have to do this."

I pulled a face, huffing softly. "Fine."

"Fine?"

"I'll do it." My hand shook as I lifted the marker to the board. I added a slash at the end of Emmie Franklin and began to write. I dropped my hand, stepping back.

We were both silent for a long moment.

"Abishag? Am I saying that right? A-bi-shag?"

I nodded.

"I… Is it a Bible thing?

I nodded again.

"Am I meant to know it?"

I quoted from memory. "When King David was very old, he could not keep warm even when they put covers over him. So his attendants said to him, 'Let us look for a young virgin to service the king and take care of him. She can lie beside him so that our lord the king may keep warm.' Then they searched through Israel for a beautiful young woman and found Abishag, a Shunammite, and brought her to the king. The woman was very beautiful; she took care of the king and waited on him, but the king had no sexual relations with her. 1 Kings 1-4." I sucked in a shaky breath. "David used to say I was his Abishag. I would keep him warm in his old age. He used the quote at the wedding. In the weeks before, he'd whisper that, unlike the story, I would not remain a virgin."

Luc's hands turned me, one pulling me into him, wrapping around my back. The other lifted to my face, wiping away tears I hadn't realised were falling.

"I'm sorry." I whispered the words, my voice unsteady. "I don't mean to be a wuss."

"You're fine." He offered a comforting squeeze. "This is good. You should talk this out."

I laugh-sobbed. "No, I really think I shouldn't."

"Have you ever told anyone?"

I shook my head. "Not till now."

He pulled me in, crushing me against his chest.

"Em…" He trailed off.

"I'm okay, Luc."

"You're not. But we'll get you there."

I pushed against his chest, forcing him to move back and let go. "I won't break."

"But maybe I will."

I stopped, looking at his face. Blank but for his furious eyes. I read in them rage.

Pure and utter rage.

I blinked.

"Why are you…?"

"You were raped, Emmie. You were fifteen. A child. Your first time should be with someone you lust-love. Someone you trust. Someone who makes it awkward, but you both enjoy it anyway. Hell, it may be in the back of a car during a drive-in, or while your parents are at work, or maybe it's after you get married. Maybe you're seventeen, or twenty-three, or maybe it's when you're forty. Maybe it's none of them. Who knows? But it should be your choice. Yours. No one had the right to take that from you."

"You're angry."

"Angry is a weak word for what I'm feeling." He stepped away, letting me go, as he began to pace.

"I'm fucking furious. I want to kill him. I want to fly over today–now. I want to call some friends who owe me favours and have certain skills and get on a plane and go and raid their property. I want to force him to eat dirt for days, no, months. I want him to die from a million cuts. I want to wash his filth from the face of the earth, knowing he'll never so much as set eyes on you again. Knowing that once he's finally dead, you can live the life you want. Not one controlled by a maggot who doesn't deserve even a thought from you."

I reached out, fingers wrapping around his forearm. "Luc?"

He immediately stopped, turning back to me, his free arm coming up to cover my hand with his.

"We'll get him, Em. I promise."

I looked at him. This man who felt so much.

"We need to work on our other cases." The words were soft. I was asking him to let it go for now. We're both too raw, too angry. The emotions were pouring out, and I feared I could never rebuild the walls he was so determined to break.

"Right." His mouth quirked a little, the flames in his eyes calming.

"You good?"

He nodded. "We'll talk more tonight."

We left the room, our hands clasped. I didn't let go.

EMMIE

Moving my things took an embarrassingly short amount of time. Most of my furniture was deemed, by Addie, as being ready for the junk pile. As such, that is where it ended up. My protests were met with a furious dismissal from Addie.

"When this is over," Jarrett told me, as he and Luc tossed my couch in the donations pile. "You're getting a new apartment and that Scandi three-seater I know you've been eyeing off for months."

The rest was boxed efficiently by a team of friends who'd rapidly assembled. Pax brought Jetta, who'd brought pizza. Within two hours bare walls and clean floors were all that remained in my once packed apartment.

At Luc's, they took my stuff to the room across the hall from the master. A guest room with its own ensuite, my furniture, the items I'd been allowed to keep, were unpacked and quickly assembled. My bed and mattress sat in the middle of the room, one bedside table and a lamp at the ready. My clothes were picked over by a clucking, judgmental Jarrett, and hung in the wardrobe or folded into a spare set of drawers.

My comics were placed in the built-in bookshelves in Luc's study, my herbs on his kitchen windowsill.

A reverent Luc and Pax carefully positioned my TV in the living room, his smaller one moved to the downstairs basement/rumpus room.

The move was of little inconvenience to myself. My main job appeared to be vetoing any decisions Addie made regarding my junk pile and trying to not feel like a too-stupid-to-live heroine in a B-grade horror film. I had little success with either option.

Things I'd learnt in the last two hours? Luc was a pig. His house overflowed with clothes, instruments, and papers. Addie had tasked herself with cleaning, wrinkling her nose and making comments every time she found another dirty sock in a strange place.

How did socks end up on top of the fridge?

Kel and Jetta had gone grocery shopping. They'd emptied my fridge and cupboards and still felt I wasn't equipped to be moving in with a hungry, hungry male. As such, Luc's house now overflowed with food and beer.

I had a headache building when the team finally decided to call it a night. Hugs, backslaps, and handshakes were dished out, as we walked them to the door for a send-off.

Kel pulled me in tight, the last to exit. "I've put sanitary items in all three bathrooms. And condoms. Just in case." With that parting gem, she quickly let me go, winked, and closed the door.

Death by kindness.

EMMIE

Morning saw me in the kitchen pouring coffee for Jack, Luc, and Sawyer. It appeared that, despite my best efforts, Luc had decided to inconvenience people. Unbeknownst to me, Jack had pulled the first shift last night, patrolling the streets and Luc's yard. His tired face grinned at me over a bowl of cereal.

"Don't look so glum, I do my best work at night." He winked. I rolled my eyes in response as Sawyer sat tapping on the laptop next to me.

I didn't own anything that could be considered smart technology. My mobile was analogue, able to receive only text messages and phone calls– no photos or emojis to be seen. My TV had zero connectivity, and I didn't own a laptop. Netflix was a foreign entity.

Fear had led me to separate private and business. I was good at my job. I knew it, they knew it. But my private life needed to stay private and to achieve that I required complete freedom from the possibility technology could be used to find me.

Referred to as the Internet of Things or IOT, it was the idea that smart devices— things like phones, computers, vehicles, buildings, and other items— could eventually be sensed and controlled remotely in a way that would result in improved efficiency, accuracy, and economic benefits. So imagine a doctor is an expert surgeon in America. IOT meant one day he may be able to log on to a computer or other system and perform surgery using a robot in the UK. Or, say I'm at work and suddenly realise I've left my bathroom light on. I could open my app and turn it off. Brilliant.

The problem with this is it doesn't take into account nefarious purposes and peoples' general lack of security awareness. When you go online it's like you're inviting people into your lounge room. You enable geolocation, I can find you. You use online banking, I can see your bank in your browser history. Have a webcam? Why don't I enable it with the help of your terrible 123ABC password so I can record you and your partner having intimate relations and use that to blackmail you?

My paranoia was evidence-based. Every example was a technique I'd used either while in the God's Patriots or in the years before I'd gone legit. In an interconnected world, I was an anomaly in my desire to be disconnected.

Sawyer, on the other hand, let it all hang out. He believed privacy was no longer a guarantee and that to cut off interest, the best thing was to construct people's understanding of who you were. He had multiple personas online, each more elaborate and creative than the last. A brief google search would turn up every personality from a transgender burlesque dancer to a conservative church-going anti-gay minister. And he used each to extract the information he needed. As abhorrent as we both found some of the personas, they worked because they were cultivated to be believable.

His real persona sat under layers of lies. It was brilliant in its simplicity and execution. The only problem was the amount of effort taken to construct and maintain the rouse. But for that, Sawyer and I had written code designed to mimic and interact in such a way to appear human. It worked 86.3% of the time.

Nothing was perfect.

So, seeing Sawyer sitting at Luc's kitchen bench, typing away, muttering to himself as he troubleshot, made me uneasy.

"Could you do that elsewhere?"

"Settle, petal. I'm routing this through eight countries, and I built the bloody thing without microphone, speakers, or camera. We're safe."

I sipped my tea, still uneasy.

"Here." He spun the laptop around, showing a birds-eye view of a bunch of buildings. I squinted for a moment, trying to work out what he was showing.

"Shit," I whispered as I stepped closer. "It's The Front."

"The what?"

"The Front. It's our... the commune." My hands flew across the key pad, moving in, zooming around. The outer living quarters were the same, basic weatherboard white, tin-roofed shacks, hot in summer, freezing in winter. The church took centre stage, a large limestone airconditioned three-storey building with its own basement servers and computer labs. The deacons had a higher standard of living. The houses were large, each wife and child honoured with their own room. It was part of their psychological hierarchy, a way to make people strive to be better. It worked. I'd witnessed newcomers do whatever was asked of them in a bid to move up the ranks.

My family among them.

"Emmie?"

I lifted my eyes from the screen and looked at the three men watching me.

"How?"

"I have friends who owe me. Some of them still work in certain areas that are of use to me."

I looked at the perfect satellite images. "Must be one hell of a favour," I murmured. There were new buildings, new areas that had been cleared for some kind of large outdoor field. Animal pens and barns occupied land that had previously been covered in thick brush.

"Look at the solar farm. My God." I ran a finger over the screen. "It's massive."

"Yeah." Sawyer kicked back, frowning. For a man who normally embodied a human Labrador, he looked distinctly less-than jovial.

"It tells me they're running more than they were when you were last there."

"Like what?"

He lifted a hand, running it through his hair. "Canberra has a few solar farms that size. One can generate enough electricity to power over three thousand homes. There ain't that many people living on the commune. Not based on the heat readings from the buildings."

"Why would they need it then?" This came from Jack, the coffee obviously kicking in.

"Bing, bing, bing! That's the million-dollar question," Sawyer replied pointing finger guns at Jack and firing.

I glanced at Luc who remained silent, finding his eyes on me.

"What?"

He remained silent.

I turned back to Sawyer. "This is creepy, right?"

"Totally."

I scratched my cheek. "How did they build it? I mean, apart from it probably being illegal, someone had to notice, right? You can't get that kind of infrastructure into a remote area without passing at least a few towns."

"I've tasked some of our guys with checking it out. The orders had to come from somewhere. This required serious investment. I'm talking $100 million easy."

"Christ." Jack coughed, raising his hand to his mouth. "Where do you even get money like that?"

"Depends," I answered. "Hackers have options. Put out an ad for services on the dark web. You can hack bank accounts, blackmail people, push out some ransomware."

"Ransomware?" Jack clarified.

"Yeah," Sawyer answered for me. "It's a type of virus that basically locks your computer until you pay the ransom. Sometimes the demand is set in bitcoin to make it harder to trace back to an individual."

"Geeze. You ever do that, Em?"

"Not to individuals. Big businesses when they forced me."

"Forced?"

"Yeah." I shrugged at Jack's question, eyes back on the computer, fingers navigating around the images on the screen. "We'd be punished if we didn't complete our tasks."

"Tasks?"

"Mm."

"Like what?" Luc asked.

"I don't know... Hack some websites. Steal some cash. Code a virus. See who can shut down a power grid. You know, stuff." I glanced up in time to see Sawyer, Luc, and Jack all exchange a glance.

"And if you didn't complete them?"

"If you failed or refused, you'd be punished."

"What was the punishment?"

I pressed my lips together, not wanting to answer. The pause drew out for several long moments.

"Emmie?" Luc asked. "You gonna answer Sawyer?"

I drew in a breath. "Punishments depended on the crime and the teacher. Sister Ruth would make us clean toilets. Brother David would force us into the pit or cane us."

I pulled my shirt up and twisted to show my back. Faint white marks crisscrossed here and there. You wouldn't notice unless you looked closely. "I wasn't often bad, but when I was, I didn't go to the pit, I got the cane."

"Jesus."

"Fuck."

"Em–"

I dropped my shirt and turned back to the computer shrugging. "It's over, it's done. Let's get on with it."

"Bravest woman I know."

I blinked looking over my shoulder at Luc.

"What?"

"And that's our cue to leave." Sawyer reached across, grabbing the laptop as he and Jack stood.

"Later, kids." He pressed a kiss to my head. Jack raised a sleepy hand and followed Sawyer out.

We listened as they left, the door shutting behind them. A blush worked its way up my throat flushing my cheeks.

Our eyes locked.

"Bravest woman I know," Luc repeated, his voice loud in the quiet house.

"Luc..."

"Every moment I think you're about to break, you stand tall and strong and just beat it back. I am in awe of you, Emmie Franklin."

His hands crept up my neck and his lips descended. The kiss felt quiet, warm, comforting.

He withdrew only slightly. "The real you is beautiful."

Then he kissed me again.

EMMIE

Work was difficult for a number of reasons. An hour in, I still couldn't concentrate so I did what I normally did when stuck. I made a list.

Reasons why I am distracted

1. David has found me

I closed my eyes. If I wanted to, I could leave. I could literally get up out of my chair, grab my bag, and leave. No one would know, at least not for a while. I could hide, jumping around cities, doing what I'd prepared for.

2. I don't want to leave

It was true. I didn't. I was tired of the fear and the planning and the need to leave. I wanted a home. I wanted a new couch. I wanted a dog. I wanted a family.

I wanted *this* family. This crazy family full of beautiful, crazy people who all lived incredible loving lives. I wanted this family of friends, chosen by me. My family.

3. Luc kissed me

I underlined it three times, added an exclamation mark, then circled it in blue highlighter. Damn. Damn that man. When I most needed to be level-headed and sane, he messed me up. He destroyed me. I couldn't lie to myself, I wanted to stay because of him.

After we'd kissed the second time, he'd gently withdrew, his forehead pressed against mine. We'd stood in each other's arms, heads pressed together, no words spoken. After a long moment, he'd slowly shifted back, his smile gentle.

"Let's get to work."

And we had. We'd gotten ready, he'd driven us in, and together we'd walked into the office.

Together.

He'd turned my world upside down by moving us from a me to a we.

My head and heart didn't know what to think or feel.

4. *My friends all know*

This was my reality. My friends all knew about my past. They knew about the rape, about my upbringing, about the lies I'd told, and the thefts I'd committed. I had nowhere left to hide.

To be honest, I was surprised they allowed me in the building.

"Emmie."

I raised my head.

Our floor was bright and colourful and full of people who loved their jobs. Three of the guys stood against our plotting wall, their arms crossed as they stared at the roll out sheet.

We were updating our systems over the next two months starting next weekend. Planning had started three months ago. Patches were easy, fully reconfiguring hundreds of PCs with little disruption to people or bottom line?

Yeah, not so much.

I shoved away from my desk, taking in the whiteboard scribbles.

"I can see the issue." I pointed to the time curve which linked one batch to another. "Twelve hours? That's if nothing goes wrong. Pax will say the risk is unacceptable. You need to reduce it."

Greg grunted, his mouth a straight line, his moustache twitching. "We can't break it up. Even if we do it over the weekend–"

"We run the risk of fucking it up," Max chipped in. "If we did it all in one hit, the performance load could overwhelm the system. We'd be fucked."

"Ha. Thanks for the man-splaining." I rolled my eyes. "I meant how can we fuck it up doing a staged roll out over a weekend?"

"We'd have to take the external access offline," Max retorted.

"Why?"

"We need to get it down and done in one hit. It's too difficult to pull people in, in drips and drabs."

"Fair call." I pretended to ponder the timeline in front of me. "What if we rolled out by name?"

"Explain."

"A-J, K-O, P-T, U-Z. We roll it out one after another, one weekend between. That way we can schedule people on to cover for those who won't have access."

They scratched their chins in unison. I struggled to suppress my grin.

"That could work."

Greg nodded. "Yep. Lots of overtime though."

I laughed. "Since when has that ever been an issue?"

I twisted to head back to my desk and caught Sawyer's eye. He glanced at me, then at the guys, then back, one eyebrow raised.

I rolled my eyes in response.

I knew what they were doing. They were attempting, in their own way, to make me feel valued and show nothing had changed. Patronising as hell, I loved them for trying, in their own way, to make me feel included. These types of roll outs were standard. We did the same thing each time. But I appreciated the effort and the thought. Even if they showed it in a slightly belittling way.

The West Investments account sat open on my computer. I'd finished vulnerability testing. Luc had done physical security checks. West Investments were not coming up gold. If anything, their report card wavered at a C minus, slipping towards a D. Not good at all. I'd gotten administrator privileges two days ago and was currently running a tailored diagnostic software. It would seek out, identify, and classify anomalies. At Elliot Securities, we designed the best.

I unlocked my screen to see a small notification had popped up in my account window. I clicked, then frowned, looking at the diagnostics. Picking up the phone, I hit Luc's extension. It diverted to his mobile.

"Hey, Keys."

"Where you at?"

"I'm doing a tour of the Hitchin's building. What's up?"

"West Investments. Diagnostics came back. It's a keylogger."

A trojan keylogger was a malicious piece of software, this one logged all your keystrokes, sending them off in a file to whoever had created it. The software would record strokes that could point to specific activities, say passwords or online banking information.

"And we got it?"

"Yeah. It seems like fairly rough code. A slapdash of a

bunch of older malware someone's stuffed together. I'm not surprised our systems caught it so quickly."

"Easy fix?"

"Yeah. The West systems are terrible. This code is so old even a basic firewall should have caught it."

He laughed. "You're a code snob."

"No, I'm a security snob. It's why you hired me," I teased back.

"Nah, that was for your– Crap. Gotta go. Anything else?"

"Nope, I got this."

"'Course you do. I'll be back in an hour to take you home."

"'Kay. But we're cleaning your house tonight," I reminded him.

He groaned. "Don't. You sound like my mother."

"You should listen to her. I'm pretty sure your bedroom is a biohazard."

He chuckled. "I'll bring the hazmat suits. Later, Keys."

"Bye."

I hung up and stared at the phone for a long moment.

Bravest woman I know.

I am in awe of you.

Keys.

You're a code snob.

Unless I was mistaken, the man was hitting on me.

The kiss this morning.

The second kiss.

The endearment.

Luc isn't hitting on you, silly. He's dating you.

I sighed and looked back at my list.

Yep.

I didn't want to leave.

EMMIE

I frowned at the small white box in my hands. "No."

"Yes."

"No."

"Em."

"Luc."

"Worst case scenario."

I opened my mouth, then shut it, wrinkling my nose at him.

"Exactly." His smug face made me want to punch him.

"I won't use it."

"You will."

"I won't."

"You will because I've already set it up with my favourite apps and a lock screen of my abs."

I blinked, looked down at the phone box, then back up. "Are you kidding me?"

His smiled coyly. "You'll have to use it to find out."

I gritted my teeth. "I'm not using the phone, Lucien."

"It's Sawyer approved. He disabled the cameras, Bluetooth, and wireless. He's encrypted all calls. The microphone will only activate for calls. Location services are routed through about three different locales. It's an overseas SIM card courtesy of a friend of a friend of an acquaintance of a work colleague who owed someone a favour. I'm not joking. It's got our security loaded on it. You wrote that damn protocol."

I did. It was good. #HumbleBrag

"You know this thing is the Fort Knox of phones."

It was.

Shit.

"Okay." I spat the word. "Fine. But God forbid–"

"It's going to be fine." He reached over, pulling me against him, soothing a hand down my side. "You'll see."

"I just... I can't help..." I shook my head. "It feels weird to know it's all out. That I know that they know that they've found me so there's no need to be as closed as I was. You know? But at the same time, it's like I just... I need... I can't help it. Did that even make sense?"

He laughed. "I get you." He walked backwards towing me along. His legs hit the couch, his arse dropping to the seat before he pulled me down into his lap.

"Here's the thing. When I came back from A-stan the first time–"

"A-stan?"

"Afghanistan. Now shh, it's Lucien's story time." He pulled me closer, tucking my head under his chin. "When I came back from A-stan the first time I had trouble sleeping. I wasn't used to not hearing bombs dropping. Not having to be constantly alert. A car backfired, and I tackled my dad in an effort to protect him." He chuckled. "I'm still not sure who freaked more."

I drew back, looking up at his face, squeezing him in sympathy.

"It got better and worse. The longer I was over the more things became institutionalized. I sleep light. I automatically check for exits. I scan for threats. Did you know I have an escape plan for every room in every building I walk into?"

"Really? I do that too."

"That doesn't surprise me. When you're living in dangerous situations, you automatically look for ways to protect yourself. Things like scanning for exits keeps the anxiety at bay." He lifted a hand tapping his chest. "The old heart doesn't kill me, if up here"– he tapped his head– "thinks I have shit under control." His mouth quirked up at the corners. "Or as under control as it can be."

"So, what you're saying is...?"

"I want you to use the phone for my own peace of mind. Having said that, you're the priority. You need to be comfortable. Your modus operandi can't change."

"Oohhh, breaking out the big words."

"Let me impress you with my big mouth," he teased.

"I'd rather you impress me with your tongue."

His eyes flashed, and his smile turned naughty. "I can do that." His mouth was hot, hard, and wet as it met mine. Fingers dipped, hands glided, and tongues danced.

Oh yes.

Oh yessss.

I drew back. A little starry eyed. A little breathless. A little dazed.

A lot turned on.

"I'll use the phone."

Hair mussed, he blinked slowly, his gaze unfocused. "What?"

I hid a smile. "I'll use the phone."

"Okay." He pulled me back, one hand to my cheek as the other delved into the depths of my hair. "Come kiss me some more."

I laughed.

EMMIE

I quickly learned that a new phone was like a new pair of shoes. It pinched. It required consistent work to wear it in. You could function without it, but everyone gave you an evil side-eye.

A notification beeped, informing me that one of the numerous applications Luc had installed required my attention. Smartphones were nothing but attention sucks. I'd rather read a book.

I unlocked the screen (spoiler– it *was* a picture of his abs. Addie, Jarret, Kel, and I had already spent an inordinate amount of time in the breakroom drooling) and hit the little bubble.

Luc: I figure you've never actually dated

Emmie: Your powers of deduction are astounding

Luc: I shall ignore your sarcasm because I have decided to woo you

Emmie: Woo me?

Luc: That's right. Woo you through the ages.

Emmie: ... I have no idea what that means.

Luc: We shall begin now. With grade school.

Emmie: What the what now?

"Em?"

I looked up to find Max standing by my desk. He looked distinctly uncomfortable.

"Yeah?"

"Umm, Luc asked me to give you this." He dropped a bright pink A3-sized envelope on my desk. It landed like an atomic bomb, ballooning a mushroom cloud to coat Max, my workstation, me, and everyone within a 2-metre radius in a thin shimmer of glitter.

"What the hell is that?"

"Ah! It's in my eyes!"

"Get it off me!"

I gingerly picked up the offensive material and turned it over, ignoring the protests from my colleague. The front of the envelope featured a giant stick drawing overlapped in pink, purple, gold, and silver glitter. The back was a giant heart decorated in bright pink. I pressed my lips together to withhold the giggles that threatened to erupt.

Holding it at arm's length I ripped it open, causing another shimmer shower of glitter. By this stage, a small crowd had gathered around my desk. I raised an eyebrow at the gaggle of geeks.

"Really?"

Sawyer stood front and centre grinning at me. "Come on, Sparky. Don't leave us hanging."

I rolled my eyes, but pulled out the giant card. The handmade card was in deep ruby red while a crescent moon sparkled in gold and silver glitter. Luc's handwriting decorated the front in dark black marker.

Will you be my Sailor Moon?

My heart, already warm and gooey, melted into a puddle of warm Luc-shaped goo.

He remembered.

I opened it, jerked, then started laughing. He'd crafted a giant red pop-up rose inside the card. Green glitter on the stem, red for the petals. It wobbled precariously as I read the thick marker that proclaimed his bold statement.

I know how to do romance.

"Is this an inside joke?"

I looked up at Greg and burst out laughing. His moustache was bejewelled with all the colours of the glitter rainbow. Wiping tears, I nodded. "Yeah, he remembered something I said a while ago."

"Put a ring on it." This came from Sawyer.

"Thanks, mate." I rolled my eyes. "Bit early for that."

"If it's right, it's right." He nodded, then clapped his hands sending a new glitter cloud flying.

"Now, I think that"– he pointed at my card– "deserves a place on the winner wall."

I groaned, pressing a hand to my eyes. "No!"

"Yes!"

"Win-ner wall! Win-ner wall! Win-ner wall!" The chanting started, and the card was liquidated from my hands and positioned on our wall of pride. There, in a cloud of glittery goodness, rose now lopsidedly bobbing, Greg pinned it to the board.

I laughed, tears prickling for reasons I couldn't explain.

"Thanks, guys." I stood, brushing my hands over my top and lifting a hand to show them the obscene amount of sparkle on my palm. "I may look like a kindergarten teacher–"

"I'd say closer to stripper." The suggestion came from the doorway. Luc's broad grin and casual stance told me he'd been there a while.

"You are so cleaning this up, Falco."

He laughed. "I already paid the cleaners extra." He pushed away from the door and stepped into the room. "Besides, who do you think made the damn thing?" He shook his head like a dog, sending a cloud of shine tumbling from his hair.

We all roared with laughter. He stalked to me, pulled me into his arms, and pressed a quick closed-mouth kiss to my still laughing mouth. He dropped his arms, stepping back with a wink. My face flushed as I realised all eyes were on us. Surprisingly, I was okay with that.

I... I think I like being claimed.

"Grade school." He looked at the ruin of my desk. "My work here" –he twinkled, actually-physically-goddamned-twinkled– "is done." Turning on his heel, he left.

"Em."

I looked over at Sawyer.

"If you don't put a ring on it, I will."

I threw back my head and laughed.

EMMIE

The West Investment case niggled me again. I'd started crafting my report, outlining my findings and our recommendations for immediate, short, medium, and long-term security upgrades. My IT side would be combined with Luc's physical findings over the next few days, and we'd present a summary to Mr Stoltz and his board next week.

I'd been working through the data and spent hours analysing how the malware had integrated into the investment system. Essentially, it started with the trojan keylogger. This allowed the hacker to gain entry to the system by installing a backdoor. A backdoor was a hidden program which provided remote access to the system. They'd used this backdoor to install the algorithm and build the accounts that allowed the money to pool and then be funnelled out. Unfortunately, the accounts were shifting money to offshore bank accounts, which was beyond my legal reach. Unofficially and off the books, I could definitely continue to track the transactions.

I wasn't, because that would be illegal, but I could.

None of that bothered me. No, it was the way the money shifted. I'd moved to Fleas, our name for a series of computers that were specifically set up for testing. Their entire purpose was for us to be able to safely test new and emerging threats. This testing allowed us to identify patterns, understand how a virus would infect a system and then develop solutions and improve our own software.

I'd been scenario running to map how the algorithm selected accounts, how it gathered and transferred money, and whether we could reverse engineer it to work out exactly how much money they'd stolen and from which accounts.

The reverse engineering was easy. Now I knew about the fake accounts and how they acted, I could run a patch to search for them, and then we could track back the transactions. Easy. But there was still... something that didn't sit quite right. I couldn't put my finger on the reason, so I was running test number fifty-six while I typed up the report.

"Yo, working beauty." Luc propped a hip on my desk. "Emergency staff meeting."

"Mm?" I continued typing, frowning at the screen.

"Emergency meeting. Now."

"Uh-huh," I murmured, tilting my head as I deleted a sentence and reworked how I described my findings.

"Em."

"Mm?"

He waved a hand in front of my face. I blinked twice, turning to look up at his half-smile. "Oh, hey."

"Hey, gorgeous."

Cue my underwear miraculously disintegrating.

"Wait. Meeting? What?" I asked, ducking my head and glancing at the clock in the corner of my screen.

"Yep. Come on, Keys. Chop-chop."

I pushed off the desk, rolling the chair back. "Who called it?"

"Pax. We're headed to the war room."

In the basement, Sawyer, Kel, Pax, Brean, and Jack were bent over a table, looking at photos.

"What we got?" Luc asked, dropping into a chair. He shoved the chair beside him out, casually draping an arm around my shoulders as I settled. Kel started us off.

"Less than twenty-four hours and this is what we've found so far." She handed me the printouts. The first was a series of council applications and building approvals. "AFP pulled some strings in their WA office and managed to get the council files. They shipped them to our contact via an officer returning to Canberra last night. As you can see, it makes for interesting reading."

I flicked through the papers, looking at the information lodged. David and Edward's names were all over this, but it was the solar farm application that caught my eye.

"My father," I whispered, a shiver running down my spine.

"Yeah," Kel agreed. "As the story goes, they piggybacked off a federal grant for remote indigenous communities. The application shows they represented the commune as being owned by traditional elders who have ties to the land."

"Which, unsurprisingly, is bullshit," Sawyer interrupted. "Unless they actively recruited members from a local mob, they're lying."

"My father's name is on the application. We aren't Aboriginal or Torres Strait Islander. My grandparents were Irish." Rage simmered just under the surface.

"We have suspicions they've forged their ORIC registration."

The Office of the Registrar of Indigenous Corporations

regulated which corporations were recognised as indigenous and therefore able to apply for specific grants.

"But even with an ORIC, their application should have been denied. It's not building a community; these financials show they've used the cash for solar panels," Luc pointed out.

"This is where it gets complicated, and where the AFP are now interested," Kel replied, tapping the desk. "Page five."

I flicked to page five of the stapled documents. "They were found compliant?"

"Oh, yeah," Kel answered. "The auditor signed them off. But that auditor? He died three days later."

We all stared at Kel.

"Died how?" Pax asked.

"Suspected suicide. Only, he erased every piece of technology before the deed."

"Shit."

Goosebumps prickled along my skin.

Sawyer made a clicking sound with his tongue. "Just a friendly reminder we found all this after only twenty-four hours. One day, people. One."

Paxton rubbed his chin. "Do we think any of this was flagged? Are we worried we've tipped anyone off?"

Sawyer shook his head. "Not yet. This was all off system."

"AFP want a meeting. This shit is..."

"Big," Kel agreed. "Bigger than us. We're talking potential federal fraud, blackmail, cover-ups, cybercrime, murder, not to mention any abuse on the commune."

"We received another letter today." Jarrett held up the ziplocked bag. "It's dated yesterday."

I bit my lip.

"Delivered via priority mail. There's no evidence to suggest they've realised Emmie's aware of this shit."

"Wait." I blinked. "You think they don't know that I know?"

"Your norm is to run when they find you. You're still here. I think it's why they've ramped up the letter delivery."

Well... hell.

This completely changed the way I viewed the situation.

Mind. Blown.

Pax blew out a breath. "Okay, we need to be on guard. Here's how we play this. We go about our business as normal. Nothing strange, nothing out of place. No meeting emails about this, but we meet here every day at three. You work the case, you work it from here. Nothing out. If they don't know that we know, then our power is in their ignorance."

I watched as everyone nodded.

"How do we explain Emmie moving into Luc's?" Kel asked.

There was a pause.

"They're dating. Have been for a while. Finally coming out and moving in together." Pax looked to Luc who nodded. I opened my mouth to argue but Pax kept talking.

"Emmie, are you on rollout?" Pax asked, referring to the first round of software upgrades due that weekend.

"No, but–"

"Good," he interrupted. "This weekend, we're going to Luc's gig. We drink, we dance, we have a good time. We go to work. We go out. We pretend like nothing is happening. We good with this?"

Again, nods.

I opened my mouth to protest, but Pax ignored me.

"Kel, I want you to follow that lead. Work with AFP on

the ORIC issue, see what that generates. Sawyer, good work with the sat-images. I want more from those friends. See if you can't pull some favours. I don't care what you need to promise. I've got contacts who have a few markers they owe me. Luc, you're on Emmie duty until further notice. Brean will be days, Jack nights." He paused, considering.

"Anything else? No? Good. Dismissed."

I slumped in my chair, arms crossing as I watched them pack up papers, handing them to Sawyer to lock in our safe.

Luc squeezed my shoulders. "You good?"

"No."

He chuckled. "You're pissed. You'll get over it."

"People have *died*, Luc. This isn't some–"

He stood, ignoring me. "Let's go."

I threw my arms up. "Honestly, this is insane!"

He walked towards the door, ignoring my protestations as he exited the room.

Sawyer chuckled. I pushed up from the chair, spinning to pin him with a glare. "You know this is dangerous. You of all people know this is shit."

He shrugged, twisting the handle on the safe and spinning the lock. "No less dangerous than anything else we do."

"Bull," I spat. "This is–"

"Em." He straightened, head shaking. "They love you. I don't care how many times we all have to say it, we're going to keep saying it until it finally sinks in. We all love you. We're doing this because we love you and want to help you. We want you safe."

I blew out an exasperated breath. "But–"

"Nope. No complaints. Accept this is happening and it'll be easier for everyone involved."

I sighed. "I just..."

He waited, hands tucked into pockets.

I shrugged, battling tears of frustration. Fear. Anger.

Sawyer sighed. "Guess I need to spell it out. You're our friend. You're practically family. And now it's bigger than just you. You were the catalyst, but there are other people involved. It's bigger than just your life."

My chin wobbled, but I nodded, sniffing.

"Good. Now go find your lover boy and get him to kiss you better." His lips quirked. "I'm off to do what I do best."

"Eat too much?"

He laughed. "Save the day."

Emmie

WE ARRIVED home to Kel getting ready to exit Luc's house. I paused in the doorway, coat half-off.

"Kel?"

"Hey, babe." She came over, a quick hug for me, a kiss on the cheek for Luc, handing over his keys. "Everything's set. Have fun you two."

Her eyes shining with amusement, she disappeared out the front door with a wave of her long fingers.

"What's going on?"

Luc ignored the question, instead turning to lock the door.

"Luc?"

He made a small non-committal sound in the back of his throat and gestured for me to take off my coat, before disappearing into the house. I made a small sound in the back of my throat, one which eloquently described what I thought of this treatment before jerking the coat off and tossing it on his stand.

I paused in the mouth of his lounge room. The TV had been shifted to the side of the room, making way for a projector. Pillows, cushions, and blankets were strewn across the floor and piled upon mattresses to create a nest of comfort. An esky full of cans of soft drink and chocolate bars sat off to the side, chilling on a bed of ice.

"What...?"

"High school." Luc stood amongst the pillows looking way too pleased with himself. "I can't take you to a drive-in because The Man has shut them all down, but I can bring a movie marathon to you."

My stomach dropped, and I felt a little like I was falling. It wasn't an entirely unpleasant experience. On the contrary, it felt like living. Like I'd stopped existing and had finally begun participating in life.

My lips curved up to answer his infectious grin. "And what is the dress code for this fancy shindig?"

"Skimpy lingerie." His quick reply had me laughing.

"Try again."

"Nudist beach."

"Nuh-uh."

"Lumberjack?"

"Ohh! Sexy." I laughed, turning to go change.

"Emmie."

I paused, glancing over my shoulder.

"Be serious. Today was shit. We don't have to do this tonight if you don't want to. Is this okay?"

"Oh, yes." I let him hear just how much this meant. I wanted this. I wanted the teasing, the normality, the wooing. "You have no idea how okay this is."

His eyes warmed, and the grin slowly came back. "Good. Now, go have a bath, warm up, and when you're out we'll order pizza and watch dinner and pig out until we're both fat little piggies." He made shooing motions with his hands. "Go!"

I smiled. "Going!"

"I suggest taking the phone!"

"I'm not taking nudes!" I called back, walking away.

"Ha! The camera is disabled smartarse!"

I giggled. "See? I don't need it."

"Just take it!"

On cue the phone dinged. I opened the notification. Luc had shared a new playlist with me- *Cliché Mixtape*.

I smiled.

The power of Luc was his joy. He loved to laugh. He loved to make people laugh. He charmed everyone, and I'd fallen under his spell.

After relaxing in the bath (in which I'd spent half the time alternating between swooning and giggling at Luc's music selections) I'd dressed in comfortable PJs and come back out to the lounge room. Luc had pizza laid out and a movie I'd never seen ready to go.

He rubbed his hands together, grinning. "Ready?"

"For?" I asked, taking a slice of pizza.

"The best movie ever created! Evvvv-ah."

I rolled my eyes. "Puh-lease. Everyone knows the best movie ever created is *Wolf Children*."

"I... have no idea what that is but get ready to be proved wrong."

I sat cross-legged on the pillow pile, balancing a plate on my knee as I lifted the slice to my mouth. "Go on, then," I said, munching on the deliciously cheesy slice. "Just try and prove me wrong."

The movie opened. And I got lost in the utter ridiculousness

"How do you even know this?" I laughed, throwing

popcorn at his head as he sang along to the opening rap.

"*Men in Tights* is an institution! How do you *not*?" he replied, pulling me under him, his fingers tickling my sides. I screamed with laughter, trying to fight him off as we wrestled. He pressed a kiss to my laughing mouth before letting me go. We settled back, still grinning, still chuckling, to watch the movie.

The power of Luc. I wasn't thinking about David. I wasn't thinking about working. I wasn't thinking about running. I was thinking about lips and hands and glitter and men in very tight tights.

And perhaps that's why when I fell asleep, I dreamt of Luc in green tights.

FYI, he looked smashing.

LUC

I'd never been opposed to the concept of domesticity. I liked the idea of waking up beside my woman, sharing breakfast, maybe going for a run together.

But this?

Sign me up.

The waffles on my plate glinted temptingly with maple syrup.

"You made me waffles?" I didn't try to hide the glee.

Em placed another plate beside mine, slipping onto the stool. "Of course. You're letting me stay here."

"Wait. Are you saying you stay in my house, and I get this every weekend?"

She rolled her eyes, picking up a fork to cut through the soft pieces of carby goodness. "Maybe."

"Well, welcome roommate, rent shall be free." I sliced the waffle lifting the fluffy deliciousness to my mouth. I groaned, actually groaned.

I found Emmie staring at me, her mouth slightly opened.

"What?"

She shook her head, a small smile playing on her lips. "I just"–she shrugged– "I never knew you had a breakfast fetish."

I cut another piece, lifting it to my lips. "Oh, baby, you have no idea."

After breakfast we sat about, Emmie reading a graphic novel, me sorting through the tasks I'd neglected that week.

Music played in the background while I sorted mail. A letter killed my mellow vibe.

Dear Luc,

It's time.

Marie.

"Fuck." I blew out a breath, slumping back in my chair.

"You okay?"

I looked over. Emmie had a finger marking her place, a small frown on her face.

"Have I told you about my service?"

She frowned, closing the novel. "You were SAS, right?"

"Yeah."

"What was it like?"

"Hard. Fucking horrible. The best." I chuckled. "Seriously some of the best fun I've ever had."

"Fun?"

I stood, moving to the couch, and settling beside her. "The brotherhood. The friendship. War, for all they say, is mostly periods of boredom interspersed with shit going wrong."

She reached out, pressing one of my hands between hers. "Why did you leave?"

I rubbed my shoulder. "Paxton mostly. Do you know about the IED?"

She shook her head.

"We were on a recon run. Nothing crazy. They'd supposedly cleared the road, intel got that wrong. Our vehicle hit an IED, blew our gunner, Brick, clear of the Bushmaster. When we tried to get to him, Limo stepped on another IED. He and Brick died immediately. Pax and I took on fire from a sniper. I took a bullet to the shoulder. A damn airstrike was all that saved our arses."

I struggled for a long moment, the memories overwhelming. "Watching Pax lose it, dealing with Limo and Brick's widows. The funerals. Pax spiralling into a depression while he recovered... It was time."

"That's why Pax limps?"

"Yeah."

"Did you get hurt?" Her hands squeezed mine.

"One to the shoulder. You haven't seen the scar?"

She shook her head, biting her lip. "Can I?"

"Have at it." I pulled off my shirt, tossing it on the coffee table. Emmie raised up, shifting closer. Her fingers traced the puckered skin.

"Does it still hurt?" she whispered, eyes on my scar.

"No," I whispered back. She smelt like coconut and maple syrup. My dick twitched.

Down boy.

"Are there more?"

I turned, offering her a view of my back. I had a few scars here and there, mostly from shrapnel. Nothing serious.

Still, her fingers traced each one. I felt her breath brush the skin of my back.

I twisted back, capturing her hand. "The letter is from Marie, Limo's widow. She's kept his ashes since the incident. She says it's time. She's gonna let him go."

She melted into me, pressing close, offering comfort. "Are you ready for that?"

"I said my goodbyes a long time ago."

"Doesn't make it any easier."

"No." My lips twisted into a sardonic smile. "But he's not a bunch of dust sitting in an urn. Limo was laughter and love. He's living in his two girls."

"That's lovely." She let me be silent, processing. Her fingers gently brushed my chest. "Luc?"

"Mm?"

"Can I kiss you?"

I tilted my head down. "You don't have to ask."

Her lips met mine, offering comfort and a small amount of heat. I took. The longer we kissed, the more her fingers roamed, becoming daring.

I eased her down on the couch, covering her with my weight, feasting on her mouth, relishing the greedy sounds she made as we kissed.

Her hands danced along my sides, finger nails scraping up my back.

She slanted her head, pressing kisses to my cheek and down my neck. I rolled to my side, granting her access.

"Okay?" she asked, pulling back a little.

"Perfect." I pressed a kiss to her delicious mouth. "Just giving you better access."

She grinned, hands roaming again, dancing across my stomach and up over my chest.

My cock was rock hard, and I wasn't prepared to do a damn thing about it. I'd googled sexual trauma and called my sister, asking for advice. Sophia was a psychologist who loved dishing out advice. She'd offered me resources, explained what triggers looked like and then advised she was available to recommend colleagues should whoever I'd called her about require it.

Emmie needed to be confident and trust that I wouldn't

press her for anything she wasn't ready to give. That was one promise I could keep.

"Luc?"

"Mm." I tilted my head down, pressing my forehead to hers.

"Thank you." Her hands stilled, laying flat against my chest. "I know what you're doing."

I smiled. "Getting ready to suck your blood?" I gnashed my teeth at her. She pretended to bite my nose in retaliation. I laughed pulling back.

"No." She sobered, a little crease on her forehead. "Taking it slow."

I ran my palm down her side, flicking the bottom of her shirt up an inch, lightly tickling the soft strip of skin at her hip.

"Well, I don't know about you but-" I bent my head, lips grazing her collarbone. "-I'm not in a rush."

She shivered, moving a little bit closer. "Me either."

I traced small circles on her skin as we lazily made out, kissing, and nibbling on sensitive skin. I bit her earlobe, grinning as she shuddered. Her hips shifted closer, pressing into mine. She squirmed, panting just a little.

Fuck yes.

I dipped my hand down, sliding into the top of her pants a fraction. She froze.

"Shit." As I started to withdraw, her hand gripped my wrist, halting my movement.

"No, it's not..." She coughed. "It's the scar."

I frowned. "It still hurts?"

"Not normally. It's just that it's ugly."

"Keys..." I sighed. "There is not one goddamned thing that is ugly about you." I pointed at my shoulder. "You think this is ugly?"

"No, of course n–"

"Then don't spew that nonsense." I moved my hand back, resting my fingers on the raised scar. "This says you're alive. And I'll always be thankful for the visual reminder."

She blinked, eyes glassy. "You may be the messiest man I've ever met. But you're also the sweetest."

"Sweet?" I shook my head, shifting my hand to palm her butt and tightening my grip, pressing my body into her. "No, Keys. I'm spice and everything not nice, that's what Lucien's are made of."

She giggled, raising her chin for a kiss.

A knock at the door interrupted our play. I sighed, pulling back, rolling over her to drop off the couch. I pushed up, heading for the door.

"This better be good."

Addie stood on the other side.

I leaned against my doorway, crossing arms. "What can I do for you, Miss Addie, on this fine Saturday?"

She took one look at me and grinned. "Sorry to interrupt, but you have a gig tonight." She held up a bag. "And I have a Cinderella to get ready for the ball."

I glanced at my watch. "We don't leave for another three hours."

"Just enough time, then." She barged past, calling, "Emmie! It's your fairy godmother!"

I spent the rest of the afternoon practicing for tonight's gig and trying to stay out of their hair. Whatever Addie was doing had Emmie in fits of giggles. I found I liked the sound ringing through my house.

Hours later, the van was packed and I was getting pissed.

"Yo." I knocked on the bedroom door. "We gotta go."

Addie opened it, grinning. "She's ready." She popped on to tip-toes, pressing a kiss to my cheek. "Take care of her."

I didn't notice her leaving. My eyes were locked on the woman in the bedroom.

Jesus, Mary, and Kevin Bacon. I'm in fucking love.

Em tugged nervously at the shirt, fidgeting. "Is this okay?" she asked, her hair bouncing as she moved to the door.

"Oh, yeah." I stared at her, watching her tits move, watching her hips sway, watching the grin decorate her full red lips.

"Do we have to go?" she prompted, glancing at my watch.

"Yeah." I turned abruptly, leading her down to the garage as I tried to subtly adjust my junk.

Jesus. I mean... fuck.

Emmie chatted as I plotted. This was like every fucking wet dream, teen movie come to life. I knew she was gorgeous, but when she looked like this?

Magnif-eee-fucking-cent.

EMMIE

"Where is this again?" I asked as the van rolled to a stop down the back of a dark alley. Despite the reassurances, I felt uncomfortably exposed, in more ways than one.

The first issue was my outfit. The shirt was black, light-weight, and low cut. Way more low cut than anything I'd ever owned. The jeans were tight and dark, accompanied by a push-up bra and soft boy-cut underwear. She'd paired it with black converse and a leather bomber jacket. While I had to admit I looked fantastic, I still found myself tugging at the shirt regularly to ensure I wasn't flashing anyone.

Sex bomb I am not.

The second issue was the venue. As much as I looked forward to watching Luc play, I was having a minor anxiety attack about being in public. The risk increased in public places. Luc and Pax had worked out a protection plan, ensuring I'd be covered at all times but I still felt naked.

"This is Falling Glass." Luc slid the van door open, jumping out. I shuffled across the seat, taking his hand as he helped me down.

He squeezed, then let my hand go, moving to the rear of the van to assist his band mates in unpacking the equipment. He picked up an amp, and flashed me a smile.

"Lead on, my lady."

I grinned and walked towards the door marked Staff Only. Inside we walked through a maze of backrooms, headed for the stage.

"We're the only band tonight. We'll set up, do a check, then grab some dinner," Luc told me as he connected cables and repositioned equipment the guys were bringing in.

"Can I help?" I ran sweaty palms over my jeans, standing awkwardly while Luc crouched on the stage.

"We're good. We've got this down to a fine art." He flashed me a grin. "But thanks."

I hovered, moving this way or that as the guys came in, handing items over when directed. I felt like a seagull at a picnic, mildly annoying, but someone was always willing to throw me a chip.

Dinner was chips and a burger at the bar. Luc snagged one of my remaining fries as I swatted at his hand. He gave me a wink as he chewed. He took a swig of beer, then glanced at his watch.

"The crew should be here soon. We'll be wrapping up about eleven. You good with that?"

I nodded, mouth full of burger.

He watched me for a moment, tapping the side of his beer absently.

"What?" I tilted my head giving him a squinty look. "I know that face."

He grinned. "This one?" He pointed at it crossing his eyes.

I threw a napkin at him, laughing. "No, the deep-thought one."

He shrugged. "I think sometimes."

"Oh really?" I grinned, taking another bite of my burger

"Mm." He settled back in the chair, feet stretched out to touch mine under the bar. "Trying to work out if we've reached late teens or early twenties just yet."

I raised an eyebrow.

I enjoyed this wooing experience. Aside from glitter-bomb cards and playlists, he'd given me flowers, texted me cute messages, and sent me more pictures of his abs.

The ab pictures were slowly getting lower and, I'll admit, I was more than ready for something a little sexier.

I finished my dinner, throwing the used napkin on my plate with a happy sigh. "I'm stuffed."

"We still have some time before our set..." Luc's voice trailed off suggestively. The corner of my mouth tilted up.

"Did you have something in mind?"

His lips curled up, his eyes twinkling as he lent towards me, hands moving to my knee. "Trust me, Em?"

I ducked my head, hiding a blush. "Of course."

"Come on." He caught my hand, entwining our fingers. Luc slid off the stool, leading me through the backrooms out to the van. He slid the back open, gesturing for me to climb in.

I scrambled, settling on the back seat. He climbed in beside me, sliding the door shut, sealing us in.

The weak winter sun left long shadows in the dark alley. Inside the dim interior my eyes slowly adjusted to find Luc turned towards me. Legs clad in dark-wash jeans, his top a stone-grey long-sleeved shirt, he'd shoved the sleeves back to his elbows. Everyone knew that made a guy 1000% hotter. How was I meant to resist all his forearm hotness?

I couldn't. I really couldn't.

Beside me, he shifted. One arm came up to drape over the back of the seat.

"What are we doing?" I whispered in the quiet hush.

His teeth flashed as he smiled in the dim light. "University."

He reached out, fingers finding my hand. Slowly he rubbed circles along the back of my clenched fist where it rested on my thigh.

"Are we going to make out?" Breathless, I simultaneously relaxed into his touch and tensed at the possibility of what came next.

"Oh yeah," he growled, his voice hot with want. He made a rumbling sound in his throat. "Come kiss me."

I shuffled over, hands hovering for a moment as I hesitated. I didn't know where to position them.

He huffed out a chuckle, taking over. One hand was placed on his shoulder, the other on his thigh. He dropped his hands, clasping them loosely in his lap.

"You're in control," he whispered, breath brushing my cheek. "If I do anything you don't like, just say no or push me away."

I nodded, unable to speak. This was different to all the other times we'd kissed; granted we'd only had a handful of moments, but each had a layer of distance. When I wanted more, he'd slowed us down. He'd built the passion to a boil, then maintained it with an ease and experience I had no chance of meeting. When I wanted us to explode, to go higher, he'd withdrawn, gently, but making it clear it wasn't going any further.

Tonight, I wanted *more*.

All week, living in his house, breathing in his scent, my freedom to look at him whenever and however I pleased. I'd burned to do more. I felt frustrated. So damn frustrated.

Now, in this moment, I could see his desire. Could feel the tension of his muscles under his clothes. Could see how he held himself back.

I wanted to break that restraint.

My thumb gently swept up and down his shoulder, my hand creeping closer to his neck. We were staring at each other, breath mingling, gaze hot with unspoken words.

My thumb hit the skin of his neck, and I sucked in a breath.

Could I?

I slowly moved my hand up until my fingers tangled in his hair. Slowly, oh so slowly, I drew him down to me.

Our mouths met and for one moment the kiss remained chaste. Then I flicked my tongue against his lips and it was game over. The moment of romance broken as heat and want clashed with unfulfilled desperation.

His hands came up, one going to my neck, the other to my good hip. His mouth greedily devoured mine, our lips clashing as we clung together. He tilted my head, granting him access to my neck. His lips feasted on sensitive spots, dragging moans from deep within me. My fingers tightened, drawing him closer, pressing his lips to my neck as hot delicious shots of raw energy spiralled through my body.

"Luc..." I groaned his name, moaned it. "I want..."

My other hand, the hussy, began her ascent. Slowly, ever so slowly, she inched up his leg. His big thigh felt hot under my palm. I hesitated for a moment, only a second as his lips left my neck to return to my mouth. Hot, hard, and wanting.

Fuck slow.

I brushed fingers against his crotch. Luc reared back, panting, his dark eyes molten as he stared at me, my face clasped between his hands, my palm now solidly pressed against his bulge.

"I..." I didn't know what to say as I started to withdraw. He made a noise, a hot harsh sound of protest. One hand pulled me back to his mouth, the other shifted down to press my hand against his length.

It was my turn to moan.

As I stroked him through his jeans, his hand let go of mine, shifting to the hem of my shirt. I bucked, ignoring the twinge in my side as my need overruled any concern for my body.

I needed him to touch me. I wanted his hands, his mouth, his tongue on me. I wanted him to feel and touch every part of me.

He drew my shirt away from my body as his tongue danced with mine. Hot, wet, I wanted more.

His fingers brushed the sensitive curve of my hip. I moaned, scrambling to get closer. He pulled back, our gasping breaths loud in the van.

"I need–" I panted.

"I know." He settled back in the seat, then helped me shift to straddle him, my butt firmly in his lap. "Okay?"

"Yes." I nodded, hands moving to grab both of his. "Definitely." I pulled one of his hands, pushing it under my top. His grin flashed as he took over. His other hand I pulled up, forcing his fingers into my hair. He got it, tangling his fingers in my strands.

"Greedy," he whispered, still grinning.

I ignored him as I dropped a hand to his crotch, the other going to the belt buckle that prevented full access.

"Emmie..." He groaned, eyes closing, head dropping back as I stroked him through the material. "You don't have to..."

His hand met the edge of my bra and I stilled, waiting.

His eyes opened, head coming up as his fingers gently pushed up the bra. "Okay?"

I made a small sound of affirmation.

His eyes flashed as he palmed my breast.

Holy fuck. Holy Jesus. OHMIGOD.

I pushed into him, unconsciously grinding on his lap as he played me, his expert fingers creating a symphony of sensation.

"More," I demanded, eyes closed, mouth panting. "More."

He shoved up my shirt, mouth closing over my nipple.

Hot. Mouth. Wet.

"Oh God!" I whimpered.

He licked and sucked my right breast as his clever, clever fingers teased my left. I'd dissolved into a puddle of wet wanton desire.

"Luc," I panted, my pursuit of his cock long forgotten as both my hands kept him pinned to my breast. "Luc!"

His spare hand unzipped my jeans. He drew back, grunting. "Lift."

I rose, willing to follow any command.

He returned to my breast as a hand slipped into my jeans. Through my underwear he touched me.

"Fuck. So wet," he grunted. I groaned, pulling his head back to my breast as I pushed against his fingers.

"Luc... please."

I didn't know what I wanted. Or maybe I did. I didn't know. I just knew I wanted more. More of this, more of him, more of how he made me feel.

His fingers dipped further, pushing aside my underwear.

A knock on the side of the van snapped us back to reality.

"Yo! Luc! You in there?"

"Fuck!" Luc ripped my shirt down, hand withdrawing.

What? No!

"Jim, stay the fuck out!" he yelled.

There was a pause, then a quiet chuckle from outside as I rolled off Luc, both of us frantically readjusting clothing.

"I'm not coming in, you sicko. Just letting you know you got ten." The gravel crunched as Jim walked away.

I blushed furiously as I redid the button on my jean. My head dipped, hair hiding my burning face.

Luc gently brushed my hair back, drawing my face up to look at him. He offered a wry smile.

"You okay?"

I nodded, too embarrassed to speak.

"I shouldn't... that got a little out of hand." He blew out a breath. "Sorry."

I gave a half shrug.

"You're..." He raked his gaze over my face. "Gorgeous. Don't be embarrassed, Keys."

A small smile tugged at my mouth. "I am, but only that we got caught. I just... I'm more upset that he... stopped us."

Luc barked out a laugh. "Fuck, you're perfect." His lips came back to mine.

These kisses were slow. They weren't frantic, though they still held an edge of controlled want. When we finally left the van I still burned. I could feel how wet I remained. I desperately wanted him.

Was I embarrassed? Sure. But more than that? I was so freaking happy I wasn't broken.

Luc settled me on a table near the dancefloor. I clocked Jetta and Pax as they entered. Luc waved them over before dropping a kiss on my lips.

"Later." He winked, disappearing, his bandmates already starting to assemble on the stage.

Jetta gave me a look as she handed me a glass.

"What?" I accepted the offered soft drink, taking a long sip.

"You're flushed."

"It's hot in here." I didn't care that I was staring at Luc's hands as he picked up his guitar. Those hands were magic.

"Your lips are swollen," she accused, eyes narrowing.

I couldn't stop the grin. "Are they?"

She leaned in, staring intently at my chin. "You have beard burn!"

I chuckled.

"Spill!"

I shrugged, taking a sip of my drink. Luc smiled at me from the stage as he waited for the guys to settle.

"Fines" she huffed, settling into the seat beside me. "But I am so telling Addie."

I rolled my eyes at the empty threat. If Addie didn't know from one look at me that I'd been making out, then there was something wrong with her. Jarrett described her as a sexual savant.

The lights dimmed, and Luc stepped up to the microphone. "Evening, everybody, we're Behind Utopia, and we're your musical entertainment for tonight."

The band launched into their first song. They did covers, and a damn good job at that. Throughout the night, Addie, Kel, Jarrett, and Jack arrived.

By ten o'clock, our group was varying levels of drunk. Pax was sober, Kel also. The rest of our merry gang was everything from tipsy (Simeon) to ready to be wheeled home (Addie). I watched Jarrett eyeing off a guy on the far side of the room.

"I'm going to do that," he declared, raising his glass.

I tilted my head, squinting at the guy in question. "He's flirting with someone."

"They're not serious." Jarrett made a sweeping motion. "He's interested."

"Really?" Kel drawled dryly. "He doesn't look it."

"Oh, just you wait." Jarrett swung back to the stage, giving Luc a wave. Luc gave him a nod, finishing up the song.

"Thanks, guys, you've been great!" Luc told the heaving crowd as they screamed for more. "We've got a little surprise for you tonight. We've got two great friends of the band in the audience."

"Oh, fuck." Jetta's horrified expletive was just audible over the cheers.

"Give a warm welcome to Jarrett and Jetta!"

Jarrett calmly swept Jetta up, leading her to the stage. Luc swapped his electric out for an acoustic as the band chugged drinks, wiping their sweaty faces.

Pax crossed his arms as he glared at the stage.

"She'll be fine." Addie patted his bicep drunkenly. "You know she will."

A muscle in his cheek ticked as the crowd began to murmur. Jetta's fame as a lyricist, coupled with her recent singing endeavours, not to mention her recent brush with crime, meant the crowd knew her.

Jarrett handed her a microphone, taking the spare as they stood on stage. Jetta glanced from Jarrett to Luc to Paxton in the crowd. Jetta stared out at the crowd, fiddling with the microphone, her face pale, her eyes deer-caught-in-the-headlights wide.

Jarrett waved a hand. "This is for the hottie over in the corner. You know who you are, good looking." He winked as

Luc strummed the opening bars of Ed Sheeran's "Perfect Duet."

Jarrett sang, his eyes on the hot guy across the room. He changed the lyrics from guy to girl. As he got to the part that Beyoncé would normally sing, Jetta, her eyes firmly on Pax took over. Her voice pitched beautifully as she sang. Luc flashed a grin as Jetta and Jarrett brought it home, absolutely smashing it.

I glanced at Pax. He'd dropped his arms, hands now in his pocket as he smiled pure love at Jetta.

#CoupleGoals

They finished to rapacious applause and calls for more. Jarrett looked at Jetta, a quick conversation between them taking place as the crowd, hungry for more, cheered. Finally, they nodded, talking to the band. A moment later the opening bars of the Foo Fighters', *Everlong* revved the crowd. The dance floor packed out as Jarrett, Jetta, and Luc took turns belting out the lyrics.

"She's loving it!" Addie yelled, clinging to Pax as the dancefloor heaved. "Look at her!"

Jetta danced on stage, playing air guitar as Jarrett and Luc sang.

The band revved the crowd up, building to a peak as the set drew to a close.

"Thank you!" Luc yelled over the screams for an encore.

I fought my way back stage, flashing my wrist band at the two security guards. They waved me through. Luc wrapped an arm around my waist, spinning me around, pressing hot kisses to my laughing mouth.

"Emmie! Oh, Emmie let your hair hang down!" he sang, swinging me around until I was dizzy.

He let me slide down his body, his grin wide. "Home?"

I nodded. "But you need to pack up, right?"

"The guys can do it. They owe me." He pressed another hot kiss to my mouth, handing me his phone. "Order an Uber. We're leaving."

In the back of the car we groped, kisses hot and hard as the poor driver tried to ignore our grasping desperation. Arriving at the house, Luc tossed him a fifty on the way out, yelling, "Sorry, dude. Five stars for you!"

Laughing, I pressed the code to the high fence, permitting us access. Inside, Luc chased me up the drive, snagging me near the front door, pressing me into the brick wall, kisses landing on my lips, my cheeks, my neck.

"Inside," I whispered hoarsely, unable to bear this. "I want…"

He pulled me into him, turning me his back to the door. He flicked the pin on the lock-pad, pressing his thumb to the scanner as he nibbled my collarbone. The door clicked and we tumbled through, hands pulling at clothing, running over bare skin. His shirt dropped near the door, my shoes in the hall. We tumbled through the lounge, socks coming off, his jeans removed, my hair tie flicking across the room.

"This shirt," he growled, "drove me crazy all night."

Well, thank you, Addie.

He bent his head, delving into the deep V. He made a sound of pure delight as his beard dragged along my sensitive flesh.

Yep, I was officially dead. I'd officially died and gone to heaven because once upon a time I'd been utterly convinced there was no way Lucien Falco would ever or was ever going to take me to bed. But here we were. This was happening. THIS WAS HAPPENING.

I am dead. The only possible explanation is that I died the night I was shot. This moment is my afterlife reward. I don't even care that this isn't real. You hear that?

I DON'T EVEN CARE!

As we walked, stumbled, and fumbled our way to the bedroom– his bedroom –he finally came up for air, ripping the shirt from my body. In the doorway of his bedroom he stopped, staring at me in the new bra and jeans.

"Fuck, you're gorgeous." His voice felt like a physical caress.

I flushed, hands hovering, uncertain. He returned to me, helping remove my jeans as we tripped towards the bed. Literally tripped– his floor was littered with clothes.

"You." I pressed a kiss to his mouth. "Need." Another kiss. "To clean your room."

He laughed, pulling me hard against him. "Never."

Pantless, shirtless, we both fell onto the mattress, hands roaming, mouths searching as we teased.

His long, hard body pressed deliciously against me. His cock sat heavy against my inner thigh as we rolled around the bed, each grasping to be on top. I didn't mind when he finally won, his weight pinning me as he feasted on my mouth, his hands cupping my breasts. My bra disappeared leaving me in the boy-cut underwear.

He withdrew, pressing one last kiss to my nipple.

"You ready?" Luc asked, our gaze meeting as he stroked my cheek.

"Yeah." My hands were already on his briefs. Slowly, I pushed them down as he rose. I managed to get them to his lower thighs before he took over, quickly shedding them, his cock now free.

I took a moment to admire the fact I had done this. He was hard, and it was all because of me.

I reached out a hand, but he swatted it away, smiling. "Nope, not till I see you."

Uh-oh. Moment of truth. It was his turn to undress me. Slowly, he peeled my underwear down, revealing a part of me I hadn't thought I would ever let another person see.

When I lived in Melbourne, my housemate had given me a vibrator. He and his boyfriend had sat me down and explained that while they knew I didn't want to date, self-care was incredibly important. I'd never gotten up the guts to try it. For me, sexual desire had always had a rottenness about it. My childhood and my rape hadn't prepared me for the actuality of healthy sexuality.

Luc was helping. It didn't mean I had no hang ups, just that I was trying with someone I trusted. When I'd been by myself, I'd often found it difficult to imagine anything but that night. With Luc, he distracted me with wicked words and delicious lips, replacing the bad memories with moments so utterly perfect I had no choice but to hoard them on my soul.

As he threw my underwear across the room, I had a moment to consider if I wanted this. He was moving slow, no matter how fast and passionate this felt, he took each escalation slowly. Drawing it out. Letting me lead.

He dropped back down, this time beside me, one hand propping up his head, the other reaching out to trace soft circles around my breasts.

"What are you doing?" I whispered.

"Waiting."

"For what?"

"For the uncertainty to leave." He bent down, sliding his nose against mine, lips gently pressing a kiss to my forehead. "We don't have to do anything. I'm happy with this."

Oh crap.

Yep.

There it was.

I love you.

I opened my mouth before shutting it tight. God. He was such a good guy.

How did one tell their partner they were ready for sexy time? Did you say, *I want your penis in me?* Was there some kind of phallic-shaped bat symbol I could use? Why had no one invented mood-ring contact lenses?

I rolled towards him, tired of the distance between us. My hand immediately went to his cock, grasping it. His response was more than gratifying.

The groan, the kisses, the needy sucking of my breasts as he showed me how to stroke him.

He worked his way down my body, breaking my grip on his cock as he nipped, kissed, sucked, and licked his way down. I raised up on elbows, eyes wide.

"Relax." He winked before his mouth closed over me.

Tongue.

Hot.

Shit.

Fuck.

OH.

MY.

GOD.

He worked my clit, licking and sucking as I shuddered under him, incoherent. I clutched his—

Wait, is that his hair? Oh God, who cares? Just don't let him stop—

"Fuck," I groaned.

He curled a finger into me, rumbling a sound of pleasure.

"Tight," he told me as his finger coaxed a response. "Do you like this?"

"More," I demanded, pushing his head back down. His laughter brushed against me as he licked, his tongue doing wonderfully erotic things to sensitive parts of me.

"Like that!" I moaned, feeling it build, reaching, panting. He shifted his finger, just a fraction, and that was it. I tipped over the edge. My body squeezed around his finger as my whole reason for existing became this feeling. This wonderful, pleasure-pain.

I found myself panting, a sweaty, swearing, magnificently glorious mess. Luc hovered, one hand stroking my side as he watched.

"Hey." I offered him a shy grin.

"You're beautiful," he whispered.

"What?"

"You're so beautiful. Perfect." He replied. I felt his cock jump against my leg.

"You're pretty beautiful, yourself." I reached down grasping him. He huffed out a chuckle-groan.

"God. You're–"

"Ready," I interrupted, pulling him towards me. "So, damn ready."

"Shit," he whispered, halting his movement. "Condom."

I let him go, watching as he rolled it on. He returned to me, just as hot and hard.

His cock nudged my entrance as he slowly eased in, the vein in his neck pulsing. His blue eyes raked my face, waiting, watching, making sure I enjoyed it.

I loved how he filled me, moved in me. I loved how his weight pressed into me. My fingers raked up his back as he thrust, his growly voice whispering praises and curses, muttering filthy sentences as he drove into me.

"Come for me," he demanded, one hand reaching down to finger my clit. He rolled his finger once, twice, and I came, hard, wet and full, my body clenching around him.

We collapsed. A wet, sticky, panting mess. He made a move to roll off, but I clasped him, arms and legs tight around his body.

"No," I mumbled into his shoulder. "Stay."

He did, pressing kisses to my neck as we cooled.

The night was cold, true winter having arrived. Finally, chilled, and too tired to stay awake much longer, we separated. I went to tidy up, he disposed of the condom and secured the house. We met back in the bed.

"Good?" he asked, pulling me into him.

"Yeah." I grinned into the darkness. "Really good."

His chuckled quietly. "I'm glad."

I smiled, curling into his side. He wrapped an arm around me, pulling me closer "Me too." I hesitated, then gave in, admitting my deepest fear. "I was worried I'd freeze."

"Were you thinking about it?"

"No. You successfully distracted me."

We both chuckled. His fingers lazily caressed my shoulder.

"Thank you for putting in the effort."

"Beautiful, you are not effort."

"Still." I lifted a shoulder, shrugging. "You never rushed me. And I know you wanted to."

"I've been hard for months," he admitted.

I dropped my hand to his stomach, fingers inching further down. "I mean, do you need me to...?"

He laughed, halting my wandering by knitting our fingers together and resting our hands on his stomach.

"We can go all night another time. This is your first, and I don't want to hurt you."

He pressed a kiss to my forehead. "Sleep. I promise, you can use my body to your heart's content tomorrow."

"I'm holding you to that."

"Dear God, I've unleashed a monster."

I slapped a hand to his chest, grinning. "Maybe."

"Night, Keys."

"Night, Luc."

EMMIE

Luc delivered on his promise. I woke with a mouth on my breasts, and it deteriorated– or perhaps improved? –from there.

We stayed in bed, devouring each other, ravenous in our need. Luc finally pulled me out of bed in the early afternoon, laughing at my protests.

"I need food. You need food. We need to eat, hydrate, gain sustenance," he told me between kisses.

"Boo." I pouted, pressing myself into him. "Just once more?"

"No." He smacked my butt, laughing at my squeak. "Shower, dress, then food. Besides, I need to go to the shops. My family's coming."

I froze on the way to the bathroom. "Sorry?"

"Tonight. My parents are coming. And my siblings. And their partners. And the kids. It's my weekend."

I turned, horror dawning. "Your weekend?"

"Family dinner. We do it once a month. Tonight's my turn." He was checking his phone, eyes on the screen. If he'd been looking at me he'd have seen the abject terror on my face.

"Here? They're coming here?"

"Yeah. 'Bout seven."

I spun, running to the bathroom and locking myself in.

Shit. Shit, shit, shit, shit, shit.

Shit.

I stared at my pale reflection in the mirror, hyperventilating.

"Em? Keys?" The door handle twisted as Luc tried to enter. "You okay?"

"Fine!" I squeaked, lying through my teeth. "Just going to shower."

There was a beat of silence before Luc answered. "Okay... We'll talk after."

I showered, shaved, and washed my hair three times. I spent fifteen minutes wrapped in a towel, as I decided whether to leave the safety of the bathroom. Finally ready, I exited, returning to the bedroom to dress. I found Luc in the kitchen cooking.

"Hey." He set the tongs aside, flipping a dishtowel over his shoulder as he leaned across the laminate breakfast counter to greet me with a kiss. "Okay?"

I returned the kiss, then slid onto one of his chipped bar stools. "Sure."

One of the things I liked most about Luc was his willingness to tackle a project. He wasn't afraid of hard work or getting his hands dirty.

Mm. Luc's hands.

The kitchen was old, run down, and in need of a complete overhaul. The house had been a wreck, worn and worried from years of neglect by a hoarder. Luc was slowly bringing it back to life, turning it into a home that reflected his personality.

"When are you redoing the kitchen?" I took the offered mug, my stomach rumbling as the bacon sizzled in the pan.

"I'm taking a week in September. Gonna smash out the removal and build the cabinets. The benchtops will be longer because they're stone."

I ran my hand over the cracked lime green laminate. "You should do a wood feature for this island. Or maybe concrete. If you're keeping it."

"Good idea. I'll show you the plans once mum sends them through."

"She's an architect, right?"

"Uh-huh. Mostly commercial, but she can't help herself. I haven't actually asked her to help, but I mentioned the reno at our last dinner, and I can guarantee some will appear in my inbox in the next month."

I chuckled. He slid bread into his four-piece toaster, then removed the skillet from the flame, turning off the stove and sliding the bacon and eggs onto a folded paper towel. He busied himself hustling around, buttering the toast, and dividing the food before sliding it before me.

"*Bon appétit,*" he said with perfect pronunciation, settling onto the stool beside me.

"I met your sisters at your housewarming. I know they speak French. Do you?"

He scooped up a piece of toast, pushing egg onto it with his fork. "I speak what can be loosely termed Fren-lish. I'm fluent-ish. Mum is French so she taught us. I have long since learnt that my sisters are better than me in all things."

I grinned at his self-deprecation. "How did your parents meet?"

"She and dad met while he was over working in the embassy. He's a career diplomat. They met, fell in love, got married, he came back to Australia when his posting ended, she followed. They settled– I use that term lightly –in Canberra. Really, they had us, then moved around the globe for a few years taking different posting opportunities. I speak about eight languages, none of them well." He grinned, the edges of his eyes crinkling as he bit into the toast.

I propped my chin in my hand as I watched him eat. "That must have been fascinating, and hard."

He shrugged. "Probably why I went into the military. I was used to moving."

"But you didn't stay in the military. And now you're here." I waved my free hand to encompass the room.

"Elliot Securities offered me a job and stability. My sisters were having kids. My parents are semi-retired. It was time to come home."

"You don't advertise your ownership stake."

He paused, hand halfway to his mouth. "How did you...?" He laughed. "You found the files."

I shrugged. "It's my job."

"You're a threat." He dropped his fork, running a hand through his hair. "When Pax took over, Elliot Securities had a great rep, but the model was outdated. His dad didn't have the know-how to take it from physical security to protecting against all threats. When we introduced the cyber side, he decided it was time to retire. Cyber required capital the business didn't have. We needed to find clients, do advertising, recruit. Not to mention building the infrastructure. The banks were okay to a point, but I had the money and the time so...." He shrugged.

"So, you invested and came on as a silent partner."

"I get the benefits without the hassles," he admitted. "Eat your breakfast."

I scooped up some egg, munching as I let my mind wander. He pushed his plate back, reaching for his coffee mug. He considered me over the rim.

"You going to tell me what this morning was about? I'd been gearing up for sexy shower time, and you shut down."

I ducked my head, the blush immediate. "Sorry."

He nudged me. "Don't be. Everything we do is at your pace. Just wanna make sure you're okay."

I shoved bacon in my mouth, buying myself some time. "It's been a while since I had any positive interactions with a family."

He turned on the stool, leaning his elbows back against the bench. "Explain."

I blew out a breath, pushing a strip of bacon with my fork. Sighing, I tried to explain my apprehension. "I've met some of your sisters. But it's different now. We're together. I want to make a good impression. But I don't know how families work. Mine took a neither seen nor heard approach. When I was allowed to be seen, it was unhealthy. I interacted with my siblings, but we were like prisoners. We danced around issues, fearful of doing the wrong thing. We were surviving despite our family, not thriving in it."

I glanced over.

"You don't have to do anything you don't want to. I can just tell them you aren't close to your family. Mine will smother you with love instead, I promise."

I frowned. "But it's so much bigger than that. And I want them to see me as a good catch."

"You're not a good catch, Em. You're the only one. It's obvious you love me and I love you. That's all they care about." He picked up his plate, reaching for mine. "You done?"

He acted as if he hadn't dropped a bomb, completely detonating my world. He took the plate, scraping both before putting them in the ancient dishwasher.

"Let me clean this up and we can go," he said over his shoulder, hitting the tap to fill the sink with hot water.

I sat on a bar stool. I sat on a bar stool in Luc's kitchen staring at his back. I sat on a bar stool in Luc's kitchen staring at his back after he told me he loved me.

Luc.

Loved.

Me.

As he reached for the skillet I whispered, "I love you too."

He froze, head turning. "Keys."

"And I know you love me," I told him as he started back around the island, coming to me. "You've proved it since–"

His mouth crashed down on mine. I clung to him as he pulled me up, hands burying in my hair.

He drew back, his eyes beautiful, staring at me. "I love you. So. Fucking. Much."

Our lips met again, my arms wrapping around him as he pulled me into his chest. Slowly, we withdrew.

"Groceries?" I asked softly.

"Later."

EMMIE

Dinner was a revelation. After a session that involved a barstool, a tea towel, and chocolate sauce, we made it to the shops for supplies.

We'd made potato and leek soup with fresh bread, roast chicken and vegetables, and chocolate lava cake for dessert. We also had wine and cheese for the adults, and a bunch of fun dinner options, like feet shaped chicken nuggets, for the kids.

The only word for it was chaos. As his sisters arrived, Luc pulled out a toy box, dumped it on the floor and let the kids go crazy. I'd been handed a baby within minutes as his sister, Sophia, rolled her eyes and took me under her wing, explaining, "Mother will want to know only two things. One, if you love my brother, and two, if you want kids. If it's yes to at least one, you're fine."

Lucky for me, it was.

I rocked the sleepy baby, her sweet smell making my ovaries weep as the older kids were sent off to watch a movie Luc's dad had turned on. We'd made it through the predinner drinks, transitioned to the soup, and were now waiting for Luc to serve the main.

Luc's five sisters were hilarious. Adele was the oldest and married to John; they had three girls aged between ten and four. Bridget was next oldest. She was married to Daniel; they had two girls, six and four. Dominque was the middle child and married to Steve, who'd handed me six-month-old Pepper with a yawn. Sophia and her husband Phil, and Eloise who was single, rounded out the family. And Luc, of course. Or as they called him, *Lucy*.

I hid a smile as Dominique broke into fluent French, agitated by something her mother, Cecile, had said. Her hands flicked about in protest as her mother retorted in French. Roger, Luc's dad, gave me a wink across the table.

"Ignore them. They do this."

I offered a smile, still rocking the baby gently.

"You know, you're handling this better than me. And I only had the core family to deal with," John said from his seat next to me. He reached across the table, snatching a water jug to top me up.

"Thanks." I picked up the glass, careful not to jostle Pepper. I tilted my cup to encompass the table. "I like it."

He chuckled. "They're all as crazy as each other." He looked over at his wife, his face a picture of contentment. "It's why we love them."

Cecile bounced about, a bundle of energy, running after the children, drawing plans for Luc's remodel, pestering Sophia about grandbabies and Eloise about finding a partner. I enjoyed watching the dynamic between Luc, as the only boy and youngest, and his family.

He was obviously the apple of their collective eyes. They ruffled his hair, showered him with hugs, drew him in to every conversation. Love. So much damn love.

"All the grandkids are girls," I said, later that night as we washed whatever hadn't fit in the dishwasher. We'd waved off his family with hugs and promises that I would attend the next dinner.

"Yeah. We're male-poor on Mum's side. It's why dad took her last name."

I leaned my good hip against his counter, absently drying a glass. "I didn't know that."

"His side has thirteen boys. He felt it was his duty to carry on the Falco name. Mum is one of three girls. No males on any branch of that tree."

"So, you're the miracle?"

He laughed. "The averages were with me. Mum was determined to keep trying until there was at least one."

"How did they take your service?" I asked, reaching up to put away the glass. I turned back, taking the plate he held out for me. His forearms were covered in suds.

He dropped his head, looking at the dish as he scrubbed it, taking his time to answer. "Not great. I didn't tell them until the day before I was due for training. Mum broke things. Dad took a long walk. My sisters were in hysterics. You'd think I was dying the way they carried on."

I put the plate to the side. "Then why did you?"

"I'm not a diplomat like dad. Or an architect like mum. And all the good jobs were taken by my sisters. I wanted to work out who I was without them hovering. It seemed like a good solution."

"Was it?"

He finished washing the plate, handed it to me and started on the next. In silence, we tidied our way through two more plates before he answered. "You know, I think it was. All things considered."

He pulled the plug, draining the sink. I finished drying

the last of the cutlery, then handed him the towel. He dried his hands as I put away the remaining items, waiting for him to continue.

"It was shit, you know? War zones are fucked up. We lost friends, men I considered brothers. People talk about how hard it is to adjust when you get home, or when you leave the service. But it's only when you experience it yourself that you understand. I got friends who I counted on to save my life. They came home so broken they struggle to leave the house."

He turned, walking into the lounge, pulling me along with him. We sat, me beside him, his legs propped on the coffee table, one arm stretched across the back of the couch.

"I'm glad I did it. I served my country, I looked after my brothers, and I did a good job. I came home a different person and that's what I wanted. I wanted to test myself, and I found I like who I am." He shrugged, his mouth pulling up into a wry smile. "I guess we all have our reasons for doing crazy shit."

My lips curved. "Crazy or brave?"

"They're exclusive?" His deliciously warm body inched closer to mine.

"Bed?" I asked, my lips now inches from his.

"No." He curled an arm around my back, pulling me into him. "I'm going to fuck you right here."

Yes. Please.

EMMIE

Monday afternoon saw me struggling not to punch my computer screen. Yet again I was testing the code we'd pulled from the West Investment accounts. I should have finished my report days ago. By now, I knew the way it interacted, could predict how it would move and targeted accounts. The program wasn't sophisticated, but that damn niggle in my gut wouldn't budge.

"Okay, explain it to me again," Sawyer requested. We were both huddled over a FLEA, as I showed him the way the program manipulated the accounts.

"I can't work it out. There's just something not right." I ran hands through my hair, letting out a frustrated sigh. "This is doing my head in."

He watched as the program pulled minuscule amounts of money and transferred them into a newly created account. "The amounts are random."

"I know." I blew out another breath. "The program itself is straightforward. The amounts are randomized and mimic fees to ensure they won't flag as fraudulent. But there's... something. Something that isn't quite right."

Sawyer's leg jiggled as he tapped fingers rhythmically against the desk.

"Maybe I'm just crazy." I huffed out a laugh. "I'm probably seeing ghosts where none exist."

"What if it's not the program itself, but the way it reacts that's the issue?"

"What do you mean?"

He tapped the monitor. "This is old code. Like, really ridiculously old. West Investments deserve to have their systems taken out the back and shot. It's a wonder they're not riddled with these kind of issues. Their CIO doesn't deserve the title."

"They didn't have a chief information officer. That's how they got into this mess," I pointed out.

"If businesses these days..." Sawyer was on a roll, ranting about cybercriminals, organised crime, how privacy is a social construct that one must earn not give away. I tuned him out, having heard it all before.

Finally, Sawyer wound down. "And that's why the Illuminati are Ravenclaws." He nodded, crossing his arms over his chest in finality.

I waited, sipping my tea. He didn't disappoint. Shaking his blond mane, stretching his neck, Sawyer finally leaned towards the computer, reaching for the mouse. "Okay, where were we?"

"The code is old," I offered.

"Right." He reached for my mug, taking it and sipping the lukewarm brew. I wrinkled my nose, but he ignored me, eyes firmly on the screen.

"Old code...," he muttered to himself, drumming fingers on the desk.

A pleasant shiver ran down my back. I glanced over my shoulder, smiling as I caught Luc watching me. Today he'd dressed in a sharp navy suit complete with silver-grey tie. He'd combed his hair back, but a chunk had fallen across his forehead.

I'd sat on the bathtub that morning, watching as he'd trimmed his beard. As much as my heart had hurt watching him remove it, the scruff he'd left behind was devilishly handsome.

He'd done this in preparation of a client meeting. Pax had also attended. I'd spotted them before they left, smartly dressed, game faces on. Whoever the client was, they were big.

Luc pushed off the wall, coming to me. One hand on the back of my chair, the other tangling in my hair, he bent, lips meeting mine in a hungry kiss. We were being obnoxiously happy. Desire and the knowledge that we burned together beautifully, sparked the sexual tension. This was the first time I'd seen him today. It was an unacceptable amount of time.

I tried to draw back, but Luc's mouth chased mine. A cough interrupted our make-out session. We both turned, heads pressed together, to look at Sawyer. His eyes were firmly on the computer screen.

"Just putting it out there," he commented, mouse clicking. "There is a bed upstairs."

The blush burned away desire, leaving embarrassment in its place. I started to withdraw, but Luc stopped my retreat.

"Dude. Uncool." His hand slid forward, thumb tracing the curve of my cheek. "But thanks for the idea."

Luc pulled back, capturing my hand in his. He pulled me up, leading me toward the door. Such was his gravitational pull that I didn't think to question where he led. Sawyer, however, appeared immune to Luc's charms.

"Where are you taking her?" he yelled, seat swivelling to watch us.

"Home. We'll see you tomorrow!" Luc called over his shoulder.

"But... work!" Sawyer snapped.

"We're doing a performance review!" Sawyer's reply was cut off by the door shutting. At the elevators, Luc pressed the down button. He tapped his foot impatiently, hand squeezing mine.

"Luc–"

The elevator slid open, and he led me in. As the doors began closing, Luc crowded in, backing me into the lift wall. His hands came up, one tangling in my hair, the other caressing my breast. I groaned under his kiss, my needy, wanton body pressing closer.

Luc, I'd learned, enjoyed being in control. He loved diving his hands in my hair, directing my mouth this way or that. Holding me still as he plundered my mouth, feasting on the sensitive zones of my neck.

As the elevator descended, our hands danced, a battle to see who would surrender first. Whose desperation was such that they could no longer stand not being skin-to-skin. The doors slid open in the thankfully empty carpark.

He pulled me, nearly running in our haste. He pushed me up against the passenger door, his wonderfully filthy mouth making me think filthy thoughts. Things like where I wanted him to fuck me, how I wanted it, the raging desire a beast within me that wanted to nip, bite, and suck every part of him.

"I want you," I panted, hands pulling at his dress shirt. "I want to taste you."

"Where?" he asked, nipping at my collar bone. "Where do you want to taste me, love?"

My head lolled as he palmed my breast. "Your... cock. I want to—"

He abruptly dropped his hands, stepping back. We panted, staring at each other.

"Fuck, you're gorgeous." He hesitated for one moment, before swearing under his breath. "Get in the car, Emmie."

"But—"

He turned his back, rounding the bonnet to the driver's side. I slid in, depressingly deprived of his heat. Luc started the car, his jaw clenching as we sped out of the underground park.

I caught a glimpse of his face, as he navigated the streets.

"Luc?"

"Shh, Keys." His hand reached out, finding mine.

"Did I do something wrong?" I asked, my uncertainty, my inexperience feeding my insecurities.

His head turned, his eyes searing. He dropped the mask, letting me see raw unadulterated need.

"No." The word was a tortured groan. "Never."

I squeezed his hand before he removed it, changing gears. We drove in silence until we reached his house. Anticipation tingled, building as he drove us home. Fantasies built and, as we turned into his driveway, I plucked up the courage to ask for the one fantasy I wanted.

"Will you let me taste you?"

The tires screamed, the car skidded on the loose gravel as the car bumped to a halt. Luc climbed out, rounding the bonnet, jerking my door open, pulling me free of the car. His mouth crashed down on mine as he boosted me up, encouraging my legs to wrap around his waist.

I am not small. I am a Viking of a woman. I have tits,

arse, and stand close to six feet tall. Luc didn't struggle. He took my weight, groaning as my arse settled into his hands. He pushed me against the garage wall, fucking my mouth with his tongue, squeezing my arse with his hands as I dry humped him, my legs holding him tight.

"Fuck," he groaned, pulling back. I whimpered a protest.

"Keys, Em, love..." He tried to regain control. "Inside, we need to go..."

I hopped down, powering for the door. We reached it, hitting the locks, unarming the house. The door opened and I headed for the bedroom, Luc close on my heels. Inside, we crashed together, a frantic wave of need. His beautiful beard dragged across my sensitized skin as I stripped him of his jacket, his belt, his tie. He ripped the shirt, buttons popping across the room as I dropped to my knees, hands frantically reaching for his fly.

"Emmie."

My name sounded like a plea, and that did things to me. Things I enjoyed. I wanted to wring that sound from him again. I wanted him to only ever say my name in that needy, desperate voice.

My hands slowed as I drew out his cock. I glanced up. He panted, his gorgeous chest covered in a fine sheen of sweat. His hands were clenched at his side, as if he were trying to stop from taking over.

Oh, but I wanted him to lead.

I gripped him, using a technique I may have googled.

May have? You googled the heck out of how to tickle his pickle.

I drew his cock down, tracing its crown against my lips. He groaned, the broken sound feeding my desire.

"Emmie."

I opened my mouth, tongue dipping to taste him. Heat and salt and man.

Delicious.

LUC

Em's mouth was wetter and hotter than anything I'd ever felt. Or maybe it's just I wanted her more than I'd ever wanted anyone or anything in my life.

She stroked my length with her tongue, flicking playfully at the underside of my crown, pulling curses from me with surprising ease.

"Fuck. Jesus. Fuck. Christ. Fuck. *Fuck.*"

Her lips wrapped around me, taking me as deep as she could.

And I died. My eyes rolled back in my head as words spilled from my mouth uncensored.

"Yes, take me deeper, Keys. Suck my cock," I urged.

She moaned as she took me, getting off on my directions.

It took every piece of will power I had to keep from grabbing her hair, holding her still and fucking her mouth. But I'd spent too many months fisting my own cock to destroy this fantasy.

She drew back. "Luc?"

"Okay?"

She licked her lips, hand still firmly around my cock. She dragged her hand up, twisting just so.

I nearly came. Honest to God, this girl. This magnificent creature destroyed me.

She looked nervous for a moment, rocking on her knees. "Emmie?"

She looked up at me with those big green eyes, her long lashes sweeping down to brush the curve of her cheek. Her pink delicious lips opened to say the last thing I expected.

"*Prends-moi*, Lucien."

Holy fuck.

My control snapped, and I reached down, mindless in my need for her. I lifted her, awkwardly moving us to the bed, throwing her onto the mattress and covering her with my body. My mouth worked its way down as my hands pulled her clothes off, peeling back the shields she used to keep everyone else at bay. No one saw this. No one knew how beautiful she was, how perfectly formed. No one but me.

Possessed by my need to taste and touch, I wanted to consume her. I wanted her to burn with the same need, the same want I battled every day. It was all or nothing.

I tugged jeans and underwear from her body, my hands immediately running up her legs to part her thighs. My mouth delighted in the treasures I uncovered.

"*Tu es une déesse. Je veux te posséder*," I murmured against her core. She whimpered, putting a hand in my hair, returning my mouth to her delightful pussy.

"I don't speak French," she admitted between rapid pants, her eyes closed, her thighs clenched around my head as I teased her. "I googled."

I chuckled, my breath teasing her centre, ending her squirming. "You want me to translate?"

"Mm." Her hips thrust up as I swapped my tongue for a finger, moving up her body, pressing hot, wet kisses to every part of her that intrigued me. Lucky me, all of her intrigued me.

"It means, love," –I nipped her earlobe, enjoying her earthy groan– "you are a goddess, and I want to own you." I pressed two fingers against her. Slick, they slid in an ever-tightening circle until I found the spot that made her gasp.

"Luc!"

There it is.

I grinned, pressing a hot kiss to her mouth. She bucked beneath me, crying out as it crashed over her. I could watch this a million times and never grow tired of how she looked at this moment.

She blinked up at me, coming down from her high. A half-smile on her pretty face.

"Okay? I asked, aching to take her.

"No."

Fuck.

"No?"

She shook her head, hand snaking down to pull me closer. I heard the crinkle of a wrapper before her other hand moved to slide a condom on my length.

"No," she whispered, her hips gently undulating. "I need you."

Fuck. This girl. Perfect.

"What do you need, beautiful?" I asked, my voice rough. Her hands crept up, her hips moving higher as she squirmed.

"You."

"Say it," I demanded.

"I need you."

Her head fell back as I thrust into her. Wild from the feel

of her, I lost all control. She met my every thrust, her hands clutching, clawing at my back. I boosted her legs, wrapping them around my hips as she encouraged me to go harder, faster, deeper.

Fuckin' perfect. Fuck.

She came. Hard. Her hot, wet pussy clutching me. Squeezing. I became lost in the feel of her, in her scent, her sounds, her need. I lost control.

We crashed down in a tangle of limbs and heavy breathing.

Calming, I reached for the cover, pulling the blanket up and over us, sealing us in a cocoon of warmth.

"You good, beautiful?" I asked, pulling her into me. She snuggled down, running a hand over my chest.

"Mm. Luc?"

"Mm?"

"I like this."

"The sex?"

She waited for a moment, running her fingers gently over my chest.

"Yes, but also this." She seemed contemplative, her eyes focused on her softly gliding hand. "I've never had this."

"What? An attractive piece of man meat?" I asked lightly. She smiled, but it was bittersweet.

"Someone who touches me in a good way. Someone who cares when they touch me." She didn't look up, still determinedly focused on her hand. "We weren't allowed to touch each other, not even for a hug. They said it would make us impure." She tracked her finger, making a cross on my chest, then rubbing it out. "The only person who could touch you was a deacon. And they only did it when you were bad. They'd grab you, pull you to the room, and lock you in. If you were lucky, they'd just leave you in the pit for a few days. Most of the time they hit me."

My arms flexed, tight around her.

"I never knew why I was punished. I'd try to be good. I'd work extra hard. I'd never talk back or shirk my chores. Whatever they asked, I did it."

"Some people live to destroy. For them, to break a human is the ultimate challenge. An animal can't beg. It can't tell them they've won. They can only hurt it, making it twist and squeal until they destroy its will to live. Humans? We have a capacity, a resilience for hope. To extinguish that can be someone's entire purpose."

She blinked up at me, tears shimmering on her eyelashes. "I begged that night. I just wanted it to stop."

I brushed her tears, not shushing her, not trying to stop her. She needed to purge this horror. I would bear any burden she laid at my feet.

"He ripped the dress from me, pushed me down, and fucked me. There was no tenderness, no mercy. He beat me. I had bruises. I fought. I screamed and kicked and bit, and he overpowered me until I begged. And when he kept going, no matter how much I–" She choked. "I realised I couldn't live with that."

Fuck.

She was sobbing now, her hand stilled, her eyes big as she pleaded with me to understand. "It hurt so bad. Every part of me hurt." She pressed her face to my chest, sniffling as her tears wet my chest.

You got one chance at this. Let her get it out. Don't fuck this up. You can murder the motherfucker and burn their world down after.

"Abel, my brother, found me. He helped me escape. He hugged me. I don't remember the last time I'd been hugged before then. Addie sometimes hugs me. Kel. Even Jetta. I thought I'd forever be fearful of touch. I thought I was damaged. When you touch me, I don't think about David or Abel. I think about you and me. And I want more. I never–" Her voice broke, shoulders wracking as she sobbed. "I thought I was broken, but I'm not. And I'm so happy. I love how you touch me. How good it is. I want–" She hiccupped, pulling back to look up at me. "I want to keep doing this."

My heart ached even as I banked the rage.

I pulled her closer, hoping the reality of us would sink in, helping her fight these demons. "I love you, baby. I fucking love you. You're strong. You're Ash from Pokémon. No matter what life throws at you, you dust yourself off and keep going." I pressed kisses to her hair, to her wet cheeks, nuzzling her temple.

She hiccupped a laugh. "Does that make you Pikachu?"

"Of course. And together we're electric."

She snorted, relaxing slightly.

"First, we're going to find these bastards and I'm going to wring their motherfucking necks. Second, if you'll allow it, we're getting you therapy. You're fucking brave, but I don't want this toxic memory to taint you. How's that sound?"

"Okay." She looked up at me, her eyes bloodshot, still wet with tears. She bit her lip, ducking her head as she muttered, "I trust you."

"Marry me." I hadn't intended to ask the question. Hell, I hadn't even considered the possibility before this moment.

This woman is it. This brilliant, intelligent, hilarious, quirky woman. Emmie's my one.

I heard her breath catch, her hands flexing. She didn't answer.

Don't you dare rush her.

Finally, finally, she looked up at me, sniffling, eyes shadowed with memories. "No."

It didn't matter that she'd said no. Tomorrow, next month or next year, eventually she'd conquer her fear and say yes.

I smiled, shrugging. "That's okay. I'll ask again tomorrow."

Her lips tilted up a fraction, the shadows clearing. "I've only slept with you for a week. Don't get too clingy."

"Oh, clingy, hmm?" I wrapped my legs and arms tight around her, chuckling as she squealed, squirming in my grasp. "Like this?"

She laughed. It was edged with a hint of hysteria. I didn't mind, so long as she thought of us and not them. They didn't deserve one more moment of her.

EMMIE

The clock read 2:38 a.m.

I was curled into Luc, my back to his front when the shrill ring of Luc's phone pierced the silence of the house. I sat up, my eyes catching the glowing numbers on the alarm clock as my head twisted to look at Luc. His sleepy eyes met mine, even as his hand snaked out to the mobile on the bedside table.

"This is Lu–" My mobile's ringtone cut him off. I lost eye contact as I turned, pushing up off the bed reaching for my phone.

"You've got Emmie," I greeted, my eyes coming to rest on Luc. He scowled, glaring at the wall as he listened intently.

"Em... Shit. Shit, Em. Shit." Declan, the caller, sounded panicked, his voice breathy. He was one of the guys in charge of our software roll out tonight.

"Tell me," I demanded, watching as Luc twisted off the bed, bending to pull on the briefs he'd dropped in our earlier haste. My stomach twisted as my blood ran cold.

"It's... the whole system..."

"Declan–"

"They're in. The whole thing is fucked."

I started moving. "We're on our way." I hit the end button as I stepped towards the dresser.

"Emmie–"

I threw out a hand, halting Luc.

"I know." We shoved on clothes in silence, my brain racing a million miles an hour. How had they gotten in, what had they taken?

Who would they hurt?

Luc pulled me into his chest.

"It's going to be okay. Remember that." I nodded, not trusting myself to speak.

We got to the office in record time. As we swiped in, the first thing I noticed were the lights. Every single light was on illuminating our office.

Next was the noise. Printers, phones, people yelling. It was pandemonium, and we had walked right into the middle. I glanced at Luc, noting his tight jaw. He'd obviously come to the same realisation. We were the last to arrive.

The hair on the back of my neck rose. I glanced about, searching, automatically checking for the nearest exit.

"Pax." Luc's deep voice cut through the noise. All heads swung our way, conversation halting. My hand found Luc's.

"War room. Everyone. Now," Pax ordered.

I ignored, or tried to, the way people, my friends, looked at me, then skittered their gaze away.

My belly clenched, fear churning my gut.

Luc directed me to a seat, snagging the one next to it. Pax stood at the top of the table, his face rough.

"Okay, here's what we know. Max?"

Max stood, adjusting the papers before him.

"At 1700 hours, I clocked on for night shift. As you all

know, Declan and I were running updates on the system tonight." He paused, glancing down at his notes.

"At about 1830, we picked up an anomaly. Declan went to the affected computer and found this." Max held up a small thumb-drive. "Once removed, we started running diagnostics. The fault continued. At approximately 2000 hours Declan logged in as Administrator, at which point his profile was immediately compromised."

Declan interrupted, "I signed in as admin expecting an easy fix. I'm sorry, I thought it was a–"

Pax held up a hand. "Continue."

"By 2100 hours, it had accessed the administrator profile and locked Declan out. It was at this stage the system started to print these..." He handed a pile of papers to Ben, who took one and passed it on.

Max held up an example. Printed on the clean white paper sat a photo of me. A still screenshot from a video. The photo had me in side profile. I was laughing and clapping as Jetta danced in front of me. It was a scene from the rehabilitation clinic the night Luc and his band had performed for us. My eyes dropped to the thick black letters.

WE FOUND YOU

Bile burned the back of my throat as all heat left my body in a rush, fear turning my veins to ice. They'd never tried this. This outright attack. Insidious warnings, threats. But never like this where anyone could see.

All eyes were on me. At a distance, I heard my name being called. Luc turned my chair, filling my vision as my brain kicked back into gear.

"Emmie?" His warm hands framed my face. "Beautiful?"

I blinked at him. "I'm okay." I jerked my head away and

turned back to the table. "I'm okay," I repeated, looking back at Max. "Finish it."

He paused, glancing at Luc and Pax for permission. They exchanged a look before nodding in unison. Jack, seated on my other side, handed me the stack of print outs. I took one, blindly handing the pile on to Luc.

There I was. In vivid colour, every pixel another dot creating the shape of me.

Max continued. "By 2230 Pax and Sawyer arrived to assist." He nodded at Sawyer, who leaned forward, taking over.

"I started running countermeasures, trying to see what they were accessing. It looked like a data hack. They were after personnel information." Sawyer grinned at me. "Luckily they mistook the dummy files you created as real."

"Dummy files?" This came from Kel at the far end of the table.

Max nodded. "When we were running our pen-test last year, Emmie created dummy files. She set up a bunch of fake personnel files. Even created fake case numbers, fake clients, fake accounts. The money in them is real, she used the Christmas slush fund. At the time, it was all done with Pax's permission. After the pen-test late last year, we had Christmas holidays and they were scheduled for deletion early this year. But then Emmie was shot, and we all got extra case work, so their deletion date kept getting pushed back and"–he shrugged– "we just never got around to it."

Sawyer slumped casually in his chair, a pen spinning absently in one hand. "She did a fucking ace job on those dummies. When we did the tests last year, some of the guys didn't realise they were fakes. It's why our team"–he flicked a hand between us–"won. Leaving the dummies is actually not a bad thing. It may have just saved our company."

Max nodded vigorously. "By the time Sawyer arrived, Declan had shut down the servers. Once Sawyer got here, we didn't reboot. It was too essential to keep them out."

"So you're saying we lost nothing." This came from Luc.

"No." Sawyer shook his head, answering for Max. "No, we did lose stuff."

"What?"

"Emmie." All eyes flew to me and then back to Sawyer, who had dropped the pen and was now leaning forward. "All of your records. They targeted you."

"My client records?"

He nodded. "All of them. That's why they took your dummies. They were after anything with your fingerprints."

I closed my eyes. Dread, guilt, and fear danced like angry bees in my gut. Anxiety hit as they started talking options.

"We need to lock her down." Brean frowned.

"They've blown our deniability." Pax agreed. "This is overt. We haven't reacted the way they expected. They obviously think Emmie didn't know. They're stepping up. They'll be watching to see what we do."

"Do we keep them on the back foot? Throw them off the scent?" Jarrett suggested. "Maybe mount our own counter?"

"The thing that doesn't make sense to me is why they're warning her off?" Luc tapped the pictures. "They're tipping us off. Why not just kidnap her if they know where she is?"

No one had an answer.

"Good question but there's a bigger issue." Sawyer gestured at the briefing material. "When I got here and saw the print out, I called in some favours. Page eighteen."

We all flipped to the page. "That's images from the last three days, each spaced three hours apart."

The compound images showed no change. Three cars sat unmoved; there were no heat signatures.

"Page nineteen, it has the proceeding three days."

Cars, people, movement. Heat signatures. Lots of them.

There was a long silence as we all processed. My heart thumped loudly in my chest. I opened my mouth to speak, finding myself suddenly incapable of making a sound. Fear overrode my rational brain.

They've abandoned The Front.

When I was small, one of my older brothers had found some rope. We'd been playing in the bush. He'd suggested we play cops and robbers. I, of course, was the robber. He'd hauled me up, throwing me against a tree and roughly tying me to it. The rope squeezed my chest tightly. I'd tried to scream, tried to tell him to stop, but all that had come out were gasping breaths as I struggled to breathe. I'd passed out at some point, awakening to find Abel standing over me, protecting me.

This was exactly what that felt like. My chest constricted, my ability to speak halted. I watched black squiggles dance in my periphery. I panted; air seemed to be a struggle. My fingers tingled and my legs felt weak.

Oh God.

"They're gone." Luc broke the silence.

"Yes," Sawyer confirmed. "I alerted AFP. They're sending a team to check it out today, but..." he trailed off.

This was planned. There was little chance of any evidence being found.

"Where are they likely to go?" Max asked.

Fuck.

"I need–" I shot to my feet, looking for an exit. "Bathroom."

I ignored startled looks as I hurried from the room, Luc close on my heels.

"Emmie!"

I hit the hallway, turning towards the stairs. Fuck waiting for a lift, I needed out of here. I pulled out my pass, swiping through to the internal stairs, pounding up them, jumping two at a time, heedless of my protesting side or weak leg. I had one goal in mind, get the fuck out.

I headed for our locker room, swiping in. Inside, I ignored my own locker, instead heading for one at the back. Its door was dinted and had an out of order sign stuck to the front. It was always on the to-do-list, but no one had got around to it. I ripped off the sign, turning the handle. Inside were my bags, filled with all the things I would immediately need. T-shirts, jeans, underwear, water bottles, muesli bars. I pulled the big duffel, revealing the sealed envelope below. I ripped it open, contents tipping into my hand. Fake IDs, cash, road maps. Nothing they could track. Nothing that would lead them to me.

No trace.

I dumped the items in the pack and lifted, swinging it onto my shoulder as I turned.

Luc.

He stood in the doorway. His eyes, his gorgeous blue eyes, gut wrenchingly furious as he stared at me, arms crossed, blocking the door.

"What the fuck, Emmie?"

"I..." The panic threatened to engulf.

"You?" he snapped.

"I'm leaving."

He glared.

"I need to go."

"You need to go?" he repeated.

"Yes." I nodded emphatically.

"Because of today?"

"Yes."

"Because of one setback?"

I cracked. "It's not a setback, Luc! They've disappeared! You heard them." I dropped the bag, my hands flying about as I lost control. "The whole group has fucking gone. They're on the move, Luc. They're on their way. I know it. You know it. Everyone sitting in that room knew it. You think this is a mess now? Wait until they fucking get here!"

His eyes narrowed. "Life is messy, Em. You think we all get to pack up and run 'cause shit gets hard?"

"You haven't walked in my shoes, Luc." I stabbed a finger at him. "You don't get a say."

He dropped his hands. "No. No, I don't. 'Cause you won't fucking let me speak. This is a relationship. Not a fucking dictatorship. I love you. You love me. Doesn't mean life is a stroll."

"I need–"

"Me. You need *me*."

I shook my head, desperate not to listen. "I need to go." I tried to push past him; he threw out his arms, blocking my exit.

"No. Not again. This is your battleground. Here. Now."

"I'm not a fighter, Luc." I tried to make him understand. "I run. It's the only way to stay safe."

"What utter fucking bullshit. You are a fighter. I know it. Your friends know it. I look at you, and I see you fighting every single day. You do it by living your life. That's your big fuck you to them."

"My half life? The life I thought I wanted? The life I'd happily dump and run? That life? Do you get it, Luc? Is it making sense? Are you clued in? I leave. I don't stay. I pack my shit and I get the fuck out."

"Emmie –" He tried to reach for me. I spun, frantically dancing away from him.

"No, it's my turn now! You changed this." I pressed a hand to my chest. "You changed me! We have a home. We have a life. We have each other. Addie, Kel, Jarret, Pax, Jetta... all of you... I want to be here. I want..."

"You want what, baby?"

"I can't. I won't. Don't you get it? You *think* you know. You *think* you can fight this. You can't. They're better. You have the physical strength, but they have the power. They're smart, they know where to dig and how deep to go. They know what information will break you. And they will. They'll tear you apart piece by piece until all that's left is ruin. Sophia, Eloise, your parents, our friends... No one is safe. They'll ruin everything to get to me. To make me pay." I dropped back, my hands wrapping around my middle as I tried to keep the pain inside. "I need to *go*."

"Then let me run with you." My eyes snapped up, meeting his. He was serious.

"No." I shook my head in denial. "I won't destroy your future."

"You are my future. Jesus Christ, if you don't know that by now, what the fuck have we been doing?"

It took a moment for his words to penetrate

I threw myself at him. Lips smashed, hands grabbed, material ripped. Then down. Down onto the floor, one of his hands fisting my hair, the other wrapped around my back, clasping me to him.

I clawed at his sides, his back as we rolled, pants pushed down, breath short and sharp.

I ignored common sense. My little voice telling me to leave. To go *now*.

I pushed it back and lost myself in the man I loved.

The man who loved me.

He entered me and we both gasped. His eyes locked onto mine, his hand tightening in my hair.

"You are a fighter, Emmie Franklin. And you deserve an army behind you. I can give you that." He thrust, over and over.

I came on a sharp cry, arching under him. A moment later he followed, his grunts harsh and angry before he collapsed on me.

Our breaths mingled, and I took a moment to memorise this. Memorise the feel of his skin on mine, the taste of him on my tongue. I wanted to breathe him in. To savour every moment.

"You're going to run."

I didn't answer.

"I'll find you."

I closed my eyes, listening to the quiet confidence in his voice.

"And when I do..."

He tipped my head, waiting for me to look at him.

"When I do, we're having wild sex and getting married."

My heart skipped, and I felt a million butterflies take flight in my stomach.

"'Cause you're it. And no matter how much you wish it weren't true, Em, you know I'm yours."

I sighed, allowing myself to imagine our future. Our life. Our home. Our family. Boys with my eyes and his smile. A girl for him to spoil. Too much. Far too much.

Put it away.

"Not going to happen."

"You said that before." He pushed himself up, standing above me with his signature smirk. "And look where that got us."

I let him pull me up, straightening our clothes.

"Come back down, baby. Come back down and listen to our plans."

Twenty-four hours, I promised myself silently, I would give him that. I owed him that.

LUC

She was going to run. I knew it. Emmie fretted, clenching her fists, her eyes constantly shooting glances towards the exit.

I wanted to take away her fear, reassure her it would be okay. It burned that I couldn't make those promises.

We'd replaced the bag, sticking the out of order sign back up on the locker. It fucking destroyed me that she had these bags hidden all over the place, her fear so real she couldn't feel safe anywhere.

We returned to the room, her cold hand trembling in mine. We resumed our seats, the team deep in discussions.

"AFP are on their way." Kel tucked a pen in her high bun. "We've been keeping them updated but this is serious. We need their state contacts. See if they can put out feelers." She leaned across the table, snatching a picture. "This one shows make and model of cars. We have something to go on. Something concrete. AFP can connect with local police to track them."

Pax crossed his arms, foot tapping while he considered

options. He caught my eye, raising an eyebrow. I gave a slight nod, letting him know we were good.

"Kel, call AFP. Tell them we need them here ASAP. Sawyer, I want you and Max working on the files. Their targeted attack says they're only after Emmie, but something about that is hitting me wrong. Jarrett, I want you and Brean to work with Jack and Luc on a physical protection plan." He leaned forward, reaching for the brief. "We need eyes on these bastards. Three days is too long. We let that ball slip, that's on us."

"It's long enough to get to Canberra," Emmie whispered. "If they're not here yet, they could be soon."

I dropped her hand, pulling her rolling chair closer, looping an arm over her shoulders. "We got this, Keys."

I burned from the inside. The fear on her face, the pallor of her skin, the hopeless look in her eyes. If I had to, I would murder every single one of those motherfuckers.

Her hand found my thigh, squeezing.

"AFP want a crisis meeting tomorrow," Kel called from her corner.

"Set it up," I told her, feeling Emmie shudder. I pressed a kiss to her forehead. "It's okay. Just hold on to me, I got you."

I glanced at Brean. He caught it, glancing from me to Emmie and back. He tilted his head up in acknowledgment.

"Em and I are heading home." I pulled her up, tucking her under my arm. She was nearly catatonic, simply going where I directed. She'd detached, shut down. Her default was to withdraw. It cut me. I needed to get her home, get her settled, get her reengaged. This wasn't healthy. This wasn't the strong woman I knew. This was her fear talking.

Once I had her settled, safe, then? Then I'd go hunt these motherfuckers.

Brean casually pushed back from the table, stretching.

"You know what? We can figure out the arrangements at Luc's. It'll be easier to assess weaknesses at the location."

Jarrett followed, his face grim, his eyes locked on Em.

We settled her in the car, I slid into the backseat beside her. She curled into herself, sitting flush against the door, looking like she wanted nothing more than to disappear into the leather. Jarrett and Brean were in the front, muttering quietly to each other as I reached for her.

"Keys," I called, brushing a hand over her back. "Emmie?"

There was nothing, no acknowledgment, no recognition. I didn't try to pull her back. I didn't try to force her process. She'd come back to me when she was ready.

I pressed a kiss to her forehead. "Come on, Keys. Let's get you home."

EMMIE

I didn't remember the drive to Luc's. To be honest, I didn't remember leaving work. The blankets were enveloping me in a cocoon of warmth as I lay, listening to the sounds of Luc's house.

There were people in it. Their footsteps and quiet discussions echoed down the hall.

The bedside clock said early afternoon. I didn't remember being put in bed. Did I sleep? I felt exhausted, my limbs heavy, my brain foggy.

I shoved back the blankets, hauling myself out of bed. I pulled on pants, reaching for a hoodie. I pulled the hood up, padding silently down the hall. I paused just out of eyeline, listening.

"So, they're ghosts?" Jarrett sounded annoyed, frustrated, angry.

Sawyer answered, his normally jovial tone tight. "Yeah. They're not dumb. This was planned."

"This is because of Emmie?"

There was a pause.

"Maybe. It seems…"

"Excessive?" Luc asked.

"Mm," Sawyer agreed. "She's one person. I mean, I get sending a few guys over, but all the women and children? Leave your base unprotected? Either they're dumb, which I don't believe, or she's worth more to them than we realised. There's something else going on."

"Worth more? How?" Jack asked.

"That's the question."

I poked my head around the hall door, catching a glimpse of them in the kitchen. Jarrett, Luc, Sawyer, and Jack were leaning against the benchtops or sitting at Luc's breakfast bar, mugs in hand.

They were distracted, still thought I was asleep.

This is your chance.

I crept back to the bedroom. As silently as I could, I pulled on shoes. On his bedside table he'd left his wallet and phone. I hesitated for a moment, then snatched the items, shoving them in the pocket of my hoodie.

The bedroom window was one of those old push up wooden frames. It had a flyscreen, but the security screens weren't due to be installed for another month. I shifted the frame, slowly jiggling it from side-to-side, pausing as it scraped against the wood and metal. Heart pounding in my throat, I strained to hear if I'd been discovered.

Once open, I lifted the screen, gently tossing it outside. I lifted, wedging myself out the small opening, biting my cheek to keep from groaning as the windowsill scratched my exposed back.

Outside, I kept low, moving to the back of the property. Luc's yard was completely enclosed by new seven-foot fencing. I made my way to his garbage bins, pulling myself up, balancing, then using the extra height to pull myself over.

I dropped down to the neighbour's yard, letting out an *oomph* as I landed.

My thigh hurt, my side ached. I ignored both as I moved up towards the street. Using Luc's phone, I ordered a taxi, hiding in the shrubbery while I waited. It rolled to a stop in the driveway, the driver peered through the windscreen at the giant house.

I hurried down, sliding into the backseat.

"Where to?" The guy asked, eyes meeting mine in the rear vision mirror.

Yeah Em, where are we going?

I hesitated. I didn't have ID, I didn't have unlimited money. I had to get to one of my back-up locations.

"Civic bus station please."

The taxi took off and I ducked in my seat, pulling my hoodie over my face. I couldn't see any movement from Luc's house as we drove past.

At the station, I pulled out the wallet, using Luc's credit card to pay the driver. I headed for the bus stop, buying a ticket to Wollongong. The fifty dollars in Luc's wallet would be enough to get me through today. I'd work out tomorrow later.

The bus was departing in ten minutes. I sat in the back, looking out the window as passengers slowly boarded, their muted conversations filling the bus interior.

Luc's mobile buzzed.

I slid my finger across the screen, entering his pin.

Unknown number: It's Luc, are you safe?

My fingers hovered over the screen, uncertainty and fear warring with my need to reassure him.

Me: Yes.

Luc: Why are you running?

Me: You know why.

Luc: You promised I could come.

Me: I won't be responsible for you leaving your family. It's time to let me go.

The bus rumbled to life under me. The driver hit the lever, shutting the door and we were off, swaying down the road. The phone vibrated, lighting with another text.

Luc: I'm your Pikachu. Where you go, I follow.

I closed my eyes, choking back a strangled sob.

Me: Lucien, we're done.

Luc: We're getting married.

I fought a hysterical laugh.

Me: I never said yes.

Luc: You never said no either.

Me: I did. Twice. No.

Luc: I don't believe you. Say it to my face.

My fingers hovered. I needed to remove the SIM card, stop them from tracking me. I had no doubt Sawyer was calling in favours right at this moment.

Me: I'm sorry. This is my battle. I can't be yours when I'm already theirs.

I hesitated. My fingers typed out the words I wanted to say.

I love you.

I hit delete, erasing the text.

Luc: I'll find you. I won't stop.

Me: Goodbye, Lucien.

I turned the mobile off, pulling the back open to reach the battery and SIM inside.

I had no plans to go to Wollongong. This bus made two stops along the way, at Goulburn and Moss Vale. I'd be getting off at Goulburn.

The trip dragged, and every moment felt like a million

as the bus travelled down the highway, taking me far from the people I loved, the things I owned and the man who made me feel.

I swiped angrily at tears as they fell. Today, on this bus, I would cry. Once I stepped off, I'd be a new person. No tears. No regrets. No thinking of the past. Not even Luc. It would be too tempting.

Numb. I needed to fall back into numbness. It was the only way to survive.

The bus rocked to a stop, the door opening. I followed the flow, stepping off and down the street. The storage facility was a fifteen-minute walk. I tucked my hands into the pockets of the hoodie, keeping my head down.

Years ago, I'd learned three truths:

One, always have an exit plan.

Two, prepare for the worst.

Three, always have a Plan B through Z.

Goulburn was my Plan D. When I'd settled in Canberra, I'd planned backup options. I'd purchased a crappy car that ran well, forged a bunch of documents, and collected cash. Every three months I'd take a drive out to Goulburn, check the car was still running, swap out clothes if needed and pay up storage for the next four months.

When I stepped off the bus, Emmie no longer existed. I was now Lauren O'Connor.

The lot sat empty as I entered the storage facility. Yet another reason I chose this place —no cameras, no website, just a guy renting out sheds. Mine had two padlocks, both with number combinations rather than key locks. I'd planned for this exact scenario.

I rounded the end of the first row and froze.

"No."

Luc pulled out a phone lifting it to his ear.

"Got her." He tucked it back in his pocket, walking towards me.

"No." I shook my head, hands up warding him off. "You're not meant to be here!"

"Baby," he coaxed, slowing his approach. "Come here."

"No!" I backed up, desperately hoping he was an apparition.

"Emmie…" He approached, hands out, face gentle.

I couldn't. I was doing this to protect *him*. I'd made peace with my decision. I was determined. He couldn't be here. I couldn't have my efforts undermined like this.

I twisted, turning to run. I made it three steps before arms wrapped around me, pulling me tight against a hard chest. I thrashed, lashing out at him, screaming my frustration, anger and fear. He held me tight, letting me beat him. I drew on my training, an elbow ramming into his stomach. He doubled over, his grip loosening. I followed up with a kick to his shin. He grunted, losing his grip.

I sprinted, running two, three, four metres before a hand caught my arm, jerking me back into him. My fists pounded his chest in my struggle. Luc spoke reassurances, trapping me tight in his arms, making no attempt to stop the abuse.

I couldn't breathe. Couldn't focus on anything but the swirl of emotions– anger, fear, confusion.

Relief.

I screamed abuse, pounding while he absorbed every hit, every word. An impenetrable wall.

"Calm, Emmie. Breathe. I'm here. It's okay."

Finally, slowly, I calmed. Or perhaps I gave up. Either way, I stopped struggling, just leaned against him, his jumper fisted in my hands, my head pressed tight to his chest.

He continued to whisper fierce words while the wind whipped our clothing, the cold penetrating deep in my bones. Eventually, I withdrew enough to look at his face.

"Okay," I whispered, resigned.

Luc tucked me into his arm, and together we walked down the rows of storage containers out to the carpark. He helped me into the passenger side, rounding the bonnet and sliding into the driver's. Inside the vehicle he turned on the car, then sat watching me.

"Home or run?" he asked, gaze solemn. "Your call."

I hesitated, torn. I could take us home, but the risk... We could disappear, but I'd be taking him from everyone he loved and everyone who loved him. Either decision was selfish. There were no winners today.

"Home," I decided, feeling my gut clenching.

He backed us out of the facility, navigating the streets towards the highway. We were silent for half of the journey, his hand resting periodically on my knee, warm and comforting.

"How did you find me?" I asked as we passed Lake George, my gaze focussed on the waterless flatland.

"Sawyer. He already had a list of places you might use."

I grunted, leaning my head against the cool glass of the window. "And you just happened to choose that one?"

There was a beat of silence.

"Luc?" I turned in my seat.

"I may have done something bad one weekend. Inadvertently."

I crossed my arms, waiting. He ran a hand over his beard, swearing softly under his breath.

"Last summer, I did a bike ride. I'd just finished breakfast with some mates at one of the wineries. I saw your car heading this way. I decided to follow, thought it would be amusing to catch you, see if you wanted lunch or some-thing." His lips twisted into a wry smile. "When you got to the storage facility, I gave up. I'd already tracked you for thirty minutes. It would have been too stalkerish to follow you further."

I intellectually understood this was a funny story. Emotionally this was devastating. I'd put in place so many precautions. Worked so hard to make sure I was never followed. And Luc had done it without my noticing. He hadn't even been trying to hide.

I turned back to the window, tears burning.

You got complacent.

I was an idiot. An absolutely ridiculous idiot. I should have left years ago. Instead I'd been seduced by friends, familiarity, and recognition.

When you belonged somewhere, people saw you, they recognised you, they smiled and asked how your day was, and were genuinely interested. When you were transitory, you were just another face passing through. No one invested in you. No one cared.

I had to admit I'd ached for someone to care. I'd wanted someone to see me. And as more people did, I fell into the daydream of staying. I had convinced myself that my precautions were enough. The joy of being recognised and appreciated had overrode my rationale. I was a ridiculous idiot.

The self-recriminations continued up until we arrived at Luc's. He pulled into the garage and turned off the engine. Neither of us made a move to get out.

He shifted to look at me. "I'm laying this out now. We walk in this door, and you're stuck with me. You're in my bed, you're in my life, we seal this deal. I'm talking the whole shebang. House, mortgage, marriage, holidays, pets, kids if we want 'em. We have each other's back. I'm in this, Emmie. Hundred percent." He reached over, thumb stroking across my cheek. "That's where my head's at. My heart too." He offered me a tight smile. "If you're not ready, I'll take you to Pax."

I swallowed, wetting dry lips. My hands trembled as I wiped damp palms on my jeans. "I... It's hard."

"I know." His eyes never left mine.

"I want..." My chin quivered. I blinked rapidly to stem the tears. "I want that. I want this. I want you. Luc, I–" I cut myself off.

"What?" he whispered, head tilting closer. "What do you want, beautiful?"

"I love you," I whispered, my voice barely audible. Those words were a seal, a wish, a plea. They were everything I wanted, and everything I knew I should never have. Could never have.

"I love you too." He smiled, I expected him to kiss me, but his hand shifted, cupping the nape of my neck as he withdrew, forehead pressed to mine. "Are you in?"

I shuddered out a breath.

Was I? Could this beautiful man give me all I wanted? Am I brave enough to take it?

"Yes." No tears. No uncertainty, no regrets. I wanted a beautiful life with this beautiful man.

"Okay." He let go of my head, shifting back. We left the car, moving inside. The house stood silent.

"No one's here?"

"No. Someone will be on patrol, but they get it."

"Get what?" We reached the hall, and he crowded in, gently pushing me against the wall, his big, gorgeous body pressed against mine.

I wasn't fearful, this wasn't aggressive. It was seductive.

His hands roamed down my sides and curled around my arse.

"This." His lips met mine in a greedy kiss. He devoured me, marked me. Hours earlier, I'd been convinced I'd never have this again. I threw myself into our reunion, grasping at his shirt, licking and sucking at the salt of his skin. I wanted him to bury himself in me. I wanted to mark him as mine. I *wanted*.

We stumbled through the house, a trail of clothing in our wake. Luc pressed me against his kitchen bench, boosting me up. He stepped between my thighs and drove home, both of us gasping.

He whispered filthy promises, raining kisses down my neck, my collarbone as he kept a steady rhythm.

"Love your pussy. Milk my cock, Emmie. You like this? You want more? Come for me."

He surged in, breaking the last of my walls. I didn't need him. I *wanted* him. I *chose* him.

Luc is worth it.

"Fuck!" he groaned into my neck as he came, my pussy clenching around him, milking his release. My arse was cold, his chest warm as it remained plastered to my front. Our hands slowly roamed, gently stroking, fingertips grazing overly sensitive skin. We built back the need. This time, less desperate but no less hot.

He whispered demands, pulling from me what he needed, promises, declarations, apologies. I gave him everything, all of me.

We collapsed, breath harsh, bodies hot. Luc reached for me, pulling me close.

"*Mon coeur t'appartient,*" he whispered, pressing a kiss to my cheek. I didn't know what the words meant, but I felt the fierce way he said them bury deep. My life wasn't perfect, but I felt stronger, braver, maybe even a little less fearful tonight.

Hope, that dangerous emotion, bloomed.

EMMIE

We were back in the war room. The state leads were a bust. No one knew much, or if they did, they weren't talking.

Fierce eyes, short silver hair, immaculately pressed uniform, Annabelle Norris intimidated the beejeezus out of me. An AFP veteran, her hawklike eyes caught everything, her brain that much more evolved than the rest of us. It wouldn't surprise me if she could read thoughts.

The handful of times I'd been in her presence while handing over cases, I'd always felt like a bug under a microscope, much too visible for my liking. She led the AFP's transnational and organised crime division. Her word was law.

Pax stood at the top of the table briefing her team on my situation. As he wrapped up, her eyes came to me, her face impassive.

"And you're sure they're after you?"

I fought the urge to glance at Luc for reassurance. "The signs say yes, but..."

"It's an excessive response for one person," she agreed.

Her fingers tapped rhythmically against the conference table. No one spoke as she stared at a spot on the back wall, a small frown on her face. She nodded to herself.

"Here's what we know." She leaned forward, eyes on Pax. "Our cyber division has known about God's Patriots for the last twenty years. They've been a fringe group we're monitoring. They're good, damn good. We had nothing on them. Though we suspected the parliament house incident was them, we had nothing to tie it back." Her gaze settled on me. "Until now."

I swallowed, my tongue feeling too big for my mouth.

"Ms Franklin's information has given us some significant leads." She narrowed her eyes on me. "It would have been useful to have this years ago."

"You did," Luc interrupted. "Em went to the police when she first got out."

It was true. The first time they found me I tried to get help; that ended in the suicide of a cop and me running again. Emmie Franklin was one in a long line of aliases.

"We're aware of that situation." Annabelle's mouth pursed. "We've had words with that state."

"The leads?" Sawyer prompted from where he sat at the far end of the table. He leaned back, hands clasped behind his head, a fidget of movement as he twisted the chair from one side to the other.

"My team have worked backwards, using the time line Ms Franklin provided. It's been time consuming and data intensive, but we now have concrete links to at least three of the group." Annabelle frowned. "If we can find them."

"Do you have anything on that front?" Brean asked.

"Nothing. They've hidden themselves well."

"So your best lead is Emmie," Sawyer said, halting his chair.

Annabelle nodded. "It's only a matter of time before they make a move. We just need to be ready to go when they do."

I chewed the inside of my cheek, thinking. "What –" I coughed, clearing my throat. "What is the... the child abuse statute of limitation in Western Australia?"

She didn't miss a beat. "There no longer is one."

I hesitated. "If I have proof of-of my abuse, can it be used?"

"Of course." The room went wired, the air surprisingly heavy. Annabelle didn't look away, her face didn't shift. I was grateful to see not one ounce of pity, just calm understanding.

"You have proof?"

"I took pictures," I whispered. "And I kept the clothes."

Luc stiffened beside me.

"They have DNA?" Annabelle clarified.

I nodded, my eyes determinedly on hers. "Blood."

"His or yours?"

"Both. I bit his hand, and he smeared it on me when he..."

"Anything else?"

"No. I didn't have time to wash or collect a swab of semen or anything. I had to leave in a hurry."

"But you took pictures?"

I nodded. "They're dated. I have backups as well."

Annabelle gave me a nod. I think I caught a glint of respect before she looked down, making notes. "We'll need the evidence."

"It's in a storage box. I can get it."

"Today." Luc reached over, giving my hand a squeeze. "We'll drop it off today."

"That handles one matter, as for the rest" –Annabelle's

sharp eyes moved around the group– "we're going to lay a trap." She leaned forward, knitting her hands on the table, gaze finally settling on Paxton. "And Ms Franklin will be our bait."

"Absolutely not," Luc barked. "We're not–"

She lifted her hand, halting Luc's protests. "Ms Franklin has insight into their operating practices."

I frowned, a wisp of something tickling at the edge of my conscience. It whisked away as I tried to grasp it.

"I haven't been a part of the group for a long time. They've likely changed."

"I find people to be creatures of habit. While they think they've innovated, people revert to what works best. In this instance, they've operated without any interference, without any risk of prosecution for so long I'm tempted to say they've gotten cocky. That's their weakness."

She reached for her folder, pulling out three sheets of paper, passing them across to me. "Tell me about this."

I flicked through the papers, frowning. "Where did you get this?"

"We have our ways. Tell me what you think it is."

They were financial reports. The pages showed transfers from an account, I couldn't see the account number or the banking institution. The account had money coming in and small amounts being transferred out regularly.

"It's an account. The amounts transferring in are huge though." Upwards of tens of thousands of dollars.

"Does anything about it look familiar?" Annabelle watched me closely.

"Should it?" I handed the sheets to Sawyer.

"This is an account we set up in a small bank. They'd reported thefts to us, and we saw an opportunity to track. The money out, we believe, is being filtered by the Patriots."

I frowned. "You could trace it?"

"We traced the money to an offshore. The only way we could connect back to them was through matching financial transfers into Australian accounts held by members."

"They didn't cover their tracks?" Sawyer asked.

"No. It seems they got cocky."

Sawyer scoffed. "Idiots."

"English?" Brean asked.

"Normally you take amounts of money, pool it offshore, then transfer the money either to another offshore, or to somewhere you can access it. But you never transfer the exact amount. It's too easy to match," I explained.

"They didn't do that. The account has been in place for years. We've been tracking this for the last eighteen months."

"This explains how they could afford the solar panels."

"West Investments," Luc murmured.

"What?"

He turned to me, frowning. "West Investments. You said you knew the code. You sorted it in less than twenty-four hours."

I blinked, the puzzle clicking into place. "Crap."

I surged up from my seat, heading for the door. "I missed it. Crap!"

Together we ran to the bank of elevators at the far end of the basement. I smashed a finger to the button, jumping nervously from foot to foot.

"Damn it. I missed it. How could I have missed that?"

"You couldn't have known." Luc paced. I could see his mind racing as he clenched and unclenched his fists.

"But–"

"No." He cut me off. "Let's think this through, what information does this give us?"

"Umm... guys?" The elevator dinged as we both turned to see half the team clustered in the walkway behind us. "You want to fill us in?" Kel asked.

Annabelle crossed her arms, one finger tapping on the apex of her elbow. She knew.

I shook my head. "No time. Just... Sawyer? Max? I need..."

"On it." They shoved past, crowding into the elevator with us. Luc grabbed me, brushing a kiss against my lips.

"I'll brief them, see you up there."

I nodded, mind racing.

"We'll get them, Emmie. This is their mistake."

I nodded again, unable to speak past the lump in my throat. He let me go, stepping back as the doors closed.

"Em?"

"Right." I took a deep breath, turning to look at the men beside me. "Shit is about to get real, gentlemen."

They both grinned. Sawyer looked up at the camera in the corner of the elevator.

"Pete? Tell Addie I'm gonna need a six-pack of Red Bull and a packet of Red Frogs." He rubbed his hands together. "We're going to be like Captain America, only more attractive."

The elevator hit our floor, and we tumbled out, heading for the computers.

"Plan of attack?" I called, logging in.

"We hit small businesses. Banks, financial institutions, investment companies. Any Ma and Pa organisations with shitty security. We run the program we did with West Investments. Log everything," Max directed.

"Like Annabelle said, they were cocky. Anyone taking bets they're using the exact same code?"

It took less than twenty minutes to get our first hit. Max

found it, a small mortgage broker who'd been compromised. The code wasn't exactly the same but it had similar characteristics.

"Emmie!" Sawyer called from his side of the room. I looked up, blinking to clear my vision. "I got one. And I've worked out why we both felt weird about the code."

I stood, walking to look over his shoulder. "They're using West Investment like it's a bank. The code operates in small amounts, so in a bank, it would be harder to catch. In a place like West Investment, everything is rigorously controlled, and funds are strictly monitored to optimise savings. So how did they slip through?"

He tapped his screen. "This is Lalo Bank. The transactions are the same. The difference is, these are harder to identify when you have an everyday account." He pulled up on his third monitor the West transactions. "See? They don't deal in transactions that small."

I nodded. It was obvious now, when comparing an actual bank account to how an investment account functioned. For something like West Investments? No way it could have hidden this long. The transactions stuck out like a sore thumb.

Sawyer rubbed a finger across his bottom lip. "You said this had been going on for years."

"Three, I think. Longer maybe, but some of the accounts were closed, so I didn't bother to access them." I looked down at Sawyer. "What are you thinking?"

"I don't know yet." He waved a hand at me. "Go find a bug. I need to think this through."

What we were doing was technically illegal. Lucky for us, AFP were working rapidly to get us warrants. As soon as we identified a bank we wanted in, they were putting applications up to get urgent permissions. The turnaround was short, but we were working in the background by calling institutions directly. Permissions from the owner in exchange for a free security check. About half thought we were scammers, the rest were grateful for the assistance.

Two days. Three days. On the fourth, we had a decent picture of the issue.

Sawyer stood up, looking around the office. "Someone call a meeting. We've got a war on our hands."

EMMIE

"This is..." Luc trailed off, running a hand through his hair as he stared at the white board Sawyer and I had rolled down to the war room. On it, we had a spiderweb of interconnected lines showing the connection between God's Patriots and the various financial institutions we'd managed to track.

"Overwhelming," he finally said dropping his hands. "How did they think they'd get away with this?"

I shrugged, tucking myself into his side. He shifted, looping an arm around my shoulders as I hooked my thumb into one of his belt loops.

"Ma and Pa operations rarely have significant investment in cyber security. These guys were fat, little golden geese ready for the plucking."

Sawyer made a quacking sound behind us. I ignored him.

"The program felt wrong because of the target, not the way it functioned. The banks and brokers charge fees, all of which add up to look like how this theft functions. West Investments takes a commission on their accounts– not a fee. It looked wrong because it should have been blatantly obvious there was an issue." I looked up at Luc, watching as he followed each of the lines from one institution to the other. There was a list of organizations we were still to approach on the other side.

"This is major money."

"It's a hundred-billion-dollar industry," Annabelle agreed, her arms crossed as she too checked the board. "This is a massive crime. Based on your estimates, we're talking hundreds of millions of dollars." She nodded at me. "Good work."

I offered her a small shy smile. No matter the praise, Annabelle Norris would always freak me out.

"Okay." She clapped her hands, turning back to the rest of the room. "Theories."

"This was never about Emmie as an individual," Kel offered from her seat at the side. She'd been watching us, a small frown wrinkling her forehead. "Emmie's software was a risk to them. Considering the media attention, we got after her shooting and now with the trial, more people know about Elliot Securities and that is a risk."

"Which means–" Jack took up her thought thread, "–this was always about the money. More people using our software, higher likelihood of us catching their con."

"So, they threatened Emmie, tried to get her to leave. Threatened us as a distraction. They hacked our system, no doubt looking for the West files to corrupt them, and when that didn't work, they aimed to throw Emmie under a bus?" Kel said.

We sat at the long table contemplating the scenario.

I looked at the board, quietly reading over the names once again. I froze, my entire body on alert. The name of one bank stood out.

"Oh my God," I breathed. "I think I know what this is. They're planning the end game."

"The end—"

The door burst open and Addie stalked in, hand out to deflect the door as it smashed against the wall, bouncing back towards her. Cheeks flushed and eyes wild, she looked frantically around the room, her gaze finally locking on Luc.

"Luc..." She choked, her eyes filling. "Your house... there's a fire..."

"A...what?"

"Jack called it in. Some kind of explosion. Fire and police are—"

Luc snatched my hand, pulling me from the table. We dashed up the stairs, scrambling for his car. My heart pounded in my ears as bile burned the back of my throat.

"We don't know it was... Stay positive. It could be a coincidence," Luc muttered, weaving in and out of traffic.

It's them.

Three fire engines and five police cars blocked the street. Luc parked us haphazardly on the sidewalk three houses down. We ran down to the boundary fence, stopping when a policeman blocked our entrance.

Little remained. The roof had collapsed, the fire completely engulfing the inside. Firefighters frantically called directions as their hoses sprayed water over the inferno.

Smoke billowed out, ash floating down to coat our faces and clothes. Luc stood frozen, his eyes on the burning ruin of his house.

The hairs on the back of my neck lifted.

David.

This wasn't an accident. This wasn't a loose wire or a leaky gas pipe. They were here.

I pivoted, turning back to the road, hands lifting, ready to bolt. The keys were still in the ignition, my purse in the passenger seat. I could–

Stop.

I forced myself to turn around. Slowly, feet heavy, I walked towards Luc. I lifted my hand distantly noting how it trembled. Inside, I fought every instinct that screamed for me to run. I laid my hand on Luc's arm, and immediately he turned, sliding over to pull me to his side. I settled there, my arms around him, both of us watching his house slowly break down to embers.

I opened my mouth, words blocked by the lump of guilt in my throat.

"Don't." His eyes were still on the flames, his face dotted by ash. Our eyes watered from the smoke. "We don't know yet. The wiring was shit, it could be an accident."

But I knew. Even if he didn't want to admit it.

In the commune I'd watched David destroy people without remorse. He'd start by breaking them piece by piece. First, he'd take their home, then their job, their reputation, and finally, their family. He'd break them down until they had no options, no friends, nothing.

The fire now reduced to glowing embers and pieces of charred wood and stone, Luc turned to me.

"Your comics." Grooves I'd never noticed before scarred his face.

I squeezed him. "Comics can be replaced, you can't. Why are you worrying about my things? That's your entire life gone. Your medals? The photos of your team?" I asked.

"Pax has back-ups and the medals can be remade." He rubbed a hand over his face, smearing the ash. "Our life was meant to start in that house."

I shrugged. "We can rebuild."

"I wanted you to feel like you belong. I wanted to give you somewhere you felt safe."

"I do." I squeezed him. "It's right here."

His thumb grazed the apple of my cheek. "Forgive me?"

A cough interrupted our moment. Our heads twisted to the two police officers hovering nearby.

"Mr Falco?" one asked.

"Yes?" Luc kept his arms tight around me.

"We've got some questions, if now is a good time?"

He looked back down at me. "You okay?"

I nodded. He dropped his arms, taking my hand. "Do we need to go to the station or...?"

"We can do the preliminary here. We'll need an official statement, but I expect that can wait."

We followed the officer down the street towards a patrol car, away from the crowd and cameras that had arrived. The officer lifted a pen and notepad.

"Do you have any ID on you?"

Luc reached for his back pocket. "Fuck, it's in the car."

"I can grab it." I squeezed his hand. "I'll just be a second."

Luc shook his head. "No, we'll both–"

"I'll take her." The second officer offered. "Your friend Mr Elliot has filled us in on the potential motivation." He pointed off to the side where Pax, Brean, and Jack were all standing. They had phones raised to their ears or were talking to officers. Their eyes were on the crowds as they kept watch.

I offered Luc a reassuring smile. "See? I'll be fine."

Luc frowned, his dark brows pulling low as he looked from me to the officers and back. "It's the black Alfa up the street."

"We'll be right back," the second officer promised.

I led the way, dodging hoses, weaving between emergency crews and ducking under police tape. The scene was chaos. Luc's house was big and the fire had been fierce.

"It's arson, right?" I asked the officer as I hit the locks, pulling the passenger door open.

"They're still investigating," he said as I leaned into the car, my butt sticking out as I fished Luc's wallet from the centre console.

"What do they..." I froze, cutting myself off. Something hard and cold dug into the middle of my back.

"Here's what's going to happen," the officer explained, pressing the metal deeper into my back. "You're going to slowly get in the car. You're going to sit in the passenger seat and not make a sound. We're going to drive off and you're not going to kick up a fuss. You get me?" He twisted the metal deeper, bruising my skin.

"Yes."

"Good." He pulled back, and I slipped into the front seat. He came around the car, gun low but visible. Sliding into the driver side, he held out a hand and I placed the keys in it. With his free hand, he kept the gun trained on me as he started Luc's car.

My eyes searched the heaving mass of people. A fire truck blocked me from Luc's view. Brean and Jack had their backs to me. I couldn't see Pax. *Damn.*

The officer backed the car up, turning. We drove away from the scene, and I had a hysterical thought.

This is what a kidnapping felt like. Double damn.

LUC

"Tell me again how something like this happens?" I didn't care if I sounded like a crazed lunatic, I wanted some fucking answers.

"The guy was new, the paperwork said he'd transferred in from..." The police officer trailed off. "There's really no excuse."

Annabelle slapped her palm on the table, the officer flinching. "No, there isn't. Get out."

The guy scrambled up and out of the room. We were back in the War room. Emmie had been missing for approximately forty-five minutes. They could be anywhere. The police had issued an alert for my car, but we'd heard squat. I dragged hands through my hair, pulling at the roots. "We have to find her."

"This is about the money," Annabelle commented, walking across to our whiteboard. "Emmie is a distraction."

"Emmie is a fucking hostage, we can't–"

She cut me off. "Pull it together, Falco." She tapped the board. "You want to find them, follow the cash."

"What did she mean the end game?" Pax asked, looking from me to Annabelle.

I had no answer.

Sawyer sat at the back of the room frantically typing.

"Anything?" This waiting and wishing was getting us fucking nowhere.

Please, God, give us something.

"Maybe. Give me a minute." He waved me off with one hand. The seconds crept by as he concentrated.

I paced, eyes darting from the board, to the list of names and back.

"Shit," Sawyer muttered.

"What?" I crowded in looking over his shoulder. "What've you got?"

He pointed at the screen. To me it was a bunch of meaningless numbers and letters. "I followed the cash. They need Emmie to get the payload."

"Explain," Pax demanded, crossing his arms.

"She's good. Damn fucking good. The accounts she set up when she was one of their pawns? They're still live. She designed a program to siphon money from their accounts to her own. It took them years to realise they were losing out. They can't crack it. They need her."

"Why?"

"How do I explain? She's used an advanced encryption algorithm that I'm prepared to say even a supercomputer can't crack. And she did that ten years ago. Ten fucking years. Do you understand how extraordinary this is? These bastards can't work out which alias she used or where the money is hiding. But judging by the transfers, the account itself would have millions. Hundreds of millions sitting in it." Sawyer navigated to another screen. "And your cult has just purchased land in Russia. A country with whom Australia doesn't have an extradition treaty."

"Fuck." I ran a hand through my hair. "It was never about *her*. Emmie's just the key to their money."

"Do you have flight logs?" Paxton demanded.

Sawyer hit some keys, then shook his head. "They're either doing this last minute, are doing the private gig, or they're using aliases. Either way nothing is popping. No big groups heading out, not that I can pinpoint. But I'm stretched. Max is on it."

"You're in flight manifests? Wait, no. I don't have time right now." Annabelle shook her head. "I'll put a call out to exit ports. Immigration will be on the lookout for her."

Kel frowned. "The photo you have is current, but I doubt they'll let her leave the country. Too many people, too much risk. They'll force her to sign over the alias, kill her, then mock up some death certificates to get the money."

Fuck.

I buried the fear. I didn't have time or energy to spare on that fucking shit. I needed to be present.

"We need to find them. Now," Pax declared pushing up from the table.

"Got a lead!" Sawyer yelled.

Thank God.

I leaned close, eyes narrowing on the screen. He had camera footage. My car. "Thirty minutes ago, the guy stopped at a red light on O'Halloran Circuit in Kambah. The CCTV footage caught the license plate."

I pushed back from the desk. "Track it and call me when you have a location." I pointed at Annabelle as I passed. "Get your guys on this or so fucking help me-"

"Unlike you, we have the authority to arrest." She

followed me out. We jogged up to the carpark; she hit the locks on her unmarked vehicle.

"I'm driving." I reached over to take the keys but she held them out of reach.

"No way, Bucko, I am. This is a police vehicle. I am police. You're here for the ride."

I gritted my teeth but diverted for the passenger seat. Arguing wouldn't get us to Emmie any quicker. She threw the car in gear heading towards Kambah. My mobile rang.

"Talk to me," I demanded.

"Satellite imaging picked them up. I'm texting you the house address. We're running it through our system. See what shakes out. Pax and the rest are on their way."

"Any other cars? People?"

"Not that I can see. I'm about to lose visuals though. Satellite is about to drift out of range."

"Sat... Jesus." Annabelle shook her head as she swerved around slower drivers.

I rapidly calculated the risks. "At the very least, this is a Canberra base. At best, it's one guy with a gun. We need to prep for worst case. Who's coming?"

"Pax, Brean, and Jack are on their way," Sawyer reported.

"My people?" Annabelle asked.

"They've called it in. Warrant is in process, but your tactical guys are enroute."

"Keep us posted." I hit end on the call, directing as we flew down back streets towards the address.

"It's on this street, number twenty-seven." We drove past, a quick glance showed my car in the driveway.

"Don't need a warrant. We've got cause," Annabelle remarked, turning left onto a side street, quickly parking.

I checked my side arm. "We good?"

She withdrew her weapon. "Stay on me. Let's go."

We crept through gardens, sticking close to the houses. Up ahead, I saw Paxton's car pull to the curb a few doors down from the residence. Jack, Brean, and Pax climbed out, nodding when they saw us.

I lifted a hand, signalling our entry. Jack and Brean vanished, disappearing around the rear of a neighbouring house. They'd cover the back, leaving us to deal with the front of the premises.

We got close, Annabelle held up a hand, counting down.

Three.

Two.

One.

We surged forward, fists pounding on the door as Annabelle yelled, "Police, open up!"

The door remained closed. Silence.

"Go!" Annabelle yelled, lifting her pistol.

Pax and I lifted a foot kicking the door in tandem. It burst open, swinging back to slam against the entry wall. We surged forward, clearing the entry and scanning the hall down to the lounge. Wires and cables were sticky-taped to the ceiling, running from one end of the house to another. A large humming server stack dominated the lounge, the dining room cluttered with desks and computers. The kitchen and garage were clear.

The bedrooms.

Fuck.

We made it to the back room, the rest of the house clear. Paxton threw open the door, I surged forward as he provided cover.

Empty.

Blood.

Fuck.

Blood on the carpet, blood splatter on the walls. Fresh, red, and wet. They'd been here recently.

Emmie. Fuck. Fuck!

We should have run.

Rage and fear converged into stone cold numbness, fuelling my focus. Failure wasn't an option.

Pax's hand landed on my shoulder. "Hold it together. We'll find her." He turned to Annabelle.

"We didn't see anyone leave. Where are they?"

"Trap door?" I asked, looking around. "False rooms?"

"No," Brean answered from the doorway. "The back fence is pulled down. Looks like they use the house behind. They're gone."

"Fuck!" I exploded. I refrained from kicking the bed. This was a crime scene, if we were to catch these fuckers, I needed calm. I turned to Annabelle. "Are we good to search the house?"

She sheathed her gun, looking around the room. "The servers are still running. We need cyber here. They're our best option."

I turned from the room, tuning them out, leaving Pax and Annabelle to sort their shit. I jerked my head at Brean. He silently led me through the house, out to the backyard, across the frost-bitten grass, to the back entrance of the additional house. Inside we found a similar set up, wires running across the ceilings, servers humming from the lounge room, electronics sprawled across every available surface.

Jack rummaged through drawers, blue gloves covering his hands.

"What've you got?" I asked, coming beside him.

"Not a lot," he admitted, voice tight with frustration. "A

few bills, a bunch of receipts and some random scribbles that don't make sense."

"Show me."

He lifted the small stack of papers, laying them out across the surface. A word caught my eye.

Neglinnaya

I pulled out my phone, searching. The first result said it was a river in Moscow.

Neglinnaya AND Money

Top result: The Central Bank of the Russian Federation is headquartered on Neglinnaya Street, Moscow.

"FUCK!" I twisted, hands diving into my hair as I stared at the servers. "Sawyer's right. They're making a run for Russia."

Brean was already on the phone. "AFP have the warrants. They're not leaving the country."

"We don't have time for this. We need to find her. Now."

"We're trying. We just need a lead."

I stalked from the room, leaving Jack and Brean to search. Like Hansel and Gretel, I followed the blood droplets to the attached garage. I stood in the cool dark room thinking.

This was on me. This whole shitshow was on me. I'd underestimated the threat. Every word Emmie had ever said was truth. These motherfuckers were pure evil.

I hit the garage door, watching as it opened to the street. An older woman knelt in the front garden across the road, pruning shears in hand.

I crossed, coming to kneel near her.

"Excuse me, ma'am?"

Her large-brimmed hat flopped to the side. "Yes?" She looked wary.

"I'm with the AFP." Not entirely a lie. "We're looking for

a missing person. Do you happen to know the people in that house?" I gestured behind me.

She narrowed her eyes. "I knew those boys were trouble. Coming and going at all hours."

"Ma'am, I'm sorry to rush but time is against us."

"Of course." She lifted up, brushing dirt off her knees. "You'll want the tapes."

"The what?"

She pointed at the eaves of her house. "Cameras. Had a break in just over a year ago. My son installed the cameras. They capture everything on the street."

Fucking hell.

"Yes, yes, I would love to see your tapes." I pulled out my phone, following her into the house. "Sawyer, I got a lead."

EMMIE

A tuft of hair stuck to the carpet above my head. My eyes narrowed on the clump as the car bumped down the road, sending me bouncing. The smell of petrol, grease, and strangely, wet dog, overwhelmed the interior of the trunk. My eyes had slowly adjusted to the dim light coming from the cracks between the seal of the car's boot lid. I reached for the clump with my two bound hands. Thankfully, they hadn't tied my hands behind me. Rookie error.

The clump was sticky. Gingerly, I dropped the hair on the floor, reaching with my hands to run my thumbs over the crown of my head. A small amount of sticky wetness met my exploration. Blood. The hair in the boot was likely mine.

Good. The DNA will place me here. Try and beat that in court, you bastards!

Ignoring the protests of my abused body, I twisted, searching the interior. The car had to be old, I'd guess mid-eighties. Unfortunately for me, that meant no emergency boot lever. They'd only been mandatory since the early 2000s. But then, my luck had never been that good.

I gave up the search for a quick exit and moved to pulling at the carpet and wheel wells. Under the carpet was a spare tyre and a tire iron.

Perfect.

With much grunting and grasping, I managed to pull the iron free, sliding it to the side where it wouldn't hit me if we flew around a corner and was within easy grasp.

Another search of the interior turned up no further treasures.

Damn.

As we flew over another bump that sent me flying into the boot lid, I rotated, landing with an *oof*. New wetness decorated the back of my head as dots danced in front of my eyes.

Pull it together! You don't have time for this.

I processed my day so far. Kidnapping, beating, followed by a boot ride to what I could only assume was the end point for me. I reached out, pulling the iron into me and tucking myself into a tight, small ball, protecting the tool.

David.

The 'officer' was a relative. Related to me through marriage to one of my sisters. He was older than me by a few years. I had no idea who he'd married and didn't remember him from the commune. He'd been silent as we'd driven through the streets, his gun resting on his knee, one hand on the trigger as he kept it steady.

I'd been bundled into one of the bedrooms, tied to a chair, and immediately educated on what they did to deserters.

In a strange way I felt free. Like my years of fear and worry were vindicated. Each punch they laid on me, each kick another sign I'd been right to put my life on hold. My worst fear had come true, and yet, I was still living.

Well, for the moment.

The first punch had come from behind, hitting me hard in the side of my head. The chair had tipped, nearly falling.

"This is from my wife, your sister." The 'officer' landed a punch to my stomach. I'd doubled over, vomiting on his shoe. The three men had taken turns, beating me until I was black and blue. One of my eyes had swollen, narrowing my vision, the other slightly blurred. But I could still see, and I'd thank whatever benevolent being out there had granted me that small privilege.

They'd kept me at the house for less than half an hour. Beating me until I was barely conscious. They'd dragged me outside, across the yard and down to a waiting car. I'd been dumped in the back before they'd driven off.

The car turned sharply, sending me crashing into the side. I clutched the iron, desperately trying to avoid knocking myself out. Under me the car lurched this way and that, bumping along what felt like a dirt road, the sound of stones pinging against the metal undercarriage.

This is it.

Shit.

I curled into a child's pose, the tire iron clutched tightly to my chest. I had a plan. It wasn't great, but it was a plan all the same.

The car rolled to a stop, the engine shutting off. The car rocked as the men inside opened doors, chatting quietly. Their steps crunched on the ground as they walked around the car. I could make out bits and pieces of the conversation.

"...here?"

"Inside."

"Get her."

The voices were above me now. I curled tighter, my fingers clutching the weight of the metal. The sound of a key sliding into a lock gave me a two-second warning. The boot popped open, light blinding me. I frantically blinked, keeping my head down, body curled.

"Time to get up." Hands reached for me, digging into the soft flesh of my upper arms, hauling me out. My front was to the boot, my back to them, my bound hands clutched the iron to my stomach as they pulled me free.

One.

Two.

My foot touched the ground, and I reacted immediately, twisting violently, bringing a knee up to clock the first guy in the groin. He went down. Hands at the ready, I swung back around, slamming the iron into the other man's head. He stumbled back, falling.

I heard the other men shout as I took off, running for the first spot my eyes landed. Thick bush scrub surrounded wherever they had brought me. Thick enough I could hide in the brush if only I got deep enough. I didn't spare a glance at the men. Iron clutched tight, I bolted, my feet skittering across the dirt.

Shouting erupted behind me, the sound of pounding feet dogged my escape. I focussed, breaking through the underbrush, plunging deeper.

"Abishag! Stop!"

I tripped, stumbling.

"Abishag!"

I stumbled to a halt, my feet lead as I turned, dread, despair, and fear crashing as I watched the man approach.

"Abishag." He offered me a tight smile. "You've returned."

His face impassive as his eyes took me in. He'd aged. His

face had thinned, giving him an older, mature look. Unfamiliar marks and scars criss-crossed his cheeks.

He looked directly at me, his hand settling heavy on my shoulder.

"Welcome home, sister."

EMMIE

While tying me to a chair, he informed me it was nothing personal. This Abel was different to the boy I remembered. I'd always assumed he'd escape. Back when I knew him, he'd been determined to get out.

Now, he seemed determined to stay.

"The scars are from that night, if you're interested," he said lightly as he tightened the ropes binding my legs to the chair. "David assumed I'd helped you." He lifted one hand, dragging fingers over the light marks. "This was my penance."

I swallowed, cursing myself for my weakness. "I assumed you left."

He chuckled. "I learnt the error of my ways." He straightened, hand coming to settle on my head. "You will too, Abishag."

My tongue felt thick in my mouth. I swallowed, ignoring the pain in my cheek. "It's Emmie now."

He chuckled. "You've returned home, sister. Your place is here, your name is as it was."

The hair on the back of my neck lifted, fear tightening my chest. "I'm not returning."

There were voices outside the door. Abel tilted his head, listening. His cold eyes came back to me. "David comes."

There was a knock at the door. The man on this side, a man I wasn't familiar with, pulled it open, permitting a large body. As he stepped into the light, I could see that time had not been kind to David. Grey had overtaken the brown of his hair and middle age had left behind bald patches. His face had deep grooves and a purple-red tinge to his skin. His brows were low, as if he were perpetually frowning. The cruel twist of his mouth, cemented in the wrinkles around his lips and the drooping of his chin.

He was still large, built like an old-school boxer. His meaty hands had twisted knuckles that were thick and inflamed. As he strode towards me, I detected a slight limp on his left side. His feet planted firmly in front of me, hands immediately going to his hips as he stared down.

The man I'd feared for years stood before me. And once again I was in a powerless position. Surprisingly, I didn't quake with fear. Instead, I made a promise to Luc.

I'll hang on till you find me.

My resolve firmed as I met David's stare. I wouldn't back down.

"You've caused quite a mess, little girl." His voice sounded older, rougher than I remembered. The phrase was deliberate. A shiver of a memory whispered at the edges of my mind.

My hands were pinned to the bed, a hand at the back of my head, forcing my face down, pressing my cheek into the mattress. David's breath was hot against the shell of my ear.

"Are you a good little girl? It's time to please your husband."

I shoved the memory away, my fingers flexing. I wrapped

them around the thick wood of the chair arms, grounding myself.

"Hello, David." I lifted my chin, ignoring the fear, pushing away the memories. "I can't say it's nice to see you."

For a moment he looked uncertain, surprised. Perhaps he'd expected me to fall at his feet. Perhaps he'd expected me to beg. His face hardened.

"You've grown a backbone while you've been gone. Don't worry. We'll rid you of that."

"You can try." A little frisson of something like pride burned in my stomach.

He held out a hand. The third man in the room stepped forward, handing him a thick leather whip.

Oh God.

David pulled the plaits through his fingers. "You remember this, don't you Abishag?"

I swallowed. "My friends will–"

"Shut up!" He cracked the whip, landing the first blow to my knee. My jeans absorbed most of the impact, the skin underneath burning.

Stay strong.

Blinking back stinging tears, I glared at him. "Must make you feel good to hurt a woman," I taunted. "But then hurting women and children was always your kink, right, David?"

The next cut landed on the sleeve of my hoodie, raking heat across my forearm.

"Whore! Jezebel!" David screamed, his face now mottled as he stalked around my chair, kicking the back, knocking punches to my ears. "Eve! Temptress!"

The whip cracked down on my other arm, slashing the fabric and leaving a bloody trail.

"You perverse, rebellious woman! Respect thy husband! Submit! A disgraceful wife is nothing but decay in her husband's bones!" He spat on me, the wet landing in the centre of my chest. "I sanctify your body through our marriage! You are pure from your sins because of *my* holiness. Accept your punishment, whore. As your husband, I will make you respect me."

David quoted bible verses, raining hellfire down upon my head as he laid blow after blow on me, painting my body in blood, bruises, and fury.

"What God has brought together let no man–"

"Enough." The voice was quiet, determined, final.

David fell silent, stepping back. My head hung limp, drops of blood falling from my nose to pool in the fabric of my jeans. Gentle hands lifted my head, turning me this way and that. I forced one eye open, barely making out the familiar features.

"Oh, David." Edward shook his head. "I leave you to discipline your wife, and this is what you do? Must I remind you of our agreement?"

David coughed. "She can type. I left her hands."

Edward dropped my head, his fingers running over my hands, lifting and checking each finger.

"Yes," he said, standing. "But she is hardly able to perform like this."

"She'll do it." David's heavy hand settled on my shoulder, squeezing. I gasped as pain exploded from the dislocated joint. "She knows the consequences."

I watched, swallowing against the nausea, as feet shuffled in front of me. Finally, Edward spoke.

"Take her to the women. Have them clean her up and what-not. When she's decent, bring her to me." He turned to leave.

"But what about the–" David protested.

"Patience, brother. God's work comes first." I heard the door open. "Come, David. We have much to decide."

I listened to them walk out, their steps echoing down the hall outside. Hands tugged at the ropes keeping me strapped to the chair. In moments, I was free but unable to move. Hands gently pulled me forward and slipped under my knees and behind my back, cradling me like a child.

"I got her. Go tell the women." Abel's chest vibrated under my ear as he held me close. The other man in the room left. I fought unconsciousness, the world spinning, the nausea rolling as he shifted me higher, his head dipping down until his lips were pressed against my ear.

"You should have run." His voice was barely a whisper, his tone apologetic. "You'd run every other time." He below out a breath, hitching me higher. "When you stayed... They gave me no choice. You'd understand if you knew her." His voice broke.

Knew who? Who is her?

"Call Luc," I whispered, barely able to utter the words through the swelling. "Please."

He pulled me closer. "I can't."

"Please..." I gave in to the dark.

LUC

The registration check on the vehicle turned up more questions. The only person able to answer them sat in the interrogation room at the local police station while Annabelle and her partner drilled him with questions.

Dressed in a smart suit, Eric Flowers COO of West Investments, sat handcuffed to the desk. He stared at his clasped hands as Annabelle rounded the table.

"Come on, Eric," she cajoled. "The evidence is all there. We know you planted the software. We know you rented the two houses, and we know you bought the car. You're looking at embezzlement, kidnapping, torture, and that's just today." She lent down, tapping a hand against the sterile table. "Your choice."

"I want my lawyer."

Annabelle tsked. "Your appointed lawyer is just there." She nodded at the man in the corner of the room.

"*My* lawyer. Not some underling."

"Your lawyer is in Europe on three weeks' holiday."

Eric's fingers flexed. "I'm not talking until I get my lawyer."

The man in the corner coughed. "Perhaps we could have a moment alone?" Annabelle and the officer left the room. Paxton bumped my shoulder. "Don't worry, Annabelle will break him."

I gritted my teeth, feeling the muscle in my jaw jump. If I had three minutes alone he'd be squealing like a pig.

The sound was muted as we watched through the double-sided glass. The lawyer gestured animatedly as Eric shook his head. Finally, the lawyer stood and tapped on the door. It opened, Annabelle and her partner returning. The volume switched back on.

"You ready to talk?"

"We want a deal," the lawyer said, laying a hand on Eric's shoulder. "He talks in exchange for protection and a pardon."

Annabelle crossed her arms, shaking her head. "Protection, a new identity, but he's serving time. We could look at a reduced sentence, but Mr Flowers has too many crosses against his name."

The lawyer sat down, leaning over to whisper in Eric's ear. After a moment Eric nodded.

The lawyer held out a hand. "We got a deal. Reduced sentence, two years, and protection."

"I'm not making promises on the sentence," Annabelle cautioned. "We need to hear what he's got first."

The lawyer hesitated, then nodded. "Eric?"

The guy sighed heavily, eyes glued to his hands. "They recruited me fresh out of high school. I thought I was top shit. Knew how to hack. They honed in on me, taught me what I needed to know. I was in deep when they blackmailed me." He clenched his fist. "I couldn't get out. They shaped who I became. Paid for my university, hacked systems so I became the preferred candidate. All I had to do was plant software in each of the companies." He scoffed. "At first I thought it was intellectual property theft. They could sell the plans to the highest bidder. Sure, there was some of that. But then they had me work the financial sector. I ended up planting software that pulled money."

"How much?" Annabelle asked.

"Millions by now. I don't know how many places I've worked that still haven't found the malware."

No one spoke for a long moment as he struggled. "They sent me to Canberra two years ago. Set me up at what would become West Investments. The merger was already in negotiations. They had me plant the software, then leave it. Grant is a mover and shaker. He takes over shitty companies, flips them, then sells them for a profit. My role gave me access." He swallowed, shaking his head. "For a while, everything was fine. I did the dirty work, they got paid, and they left me the hell alone."

"But?" Annabelle prompted.

"They contacted me with a new request." He looked up, his face ashen. "They ordered me to blow the West account."

"Blow how?"

"Report it."

"Shit," Paxton whispered beside me. "They wanted Emmie."

"Why?" Annabelle asked.

"Said they had a bigger target. I was to contact Elliot Securities and ask for the people who'd worked the Sierra account."

I jerked in surprise. We closed the Sierra account the middle of last year. A local start-up that specialized in wholesale medical equipment, their website had been compromised. Shaken, the CEO had asked us to overhaul not just their online security, but all their backend and physical. The guy had sung our praises for months, referring new customers our way. Emmie and I had worked the case.

"They did their research," Brean commented from my left. "Addie wouldn't have questioned that referral, just passed them on to you."

My fists clenched. This wasn't getting us any closer to Emmie.

"Did you know the Sierra case?"

Eric shook his head.

"Did they tell you about the real target?"

Eric shook his head again. "They wanted all the information about my meetings and who would be where, when."

"And the houses? The car?"

"Last month. They wanted me to set it up. First it was two guys, then five, then ten." He paused. "Said they'd let me out once this was done."

"It was a big job?" Annabelle asked.

"Huge. People were coming and going. They kept wanting more tech, more infrastructure, more... just more. I got them what they wanted, but it was causing issues. They were... on edge. Pissed off."

"You know they've kidnapped Ms Franklin."

Eric dropped his head. "Yes."

"Do you know where they're taking her?"

He hesitated, glancing at his lawyer. The lawyer nodded.

"They gave me a fake ID. Robert Castle. The house is a rental in Bywong."

I turned to leave but Paxton's hand clamped down on my shoulder, halting me.

"Wait," he said, nodding towards the glass. "We need to know more."

"Do you know what they want with Ms Franklin?"

"Something about an account. Before she left, escaped, whatever, she transferred money."

"Fifty thousand." Annabelle nodded. "We know."

"No." Eric shook his head. "I've heard whispers it's in the hundreds of millions. Maybe more. She siphoned the money. It goes through multiple offshore accounts, never staying in one place long. They can't track it, can't work out her alias. She's covered her trail so well they can't figure it out. And they need the money."

"Why?"

"They need her to access the accounts. They're transferring cash to weapons dealers, big players overseas. They don't have the money to pay these guys off. They need her to enact their final solution."

"The final solution?"

"They never told me. But it sounded like they were planning on something big."

"I want the Bywong address."

I twisted out from under Paxton's hand. "Let's go."

Annabelle met us in the hall. "The tactical teams are approved. We're lead."

"I want in," I told her, palming my gun.

She locked eyes with Pax who nodded.

"Fine, but you stay behind my guys. I don't need a civilian contractor getting shot." We followed her up to the meeting room. Maps were spread on the table, Sawyer sat hunched over a laptop next to two analysts.

"Swayer?" I asked, entering the room.

"I got satellite and confirmation from a CCTV that they passed through the town. They're there."

"How long do we have?" Pax asked, looking over the maps.

"Maybe three hours? They don't know they're compromised, yet," Annabelle commented, taking a stack of papers from her aide, then frowning. "We've pulled the plans from the rental agency. The house is surrounded by bush. That's going to make entry difficult."

"We'll have to wait till dark," Brean agreed, running a hand over the property lines. "They'll no doubt have traps and patrols."

I stared at the plans, memorising the layout. "The house is big. Also, outbuildings." I pointed at the plans. "Based on this, they have enough room for half the commune."

"Shit." Sawyer hunched over the laptop. "Give me five. I'll see if... fuck." He slapped a hand on the table, twirling the laptop to face us. "Three buses. They passed through the town three days ago."

"That could be–"

"They're registered as being hired by Robert Castle."

"Okay." Annabelle clapped her hands together once, all attention turning to her. "This has just jumped from a hostage to a full scale takedown. We've got one opportunity to bring these guys in. Someone get me the commissioner. We're going to need support."

Her aide stood, moving to exit the room.

I looked down at my hand, feeling the slight tremor. I clenched it into a fist, impotent rage threatening.

Get it together, Luc. She needs you.

"Emmie may not have time to wait while you seek permission," I said to the room at large, my eyes still on my fist. I lifted my head, killing all emotion, my eyes completely dead.

"We need to move fast. They've got her, they're not going to hesitate using her."

Annabelle eyed me, her piercing blue meeting mine as she considered my words.

"We have one opportunity here, Lucien," she finally said, the room quiet as our wills battled. "We can take down this whole crew and nullify the threat against Ms Franklin. Or we can rush it, save her, and pray we get the rest while we're there." She lifted a hand, palm up, "What would you prefer?"

I looked back down at my hand, eyes closing as I finally choked out the words. "We'll do it your way. Just pray she's alive."

The room seemed to breathe as one, people springing back into action. I felt Brean and Pax beside me, both watching me struggle to contain my fear, my rage, my frustration.

"We'll find her," Brean whispered. "We've got this."

I ignored the pit in my stomach, looking over at Sawyer. He stared back at me, his shaggy hair standing on end, his eyes tired and mouth tight.

He gave me a sharp nod before returning back to his laptop.

I forced myself to sit, pulling the plans and maps to me. "Choke points are here and here." I pointed at the spots on the house plans.

For a moment neither Brean or Pax moved. I could feel their silent communication above me. They both sat, examining the documents with me.

"And here." Brean pointed to one of the buildings. "The real estate ad says it has a studio. I'd put her there. Easier to secure, quick access for an exit, less conspicuous."

A quick glance at the tactical lead showed they were concentrating on the house as the central point.

"I'll get us in with the group targeting this," Pax murmured, slipping away from the table.

"And if she's not?" I asked.

"We've come this far. You gotta believe," Brean told me, clapping a hand to my shoulder. "She's smart. She's resilient. Our Emmie is a fighter. She's gonna do whatever it takes to survive."

Survive, baby. I cast the thought out. *I'll find you.*

EMMIE
THE PAST

I fidgeted on the chair, watching as Edward flicked through the binder I'd compiled. My plan for the final coming.

It was simple, route money from small financial institutions. Build a cache of cash, then use that to develop a safe house for the commune. Once complete, target the major banks both physically and electronically. If the banks went down, if the stock exchanges were all taken out in one massive synchronised hit, it would cause global chaos.

Not every bank needed to be targeted. Just the headquarters of major lines and the stock exchanges. We had enough members scattered across the globe to do it.

I'd developed the final coming.

Edward finished reading, placing the binder on the desk. He knit his fingers together, considering me.

"Sister Abishag, do you understand why I tasked you with this duty?"

I shook my head. "No, Prophet."

"You are creative. You see a puzzle and break it down until it is easily surmountable." He nodded at the binder. "I will pray over this and decide."

"Yes, Prophet."

"If God decides to bless this plan, then work needs to be done."

"Yes, Prophet."

"We require guns, explosives. Your estimates are conservative?"

I nodded.

"Hmm." He leaned back in his chair, one hand tapping against the arm rest.

I waited, palms pressed to the front of my jeans.

He began muttering, mulling my idea over. "It will take time and resources to achieve our end. We must ready the chosen. Embed them in the financial institutions. Build connections and stockpile weapons."

He closed his eyes, mouth moving silently for many minutes. Finally, he opened them, turning back to me.

"Yes." He tapped the binder. "God is pleased."

EMMIE
THE PRESENT

Dark. It was my first thought as I opened my eyes. The room had deep wood panelling. Boards covered the one window from the outside, allowing no light to enter. The air was stale, hot, and smelled like mothballs.

I rolled, immediately regretting the movement as my stomach rebelled, nausea assaulting me.

The smell of blood, sweat, and vomit hung heavy as I fully woke. The nausea now under control, I gingerly rolled to my side, pushing to a sit. The small room had a bolted down chair, a mattress– no blankets or sheets –and a bucket in the corner. I assumed that was my toilet.

Despite the indignity, I forced myself to use the crude chamber pot. God only knew how long I'd be kept here.

There was no water to wash my hands or soothe my throat, no toilet paper or towels to clean myself. Despite the protests of my injured body, I explored the small bedroom, looking for weaknesses. There were none. It appeared they'd taken the tire iron to heart, stripping the room of any useful items. There was not a loose nail or screw to be found.

I'd have to rely on my wits and training.

God, help me.

After my slow circle of the room, I collapsed back on the mattress, groaning as the thin foam barely cushioned my weight. It was one of those old shitty kid mattresses which contained zero springs and nearly no actual support. It sagged into the floorboards, barely separating me from the hard wood.

Under me, I could hear people moving about. A clatter of utensils, the scrap of furniture, and the dim drone of voices as life happened around me. I didn't remember seeing a two-storey building, but then I'd been in such a rush that I hadn't paid enough attention. Unless they were in some kind of basement and I was above them?

My head spun with possibilities, each more creative and wildly implausible than the last. I drifted in and out of consciousness as I struggled to consider a plan of attack. My body required rest, healing; the concussion throbbed, and the nausea crested as I struggled to focus.

After what felt like hours, the door opened, permitting four people in. The two men entered, taking position on either side of the door. I remained on my side, watching women enter the room. The men were middle-aged with matching haircuts and beards. Both wore fierce expressions and glared down at me. I ignored them, knowing I would find no help from them. The women were a mix. One was older, her hair long and tied back in a strict braid. The other was younger, with a softly rounding belly and hair in a loose Dutch braid. The older woman placed a plate on the bolted down chair, then moved to lift the waste bucket.

The younger approached, kneeling beside me, placing a bucket of water and two water bottles down. She reached into the pocket of her skirt and withdrew a rag, dipping it in the water.

"I'm just going to clean you." Her voice was soft as she wrung out the cloth. "Please stay still."

Gently, she rubbed at the dry blood and crusted dirt on my skin, dipping and rubbing, dipping and rubbing. I tried not to move as she worked her way down my face, towards my top, the mattress growing wet from the pink water.

"That's enough, Beth," one of the men said from the door. The girl pulled a hand back, her free hand going to rest on the curve of her belly. "Edward only wanted her presentable not ready for marriage."

"Let me just clean the blood from her arms, and then we'll be good."

He made a sound but let her carry on.

She pressed the bloody rag to a deep cut in my arm. I sucked in breath, desperately battling nausea as the red haze of pain overwhelmed my thoughts.

"You're pregnant," I whispered, as the men murmured between themselves. She hesitated, and then her head dipped in the slightest of nods as she continued cleaning the deep cut.

"Was it... consensual?"

She didn't react, her eyes on my cut.

"Who's the father?"

Her lip trembled, but she said nothing.

"How old are you?"

"Fourteen." Her voice was an exhale of breath, barely a whisper.

"How long have you been here?"

"Five years."

"Do you want to–"

"Quiet!" The man at the door snapped, causing us to jump. "Beth, you're done."

She quickly packed up her rag and bucket, leaving the bottled water behind. The men and the other woman also left, locking me into the dark room.

I slowly pushed up. Clean clothes were piled beside the chair. Flat bread and a paper plate all they gave me.

Smart.

I ignored the clothes and food, instead drinking slowly from the water bottles. They may be drugged, but I had to take that chance. I could hear movement downstairs again. I drifted in and out of consciousness, tiptoeing the line between delirium and lucidity.

Footsteps echoed on the stairs outside the prison room. I forced my eyes open. The room remained dark; I had no concept of time.

Had I been here days? Hours?

Everything hurts.

Be strong. Be ready. Look for mistakes.

The door scraped along the floorboards, protesting as it opened. I couldn't summon the strength to look up.

"Abishag, damn it!" Hands settled on my feverish skin, rolling my body. My head lolled before I forced my eyes open.

"Abel." My voice was a hoarse whisper. "Why?"

A muscle in his jaw ticked as he lifted me. "Greenfields."

Ice froze the blood in my veins.

Fuck.

"They found it, sis."

I groaned as he moved me, repositioning my body. "They want the password."

"Now?"

He carried me through the door, out into glaring lights. My eyes snapped closed, vomit burning the back of my throat as my body protested the bright lights.

"Now," he confirmed, carrying me down the stairs. "Edward has demanded it."

"Why are you still here?"

He hesitated for less than a moment before continuing down the stairs. "I can leave after you deliver it."

"I'm the bribe?"

"You're my indulgence. Delivering you is the price I have to pay for my excommunication."

I was silent as he carried me through the house. An indulgence, much like those practiced by churches back in the 1500s, was a way for members of the God's Patriots to purchase an exemption. In the commune, indulgences were large amounts of money that purchased three things - wives, favours, or excommunication. Only one person had achieved the sum required for excommunication while I was there, leaving behind his wife and children because he hadn't the funds to take them with him. The wife had been forcibly remarried a month later.

Excommunication was the only way to cleanly leave. It sealed your fate, cutting you off. The church had nothing to do with you, and you were free to live your life.

Greenfields had been my ticket out. I'd worked on the program for months before David finally got his way, derailing my secretive plans.

"How much?" I choked out as we cleared the steps, moving into a large room.

"Rough estimates show over a billion."

How? How had they not discovered it? How had no one stopped it?

"Why do they need it?"

"To enact your plan. It's time for the final coming."

Oh, God. I was right.

Abel bent, placing me on a chair, arranging my body gently before stepping back. I forced my head up as I looked at the room through one squinting eye.

It was a large space, brightly lit thanks to the numerous fluorescent lights that hung from the wood beams above. I assumed it was some kind of garage, with a little loft where I'd been kept. In the garage, women and men stood or sat here and there, all watching. There was a computer in the centre of the room, cables running from outside.

"Abishag." Edward stepped forward, his smooth voice sending a chill up my spine. "Your trial begins."

"I'm not called that." I forced out between swollen lips. "My name is–"

"Quiet!" he snapped, clapping a hand down on the desk. "You're here to face your punishment."

I watched, dread a heavy rock in my belly as he called out my charges.

"Spousal abandonment, extramarital relations, treachery, theft, lust, greed, deceit..." he paused, arms sweeping to engulf the room at large. "And worst of all, dishonour to God."

He turned back to me, folding his arms over his chest. "How do you find her?" he asked his eyes boring into mine.

"Guilty." As one, the disciples spoke my sentence.

Edward smiled. "And her punishment?"

Able stepped forward. "Excommunication."

Another stepped forward, a young woman I didn't recognise. "Concubine."

A third. "Stoning."

Finally, after each had spoken, Edward walked the room, considered their words. "Is Abishag not a daughter of Eden?" he asked.

"Yes," came the response.

"And does God not punish, then forgive those who abandon Him?"

"Yes," came the reply.

"Do we believe Abishag worthy of forgiveness?"

There was a mixed response.

Edward tapped his lips with a finger as he strode around, circling my chair.

"Can I say something?" I asked, fighting to get the words out. All eyes came to me.

"Speak, Sister Abishag," Edward invited.

"You guys want the cash, I want out. Abel delivered me to you. He also wants out. I'll give you what you want if you let both of us go."

Edward propped a hip on the desk, crossing his arms as he considered me. "Your husband has asked for your return."

I swallowed the bile that rose at his comment. "He has other wives. And like you said, I've been with other men."

One man. I've only been with one man because you fucked me up. You told me I was useless. You made me think sex was dirty. You made me associate pain with love. And that one man helped me blow away all the hate and disgust you'd built.

David shoved his way through the crowd, face flushed. "I'll take her!"

Edward considered his brother.

"The code has a kill switch." I dropped my last bargaining chip. I looked directly at Edward, speaking just to him. "You make me stay, and it's all gone."

"I'll make her–"

Edward raised a hand to silence his brother. "You wish to take her back. I understand." Edward remained focussed on me, his head tilting slightly to the left.

"You would deprive your brethren of their dues? Your God, His glory?" he finally asked.

"You aren't my God, and you have never been my brethren. I abandoned the church long before I physically left."

There were gasps. David surged forward, slapping a hand across my face, sending me sprawling from the chair.

Groaning, I pushed myself up, spitting blood. Hands gripped me, hauling me back into the chair. Edward hadn't moved.

"You rape children, impregnate teenagers, beat those who are different to you." My head drooped, too heavy to lift from my chest. "You're all monsters."

A fist landed in my stomach, doubling me over. My hands clutched at my middle as I rapidly swallowed against the bile filling my mouth.

"Quiet, whore," David threatened. "Edward?"

The silence was filled only with the sound of my laboured breaths.

"Brother Abel, what say you?" Edward finally asked.

There was shuffling, and then Abel's strong voice filled the room. "I have no loyalty to my sister. I simply wish to be with my wife."

I struggled, lifting my head as I blinked to clear my fuzzy vision. Abel's hands clenched and unclenched, his jaw rigid.

"Sister Margery chose to leave us," Edward pointed out. "She put her faith in man and not God."

Abel's hands relaxed. "That does not mean I am not still her husband."

"You would leave our Church?"

Abel nodded once sharply.

Edward tsked. "You delivered on your indulgence. You may leave." He waved his hand dismissively. "Take nothing with you but the documents we've approved. When the Final Solution comes, you will find no pardon from God. From this day, you are dead to the church."

Abel's knees buckled, and I watched the painfully stark relief etch across his face.

"I understand. Thank you, brother." His eyes briefly turned to me before he looked away. "God bless you all."

He turned on his heel, heading for the door. Edward gestured to me, beckoning me forward. Two men hauled me up, heedless of my injuries.

They pulled me forward, my feet dragging loudly on the concrete floor. They dumped me in front of Edward. My legs, unable to sustain my body weight, collapsed and I fell in a heap at his feet.

"Sister Abigshag. God, the Father of mercies, through the death and resurrection of His Son has reconciled the world to Himself and sent the Holy Spirit among us for the forgiveness of sins; through the ministry of the Church I will cleanse you from your sins in the name of the Father, and of the Son, and the Holy Spirit."

"Amen," murmured the crowd.

Dread and fear clawed at my throat, as a heavy weight settled in my chest, constraining my breathing.

"David. You are to discipline your wife. Under your hand, she is to give us the password, transfer the money, then follow your instruction. You are to cleanse her however you see fit." Edward squatted down, his fingers wrapping around my chin, lifting my head until my eyes met his. "You are our greatest asset, Abigshag. God has returned you to us. You will learn your place, and you will rejoice in the love of your husband, your family, your brethren, and your God. After today you will serve us. Your place is here."

I smothered the whimpers that threatened to escape.

"They'll come," I whispered. "You won't break me."

His lips twisted up at the corners. "They can try."

LUC

The bush land around the farm lay in shadows. Nocturnal animals prowled, and the noises of the night played soundtrack to our activities.

I'd been lying in this hole for three hours, my gaze trained down the scope of the .50 calibre rifle.

Back when I'd served, this weapon had been an extension of my body, as familiar to me as my hand.

Activity at the farm had slowly reduced over the last hour. A flurry of movement to and from an outhouse, a patrol of the immediate grounds by some armed, but ultimately undertrained militia, and then quiet.

I didn't like this.

The leaves crushed beside me as Paxton settled back into place.

He tapped my leg once. An hour to go. I lifted my shoulder slightly in acknowledgement, gaze never wavering.

A door from the outhouse burst open, a young man stumbling out. Pax and I tensed, alert as we watched. He closed the door, hands immediately going to his knees as he doubled over, sucking deep breaths. After a long moment he straightened, quickly moving toward the main farmhouse. He disappeared inside for less than ten minutes before returning with a backpack. He glanced back and forth before making for the road.

Our ear pieces crackled. "DELTA, there's one headed your way. Follow and bring him in when able."

My gaze remained trained on the outhouse. Paxton tapped my thigh three times. Thirty minutes to go. The door from the outhouse opened again, people streaming out. They were chattering, laughing as they headed for the farm-house or another outbuilding.

Fuck.

We'd assumed the outhouse was a sleeping quarter. When they'd left the main house, the assumption had been they'd headed for bed. It was now late. Emmie had been missing for over ten hours.

My argument for early entry had been shot down. They'd said night would provide us with better cover and a higher degree of surprise. With this many people still awake...

This wasn't good.

"All teams, hold for further orders," Annabelle said over the radio.

The only external sign of my frustration was the tightening of my shoulders. I breathed out, forcing myself to relax. Stressed snipers made mistakes.

My shoulders relaxed, my breathing evening as I continued to watch the outhouse. I'd been in worst situations before. Life and death situations. Situations where, if I didn't get the target right, my whole team would be dead. But I'd never been in a situation where the woman I loved was in danger.

Fuck.

I'm here, Keys. Stay strong.

Time slowly trudged on. The farmhouse settled. The outhouse remained lit but quiet.

Thirty minutes.

Forty.

Forty-five.

I breathed in and out, concentrating on the air in my lungs, ignoring the questions of what if. Of what was happening. Where she was.

If she still lived.

Our earpieces crackled to life, "T-minus ten minutes." I repositioned slowly, getting ready for the surge. Beside me, Paxton tensed.

We're a go.

A roar split the silence, followed by screams. Lights began to flick on in the farmhouse.

"Go! Go, Go, Go!" Annabelle yelled over the radio.

Pax and I surged up, heading directly for the outhouse. The scream abruptly cut off as we reached the door, our team not far behind. We fell beside the door, waiting for the tactical guys to arrive with the battering ram. They did the count, hitting it once, twice, and then it swung in, permitting us entrance.

I entered, skidding to a halt in the near-empty room.

Lights.

Blood.

Emmie.

EMMIE

The door clicked shut, sealing me in with David. His big body was off to my left as he waited for the others to leave. I kept my head down, pretending to ignore him as I assessed the situation. Fear infused my body with adrenaline.

This is my time.

Years ago, I'd swore he would never hurt me again. Never degrade me the way he'd tried so long ago. I'd worked hard, trained for this moment.

I watched him from under the strands of my hair. He went to a closet off the side of the room, pulling out a large broom. With a quick twist he removed the head from the handle, tossing it away. He turned back to me, judging the weight of the pole in his hands.

"Now, you're mine." The handle came down, heading straight for my side. I rolled, ducking out of the way, scrambling to my feet just out of harm's way. The sharp crack of the wood on the cement ripped through the room. He pulled up, his face mottled with rage.

"You've been a naughty girl, Abishag." He stalked me,

and I danced back, adrenaline overpowering the weakness in my legs, suppressing the aches and pains.

Hands up, look for a weakness, get the advantage, eyes on his face, look for his tell.

The wise words of each of my trainers came to me. My body fell into the natural stance and movements, reflexes honed from years of repetition.

There.

David's eyes flickered to my right side before he shifted the handle, swinging to that spot. There it was. His tell.

Emboldened, I waited, trying to tire him as I circled, and he followed, swinging and missing. The occasional swipe caught me, but I stayed, forcing myself upright, forcing strength and courage into limbs that wanted to fail.

"Submit to your husband!" he screamed, spittle flying.

"Never!" I yelled back, dancing back towards the centre of the room.

Enraged, he let out a roar, swinging wildly, charging towards me. I ducked low, sliding under the broom handle, coming up close to him. Using his momentum, I grasped his wrist, pulling him over my shoulder and body slamming him into the floor.

His grip on the handle loosened, and I wrestled it free, turning it back on my aggressor. I beat at his head, smashing the handle into it as he screamed for mercy. I ignored his pleas, beating mercilessly at his body, heedless of the blood that arced into ever-widening patterns, covering the walls and floor.

This is my moment. Today is my revenge.

I vaguely registered pounding on the door at the same moment I realised David was silent. I dropped the broom handle, my legs finally giving out. I fell to my knees, slumping as I struggled to stay conscious.

The door burst open, and I watched as Luc cleared the entry. His beautiful eyes swept the room, coming to rest on me, then David. Blood soaked the legs of my pants.

"Emmie." He took two quick steps, falling beside me, pulling me into his arms, his hands running up and down my body as he pressed urgent kisses to my cheeks, my lips, my hair.

"I think I killed him," I whispered, clutching desperately at Luc's vest.

"It's okay," Luc assured me, his hands still moving over my body. "I've got you."

I struggled against his chest, watching as men surrounded David. Paxton rolled him, a hand coming to his neck. After a long moment, Pax looked up.

"He's dead."

Good.

Not a part of my soul grieved. I felt no guilt, just relief.

"Thank God," I whispered as black squiggles clouded my vision. "Thank God."

The last thing I remembered was Luc pulling me closer.

EMMIE

Hospitals, I'd learned, each smell alike. Both sterile and rotten. The strong smell of anti-bacterial cleaner rarely covered the stench of illness. I didn't like how the obscure scent permeated my pores, leaving me feeling cleanly dirty. It was weird.

"And tomorrow you have the meeting with AFP, if your doctor approves." Luc sat at my bedside reading from the calendar he'd installed on my new phone. Turned out, with no crazy cult to fear, I was free to embrace all the conveniences technology had to offer. Which, according to Luc, included playlists, shared couple calendars, and sexting.

Lots and lots of sexting.

Luc, it seemed, felt the best way to encourage my body to recover was to offer sexual rewards.

"I've been here three days," I grumbled, pushing the tasteless cube of jelly the hospital described as dessert around the bowl with my spoon. "Isn't it about time I go home?"

"Eat your meal," Luc instructed from his seat, eyes still on our calendar.

Our calendar.

As much as I complained, a pleasant little spark shimmied up my spine every time I said our.

Grumpily, I scooped the jelly, stuffing the red mess into my mouth. It didn't taste pleasant. I really wanted a cheeseburger and giant fries. Instead I had clear broth and jelly thanks to my bruised jaw. Fun.

"Knock knock!" called a cheerful voice as Addie, Kel, Jarrett, Jetta, Paxton, Brean, and Jack entered the room.

"Jesus." Luc stood, shuffling to make room. "You guys bring the whole tribe?"

"Sawyer and Courtney are parking the cars. They'll be here shortly," Brean reported.

Addie hip-bumped him as she leaned over my bed, pressing air kisses to either side of my face. "How are you today, sunshine?" she purred, dumping socks, clean shirts, and three books on my lap.

"Good," I muttered distracted by the abundance of gifts.

"We've been down to see your sister-in-law," Kel told me, dropping into Luc's vacated seat. "She's doing well."

"Is it sister-in-law or sister-wife?" Jarrett asked, perching on the arm rest.

"Sister-wife," Addie confirmed, starting to fuss with my blankets. "She's considering her options."

"She was never married to that fucker," Luc interrupted, his face darkening. I offered him a small smile.

"You know what I mean." Addie waved a dismissive hand. "All we're saying is, Beth is doing well and child services have agreed to place her with Kel."

All eyes went to Kel who shrugged. "Seems like the best solution."

Jarrett clasped a hand on her shoulder. "It really is," he

agreed. "Though the baby is going to be an added pressure in the next few months."

Kel shrugged, a small smile playing on her lips. "We'll work it out."

"Does Beth want to keep it?" I asked.

Beth, the young girl who'd helped me, was David's most recent wife. Like me, she'd been raped. Unlike me, she hadn't had an opportunity to escape. The baby was David's.

"No." Jarrett shook his head. "Said she's too young for this and wants to start over somewhere new. Somewhere she's not known as the"–he raised his hands making air quotes– "pregnant cult girl."

"Fair," Jetta said from her seat on Pax's lap. "She's going to have enough baggage without adding a kid to the mix."

"And Abel?" I asked, ignoring Luc's reaction. Luc wasn't a fan of my brother, no matter that he now understood Abel's desperation.

"Grieving," Addie said, moving to my feet. She fussed, pulling up the blankets to change my socks. "That poor boy."

"Poor boy, my arse," Luc muttered. I reached out a hand giving him a squeeze.

My brother had stayed because he'd fallen in love with Margery, a young woman in the commune. He'd worked hard and been granted permission to marry her. They'd been like me, desperate to get out. They were working on it when Margery got sick. The church didn't believe in healthcare beyond basic first aid, at least not for the plebs. Edward preached that God would heal. Abel had pooled their money and gotten her an indulgence. She'd left to get treatment. It had been cervical cancer. She'd passed away over two years ago.

Abel, unaware of her new identity and with no way to contact an excommunicated member, hadn't known.

"At least he tried to warn Em," Jetta pointed out.

Luc snorted in response, crossing his arms, a scowl still marring his forehead.

Abel had been the one to send through the messages. While tasked with bringing me back into the fold, he'd resisted in the only way he knew how– by threatening me. He'd hoped the threats would give me enough time to escape. Luc, having watched me freak the fuck out, didn't appreciate the gesture.

"We're here!" Sawyer announced, entering the room. He carried what I can only describe as a silver phallic-shaped balloon.

"The fuck is that?" Luc asked, pointing at the atrocity.

"It's a Zeppelin!" Sawyer enthused, dancing from one foot to the other. "You know? 'Cause Emmie's had such a disaster of a year."

I took the string of the offensive plane, watching it bob above my head.

"That is no blimp," Addie drawled dryly. "It's a goddamed penis."

Everyone sniggered.

"I guess... thank you?" I asked, tugging on the sting.

"You're welcome." Sawyer reached over, ruffling my hair. "Only the best for our Em."

Courtney gave me a small smile. "I heard they've arrested the last of them."

"Yeah." I blew out a breath, holding out the string to Luc, who led the balloon over to the other side of the room. "Annabelle wasn't mucking about."

"The confiscated servers were damaging, but the abuses are what will push the charges up," Paxton offered, his hand absently stroking Jetta's leg. "The body count is pretty high."

"Not to mention the money," Sawyer said, as he flicked

through the multitude of well-wisher cards piled on my dresser. "Our Emmie is now legendary."

I blushed, looking down at my hands.

"I don't know if I want to be known for the biggest theft in the world," I muttered.

"Only behind closed doors." Luc laughed. "AFP returned all the cash with a recommendation to get in contact with us. We're going to be swimming in clients for the next few years."

"Hear, hear!" Sawyer raised his hand as if he were holding an imaginary drink. "To Emmie!"

With laughter, the rest of the group tipped fake cups towards me.

"To Emmie!"

My blush deepened.

"What happens to your siblings and the others from the cult?" Courtney asked when we'd settled back down.

"Some of them are going away, others will be on release, provided they abide by the terms of their bail. Most of them have to go into a deradicalisation program, but with Edward incarcerated their heaven on earth ideology is broken," Luc said. He'd moved to sit on the bed, his arm around my shoulders as his hand lazily drew circles across my skin.

It was distracting.

"Are you worried?" Courtney asked, her face sympathetic.

Am I worried?

"Surprisingly, no," I said slowly. "I think my core fear came from David, and he's... gone. Which means I'm free to work out what I want to do with my life. If the others target me, I know now I can work through it. I have backup." I squeezed Luc's knee. "I have Sawyer watching my shit." He took a bow. "And I know I can take care of myself." I shrugged. "Taking a life was... horrible. But I can't feel anything but relief. I no longer feel like I have to run away or have anything to fear. I know I'm strong. I protected myself."

Luc's hand squeezed my shoulder.

Courtney nodded. "You have closure."

I smiled. "Yeah, I guess I do."

Luc pressed a kiss to my forehead. I tilted my head back, offering him a smile.

The click of a mobile camera shattered the moment. We both looked over at Sawyer who waved back.

"Don't mind me. Keep being adorable. I just want to commemorate this moment in picture form."

"Sawyer," Luc drawled, "never change."

EMMIE

Spring was finally emerging. I'd reclined by the pool, music playing in the background as Luc sat beside me, quietly plucking at guitar strings.

With Luc's house destroyed, we'd moved into an apartment. Luc had put his foot down when I'd suggested moving back into mine.

"One, it's a shit box. Two, it's a shit box. Three, it's tiny as fuck with a coffin-shower shit box."

I'd laughed. "Well, what do you propose?"

"We move into a rental while the house is rebuilt. One with a shower big enough for me to fuck you every morning."

We'd gone apartment shopping that afternoon.

Cecile, while devastated for her son, hadn't been able to contain her glee at designing us a new home. We'd finalised the plans last week. Construction would begin in December.

We'd spent the last few weeks clearing debris from the block. His house may have been decimated but his pool and gardens were still beautiful, if not slightly charred. We'd finished today's cleaning and were hanging out by the pool.

I dropped the book I was reading with a satisfied sigh, curling onto my side, turning to look at him. He shot me a smile. That toe-curling delicious smile that had lured me in from the start.

"What?" he asked as I continued to watch him.

"I'm happy." I gave a little shrug, offering him a smile. "And I like watching you."

He put his guitar aside, moving to lean over me on the sunbed. "You do, hmm?"

He dropped his head, tickling me with his beard.

"Yes!" I laughed, shrieking as he rubbed his face across mine and over my chest.

We wrestled for a moment before his body finally collapsed gently on me, holding me down. His tickling turned to caresses as he captured my mouth with his deliciously deep kisses. It had been weeks since I had returned home, my body healing as my heart overflowed.

As his hands slipped under the thin cotton of my shirt, I groaned, placing a hand on his chest. "Luc, stop."

He paused, moving back a little. "Okay?"

I slid back to sitting, watching him rock back to sit. "We need to talk."

He didn't look mad, just concerned.

I reached across, pulling his big hand into mine, running my thumb across the lines of his palm. "I have a question."

"Mm?"

I finally looked up, offering him a small smile. "Marry me?"

He froze, completely. For a moment my smile wavered.

"I mean... if it's... you don't have–"

His lips crashed down, halting whatever nonsense was about to come out of my mouth.

"Yes," he whispered, pushing me back down on the daybed. "Fuck, yes. Any day. Every day. Today!" He pressed kisses to my lips, my cheeks, my eyelids. He sucked and bit his way down my body, stripping clothes from me as he whispered yes over and over.

Naked, he claimed me. There in our yard under the warm sun. And when we were done, he laughed at my weak protest that we'd get sunburn on our butts if we did it again. He convinced me with lazy kisses and seductive words that I had no hope of withstanding, all whispered in his deep, gravelly voice.

Later that night, in our bed in the rented apartment, he slid a ring on my finger. A rose cut grey diamond set in a rose gold band. It looked a little like a crown.

"I didn't get you a ring," I whispered staring at the setting.

He shrugged, pulling me closer. "I can get a tattoo."

I blinked up. "Tattoos are permanent."

"So are you."

I shoved him in the face, laughing. "That's so corny."

"But true." He pulled me back, kissing me again. "We're going to have a beautiful life."

"I want to travel," I admitted. "I want to see and enjoy, well, everything."

"Of course." His fingers tangled in my hair as I drew patterns on his chest with the tips of my fingers. "Where should we go first? I hear you've always wanted to live in London."

We both chuckled.

"Italy."

"Not France?"

I pressed my lips together, hiding my smile. "I thought you didn't like Paris?"

"God, no. But we can go to my mother's family in the south. I want to show you the beauty of provincial France. I want to drink champagne from your breasts."

A quiver of desire lit in me. "We could do that."

"Six months. We're taking six months as our honeymoon."

I tilted my head back. "I'm not sure my boss will let me."

He laughed. "Only if you ask nicely."

"Oh?" I ran a hand down his front, dipping it into his boxer shorts. "Like this?"

He groaned as my fingers tightened around his cock.

"Maybe," he grunted. "Jesus, I'm hard again."

I huffed out a laugh. "I won't hold it against you."

"I will." His hips jerked in my hand, pushing him closer.

"Luc?" I asked, still stroking.

"Mm?" His eyes were closed.

"I love you."

His eyelids lifted, his beautiful blue eyes staring directly at me. He reached down, pulling my hand away, twining our fingers together. "I love you too."

"I know."

EPILOGUE
LUC

I didn't want to point it out, but one couldn't argue with the truth. My wife was hot. I was a thousand percent sure on a regular day, she had to be the sexiest thing I'd ever laid eyes on. But today?

I'm about to lose my mind.

She was on the dance floor with her girls, laughing as she shimmied in her wedding dress. A frothy thing, I couldn't wait to strip it from her later that night. She caught my eye, sending me an air kiss.

That, ladies and gentlemen, is my absolutely, stunningly gorgeous wife. God, I'm a lucky bastard.

Pax handed me a bottle, tipping the neck of his towards the dance floor.

"You did good. Lucky bastard."

I chuckled at how closely he echoed my thoughts. "Don't tell her. She's convinced I'm a catch."

Jetta popped up beside Pax, wrapping an arm around his middle. "What you two talking 'bout?"

"How lucky we are," Pax said, dropping a kiss on her cheek.

"Glad you both know it." She reached out, squeezing my forearm. "Congrats, Luc. I'm thrilled for you two. Now, excuse me. I'm getting my dance on!"

She headed to the floor, joining the fray. There were screams from the girls as they welcomed her. She made a beeline for Emmie, whispering something in her ear. Emmie turned to look at me. I winked, causing her to throw back her head, laughing.

I wanted to join her, taste the laughter on her lips, whisper naughty promises in her ear just to make her blush.

But first, I had a promise to keep.

I nodded at the lead guitarist. He gave me a head lift, wrapping up the song.

"Ladies and gentleman," called the lead, "the groom!"

I climbed on the small stage, accepting the acoustic guitar and perching on a bar chair they positioned for me. All eyes came to me, but I only cared about the woman with the prettiest green pair I'd ever seen.

"Keys, in the last year life has thrown more shit at you than even I know how to deal with."

The crowd chuckled.

"I've watched you work to recover from a bullet. I've watched you battle pain to regain your life. I've watched you deal with mental demons and slay every single one. No matter what happens, you battle on, and I've never been prouder. Emmie, a year ago I made you a promise. I love you, beautiful, and I've never been happier to deliver. Here's to you, wife."

I played the opening chords to One Direction's *Little Things,* winking at Emmie as I crooned the opening lines into the microphone. Her heart in her eyes, her joy burst out as she doubled over laughing. The cheers drowned out my first line, but she caught it. Propelled forward by laughing, cat-calling wedding guests, she ended up right in front as I transitioned from one song to another in a mash-up that told the tale of my love for this amazing woman.

As her laughter turned to happy tears, I sang to her about being beautiful, about how I needed her, how she lit up my life, about the little things I loved about her, how I would carry her through the dark, finishing with the promise that I would never need anything but her. As the final note died out, I swung the guitar behind me, jumped down from the stage and pulled her into my arms.

She pressed her face against my chest, her shoulders shaking as she cried happy tears.

"Don't cry, baby," I whispered into her ear as the crowd cheered behind us.

"I never thought my life could be so full," she admitted, turning her gorgeous face to me. "My heart doesn't know what to do with this much love."

I grinned. "I have a few ideas."

She laughed, pulling my head down, letting me taste the joy on her lips. She tasted like the best kind of promise.

ABOUT THE AUTHOR

Evie Mitchell is a thirty-something romance author (she/her/hers) living with disability. She believes in inclusion, accessibility, and fierce romance. Her loves include steamy romance novels, her husband, their THREE sausage dogs (heaven help her), and her ever-growing collection of book-related mugs.

As a woman with a diverse work history including in areas such as emergency response, event management, human rights, disability access, and security - her books are filled with true stories (bridezillas), worst-case scenarios (malfunctioning dresses), and her favorite tropes (one-bed).

Evie specialises in fiercely inclusive happily ever afters.

ALSO BY EVIE MITCHELL

Capricorn Cove Series

Thunder Thighs

Double the D

Muffin Top

The Mrs. Clause

Beach Party

New Year Knew You

The Shake-Up

Double Breasted

As You Wish

You Sleigh Me

Resolution Revolution

Meat Load

Thor's Shipbuilding Series

Clean Sweep

The X-list

Reality Check

The Christmas Contract

Dogg Pack Books

Puppy Love

The Frock Up

Pier Pressure

Bad English

Nameless Souls MC Series

Runner

Wrath

Ghost

Elliot Security Series

Rough Edge

Bleeding Edge

9 781922 561794